NIGHT OF THE GOLDEN BUTTERFLY

D0807617

By the same author

NIGHT
OF THE
GOLDEN
BUTTERFLY

Tariq Ali

VERSO

London • New York

This paperback edition first published 2010
First published by Verso 2010
© Tariq Ali 2010
All rights reserved

The moral rights of the author have been asserted

1 3 5 7 9 10 8 6 4 2

Verso
UK: 6 Meard Street, London W1F 0EG
US: 20 Jay Street, Suite 1010, Brooklyn, NY 11201
www.versobooks.com

Verso is the imprint of New Left Books

ISBN-13: 978-1-84467-654-5

British Library Cataloguing in Publication Data
A catalogue record for this book is available from the British Library

Library of Congress Cataloging-in-Publication Data
A catalog record for this book is available from the Library of Congress

Typeset in MT Fournier by Hewer Text UK Ltd, Edinburgh
Printed by Scandbook AB in Sweden

For Aisha,

who suggested the title twelve years ago and now thinks it unsuitable

TARIQ ALI

NIGHT OF THE GOLDEN BUTTERFLY

ONE

Forty-five years ago, when I lived in Lahore, I had an older friend called Plato, who once did me a favour. In a fit of youthful generosity, I promised to return it with interest if and whenever he needed my help. Plato taught mathematics at a posh school, but hated some of his pupils, the ones he said were there only to learn the fine art of debauchery. And being a Punjabi Plato, he asked whether I would repay his favour with compound interest. Foolishly, I agreed.

I was in love, much to Plato's annoyance. In his eyes love was simply an excuse for juvenile lechery and, by its very nature, could never be eternal. A chaste friendship was much more important and could last a lifetime. I wasn't in the mood for this type of philosophy at the time and would have signed any piece of paper he laid in front of me.

For a man whose judgements were usually strong and clear, Plato's dislikes could be irrational and the border that separated his irony from his hatred was always blurred. He would, for instance, be deeply offended by students who clipped their fountain pens to the front pockets of their nylon shirts during the summer months. When asked why, he did not respond, but when pressed would mutter that if these were their aesthetic values while in the flower and heat of their youth, he feared to think what values they would espouse when they grew older. Even though this is not a good example of it, it was his wit that first drew one to him, long before he became known as a painter.

Once, a friend of ours who had recently graduated and had been inducted into the foreign service sat down at our table, only to be confronted by Plato: 'I'm going to change my name to Diogenes so I can light a lantern in the daylight and go in search of honest civil servants.' Nobody laughed, and Plato, accustomed to being the hero of every conversation, left us for a while; the target of his barb asked how we could mingle with such a foul creature. We turned on him: How dare he speak in this fashion, especially as we had defended him? And anyway, muttered my friend Zahid, Plato was worth ten foreign-office catamites like him. A few more reflections along similar lines and the figure rapidly escalated to 'at least a hundred foreign-service catamites and braggarts like him.' That got rid of 'him'. Then Plato returned and sat pensively for the rest of the afternoon, tugging at his black moustache at regular intervals, always a sign of anger.

The manner in which Plato discussed his amorous conquests with close friends was never totally convincing. His sexuality had always remained a mystery. He was often withdrawn and secretive and it was obvious that he had depths that we, a generation younger, could never hope to penetrate. There is much about him that I still do not know, though for almost a decade I was probably his closest friend. If only mirrors could reflect more than a clear and unwavering image. If we could also see the innermost character of the person gazing at his own reflection, the task of writers and analysts would become much easier, if not redundant.

Plato never projected any extravagant self-image, and he always made a big deal of avoiding publicity, but in a fashion that sometimes led him to step right back into the limelight. When in windy phrases one of the older and highly respected Urdu poets who regularly assembled in the Pak Tea House on the Mall exceeded the limits of self-praise, Plato would mock him without mercy, hurling epithets and Punjabi proverbs that amused us greatly but made the poets nervous. When the poet under attack suddenly turned hard and contemptuous and denounced Plato as a mediocrity, jealous of his superiors, Plato would become extremely cheerful and insist on a test so that all assembled could determine which of his opponent's poems were second- and third-rate. He would begin to recite one of the more obscure verses in a hilariously hideous fashion, and when the poet and his sycophants left, Plato applauded loudly. He never really believed that the poet in question was a bad poet, not even for a moment, but he was annoyed by the narcissism and mutual-admiration sessions that took place in the teahouse every day. He hated the vacant expressions that marked the faces of the sycophants who shouted 'wonderful' to each and every line that was recited. Like many of us, he did not fully appreciate what some of them had gone through in the preceding decades. Disappointments had worn many of them down, drained their strength, and some were now broken reeds, frittering away their energies in cafés and acting as cheerleaders for those who had acquired reputations in the literary world. Plato was well aware of this, but his own central core, a wiry steel rod, had remained unbent, and this made him intolerant towards others less strong than he was.

What had caused Plato to demand his pound of flesh now, and why in the shape of a novel based on his life? For that is what happened. A certain chain of events triggered a phone call conveying a request that I ring him in Karachi. This was odd in itself, since Plato had always loathed Fatherland's largest city, denouncing it intemperately as a characterless, hybrid monstrosity. When we spoke, he was in no mood for a lengthy conversation, merely insistent that old debts of honour had to be repaid. I had no other choice. I could, of course, have told him to get lost and I now wish I had. Not so much because of him, but because of others whose stories intersected with his. The mystery bothered me. What was it that had tightened itself into a knot in him so rock-hard that the only way of undoing it was by calling in a barely remembered debt? Was it a nagging discontent over what he had not managed to achieve, or simply the tedium of artistic endeavour in a country where the vagaries of the art market were determined by what appeared in the New York or London press? Praise abroad, profits at home.

Long before I began the awkward task of composition I would have to research certain aspects of his life, and it was not going to be smooth sailing, either. Plato had kept large tracts of his life hidden from view, or perhaps repressed them. Either way, cataracts lay ahead. How could I write about him unless he let me uncover his dormant past?

Friendships are ridiculously mobile. They flow, change, disappear, go underground mole-like for long spells and are easily forgotten, especially if one friend has shifted continents. During a lifetime we are surrounded by people in clusters, some of whom crystallize into friends of the moment, then melt away, vanish without trace, to be encountered again by accident in the strangest of places. Some political or work friendships endure much longer; a few last forever.

When I agreed to write his story, Plato was thrilled and roared triumphantly. This laughter was so unlike him that I was slightly unnerved. Irritated by my attempt to unearth the reason for this strange request, he added a rider. I would do as he asked, he knew that, but could I do so without employing any of the cunning devices or overblown phrases considered obligatory these days? It must be plain storytelling, without frills or too many digressions. I agreed, but warned him that I couldn't write a book that was only about him. He was the best person to do that, and could simply dictate a memoir if that was what he wanted. Nor could I simply portray his development in terms of his interactions with other people. The period would have to be evoked, the social milieu excavated, and navel-gazing resisted. I reminded him of Heraclitus: 'Those who are awake have a world in common, but every sleeper has a world of his own.'

Plato accepted this gracefully, but couldn't resist sharing a thought in return, I suppose, to encourage me. A setback, he informed me, could be transformed into a victory through a work of art. I disagreed very strongly. Artistic consciousness, even at a high level, could never roll back the realities imposed on a society after a historic defeat. His voice grew louder as he responded by naming painters and poets whose work, in bad times, had lifted the people to unimagined heights. They had done so, I agreed, they had enriched the cultural life of the poor and the defeated by providing them with a useful cultural prop, but that changed nothing. The world of visual art and the realm of literature remained tiny islands. The sharks still controlled the oceans. He became angry. He was working on a triptych that would be a call to arms. He would prove me wrong. His work would set Fatherland on fire. I expressed scepticism.

'Great Master Plato, your visions will hit Fatherland like thunderbolts from heaven.'

'Talking to you in this mood is wasting time. Do something useful. Go and start the book. Go now, and where the truth can't be shown naked, dress it in humour and irony. Can you manage that?'

I will try.

TWO

Zahid was in light sleep mode, dreaming. It was the pissing dream, he told me later, the bladder-full alert dream, the core of which had remained constant throughout his life. Water, forever flowing. Usually, he was having a shower, but sometimes it was a running tap or, on a few rare occasions, a turbulent sea. At school and in the mountains where our families spent the summer, he would describe his affliction in some detail. It was, he explained, a crude, effective internal alarm system. If he delayed too long, his tap began to drip. His mother once provided a more Jungian explanation, but it must have been forgettable, since she could not recall it a week later.

Zahid himself was convinced that he was unique. When he was a baby, his amah had patiently weaned him off the muslin nappies, training him to pee by turning on a tap and whistling the national anthem. It worked – the muslin nappies were permanently discarded when he was only a year old – but it must have left a mark on his psyche. He would often joke that, Allah be praised, it was water that had entered his dreams and not

nat'l
anthem

the national anthem, though after a brief discussion, we agreed it might have been better the other way round. At the end of a movie or a radio broadcast he could always find a pissoir. Much better than bed-wetting.

Later, when he was already a distinguished heart surgeon in the United States, treating important people, Zahid discovered that his dream was not as unusual as he had once thought. The revelation came as a disappointment. He used to joke that it was the end of all illusions. It was then that he decided, against the advice of his son, to invest some of his savings in banks and properties in undesirable locations all over the world: Marbella and Miami, Bermuda and Nice as well as – and this very much for old times' sake – a mountain retreat in the Kaghan valley, sadly destroyed by the earthquake of 2004. All this I discovered later. I had heard, of course, that he had become a Republican and was head of the medical team that operated on Dick Cheney in 1999, saving his life, but had not known that he had moved from DC to London after the explosions of 9/11 or that he was now in semi-retirement in a palatial villa in Richmond, overlooking the Thames. We had lived in different worlds for almost half a century.

When the phone rang, soon after dawn, Zahid automatically groaned and stretched an arm out to grab the clock. Must be an emergency at the hospital, he thought, before realizing he was no longer working. It was ten past five in the morning; must be someone from the east. Early calls upset him. They were invariably from Fatherland and it was usually bad news: another death in the family, a new military coup, an expected assassination, but still they could not be ignored. His wife was still asleep. He rose and lifted the phone, and went over to draw the curtains. Dark clouds. Like him, the city suffered from a weak bladder. He cursed.

The caller heard him swearing, chuckled and hailed him in Punjabi, the mother tongue to beat all other motherfucking mother tongues, or so its partisans boast. No translation can ever do justice to this multilayered language, so rich in puns and double entendres that some scholars have argued that virtually every word of every Punjabi dialect has a dual or hidden meaning. I'm not sure this is the case. That would have created insurmountable problems for the Sikh religion, whose founder, the visionary mystic poet Nanak, a great master of the language, would never ... I mean, he must have known what he was doing when he elevated his native Punjabi into a divine language for the new faith, split off from the caste-ridden Hindus.

Nor are the problems of translation simplified by the profusion of dialects. The voice that addressed Dr Mian Zahid Hussain spoke in the guttural dialect common to Lahore and Amritsar. As the narrator, I will keep the translation literal as far as this first exchange is concerned; but, wishing neither to tax the reader's patience nor to expose my own limitations, I may be compelled to revert to a less louche mode in the chapters that lie ahead. Or I may not.

'I say, Zahid Mian. Salaamaleikum.'

The recipient of the greeting cursed again, but inwardly. He did not recognize the voice. Clumsily unbuttoning his pyjamas with one hand while holding the phone in the other, he stumbled into the bathroom and gave much-needed relief to his neurotic bladder, just as a delightful drizzle began to water London's numerous parks and private gardens. Despite decades of wisdom accumulated at the George Washington Hospital in Washington, DC, he did not know that speaking on the phone directly above the commode creates a slight distortion, an echo easily recognized by an alert person at the other end. And this particular caller relished embarrassing his friends.

'So frightened by my voice that it makes you piss, catamite?'

'Forgive me, friend. It's early here. I don't recognize your voice.'

'I won't forgive you, catamite. The only friend you have is in your hand. Why not put some soap on him and fuck your fist? Then you might recognize my voice, you frogfucker.'

That last was not a common abuse in Lahore but unique to an old circle of friends. Zahid smiled, struggling to identify the now familiar voice and hurriedly getting rid of the after-drops, with only partial success. The traditions of our faith, alas, are divided on this crucially important Islamic ritual. The Shia insist on the Twelver: the penis is shaken vigorously twelve times to get rid of everything lurking inside. The Sunni are more relaxed: six shakes are considered sufficient. In his hurry, Zahid had taken the Sufi path – one strong existentialist tug – and spattered his pyjamas as a result. Simultaneously, he recognized the caller's voice.

'Plato! Plato. Of course, it's you.'

'Glad you recognized your name, frogfucker.'

Zahid's loud laugh, slightly tinged with hysteria, was typical of the city where he was born. He responded in kind.

'For twenty-five sisterfucking years you disappeared yourself, Plato. Did you climb up your own arse? You ring while it's barely light in this fucked city and complain I don't recognize your voice. I thought you were dead.'

'Mean-spirited catamite, why aren't you? Your mother's pudendum.'

'You vanished, Plato. Just like your motherfucked paintings.'

'Only from your dogfucking Western world. My exhibitions here are always packed.'

'Where are you?'

'Lahore, but flying to Karachi later. I have a studio there.'

'Long live Puristan. Never fucked there, is it? Why are you ringing me at this hour? Are you dying? Been working it hard? Need an arse transplant?'

'Shut your mouth, catamite. I thought you'd already be up. Aren't you fasting? Too early to say the morning prayers? Heard you'd gone religious and abased yourself in Makkah.'

Zahid was angered. 'We've all changed, Plato. You, too. Fasting is going a bit far. Better not to than to cheat, like we did when we were kids?'

'Many of our old friends are fasting now. Try calling them catamites. They're ready to kill. Why not you? Listen, Mr Big Surgeon or whatever corrupt business you're screwing up these days, I rang for something special. My arse is torn, friend. Torn. Badly torn.'

'Tell me something new.'

'Love has happened. I need your help. No jokes or cuntish questions about my age. It's happened.'

Plato was seventy-five, exactly fourteen years older than his country, as he never tired of telling us when we were growing up. He was ten or so years older than us, too, and used his seniority to boast about his sexual exploits, real and imagined, without restraint. About how he disliked docile and gentle middle-class women, obsessed with pimple removers. How he preferred the raw energy and rough hands of peasant wenches. All this we knew. But love? What depths had unleashed this monster? Wondering whether this was real or yet another Plato fantasy, Zahid decided to strike a lighter note.

'Woman, man or beast?' Abuse polluted the phone lines, lashing the recipient like hard rain. By the time the monsoon ended, Zahid was laughing so hysterically and stupidly that he woke his wife. From the way he was laughing, Jindié knew the call must be from Lahore, and that it was neither bad news nor his mother. She immediately demanded to know who was ringing up so early. By now it was pouring outside. Plato overheard her melodious voice.

'Ah, the *sunehri titli* has arisen. My salaams to the great lady. She was created to inflame the imagination of painters. Tell her that after she left, our city never recovered. Why didn't she dump you and find a better person? Like me, for instance. Catamite, I'm really pleased you haven't abandoned her for a younger wife. Some young nurse with milkmaid breasts—'

'Plato, it's early and I—'

'I'll be brief. The woman I love is Zaynab. She's married. No children, but adores her nieces. She needs help. She asks me for only one thing: my story and hers, collated in one manuscript, with my colour illustrations. Never to be published. Don't ask why. I don't know. It's her only request. How can I refuse? I only rang you because I can't track down that catamite who once was a friend of ours – Dara. He'll remember me. We spent enough time together in the kebab shops and the teahouse, especially during Ramadan, when we always broke the fast early and often. Remind him that I once did him a very big favour at some cost to my self-esteem. He promised me one in return whenever and wherever. The time for that is now. I need him, Zahid Mian. I can paint and sign my name. Someone else will have to write the stories. Or has Dara become too grand for Fatherland friends?'

'Plato, please try and find Dara's e-mail address. I don't see him. The motherfucker still treats me like a traitor. The last time I met him was at a Punjabi wedding in New York. I smiled politely in his direction, and he turned away contemptuously. Always an arrogant motherfucker. He might respond better to a direct request from you.'

Plato erupted. 'Hockey stick up your arse, catamite . . . and his. I never use e-mail. That stuff is for catamites and impotents. Just give him the message and my number. Tell him mine is badly torn. I really need that fistfucker's help. If you're too shy, ask the Golden Butterfly to ring him. She'll do it for me.'

The reference to the hockey stick revived memories. Plato was an elephant. Trust him to remember Zahid's distaste for the sport. Zahid's father had captained the Punjab university team in the late nineteen-thirties, and some years later scored a goal in the Olympics that won the silver for Fatherland. National acclaim followed, but not from his Communist friends. Moved by their disdain, he had turned down the offer of a medal and money from the government. Zahid was six years old at the time, but growing up surrounded by sports medals and cups only increased his aversion to hockey. His father had turned equally successfully to business and set up an import–export agency, which, with the help of civil servants in need of a commission, had prospered. Zahid's reaction had been to join an underground Communist cell, cementing our friendship. But nothing is ever really underground in Fatherland. Everybody knew.

Reluctantly, Zahid agreed to make the fatal call. A few hours later, as I was carefully tamping the coffee to make myself an espresso, the phone rang. My first instinct was to hang up. It was only the mention of Plato's name that stopped me. I hadn't spoken to Zahid for forty-five years – not since his departure from Lahore in the mid-Sixties to read medicine at Johns Hopkins University in Baltimore, after his marriage.

To leave the country, he had had to obtain a No Objection Certificate from the Ministry of Interior. In order to do that, we later learned, he had revealed the whereabouts of Comrade Tipu, a Bengali Communist from Chittagong who was at college with us in Lahore. Tipu was much better educated than we in both the Marxist classics and pre-marital sex, and we learned a great deal from him. That cursed spring, he was warned by a friendly bureaucrat that he had just been put on the wanted list for subversive activities against the state. Tipu felt honoured, but also scared. Nobody likes to think of electric rods, icicles or the penises of the secret police being shoved up his arse in a dingy cellar of the Lahore Fort. Someone we all knew had been tortured to death a few years previously and fear was not an irrational response. Tipu decided to go underground. An aunt of mine in a remote and mountainous part of the country was looking for a gardener. I suggested Tipu, who borrowed a few gardening manuals and left for the hills. A few months later he was tracked and arrested. The CID had been tipped off and a senior police chief was heard boasting after a few whiskies in the Gymkhana Club that it was the hockey star's son who had obliged them. A second cousin present at the occasion made sure that I was informed about it, but only after Zahid had left for Baltimore. The news spread in the city and I broke off all relations with him. Youthful arrogance, now conformist, now rebellious, rarely permits any serious questioning or re-evaluation of actions, events, experiences. We were no different. Zahid was a traitor. I cast him out of my mind, though I could hardly avoid hearing about his success as a surgeon.

Since Zahid moved to London we had exchanged curt nods at the odd wedding reception and a funeral or two, including that of an old Fatherland Communist whose son had insisted on prayers in the lavish but ugly Regents Park Mosque. Tipu himself was there. He had led a chequered career as an arms dealer, and I saw the two embrace. By then I had come to know innumerable, deeper, worse betrayals. If Zahid's was not to be forgiven, it might be qualified. But above all I wanted to hear about Plato. And suddenly, after all these years, I wanted to know about Zahid's wife. Somewhat impulsively and to my own surprise, I agreed to have dinner with them in Richmond.

◖◖

We had not spoken for almost half a century. Old age circumscribes the future, the laws of biology push one to reflect mainly on the past, but if anything, I have tended in the other direction. Why concentrate exclusively on the past? Some friends have become testy and ultra-pessimistic, seeing no value at all in the postmodern world. Biological conservatism or old hopes gone musty, in both cases inducing melancholia, despair-filled days and alcohol-fuelled evenings.

School friendships are notoriously fickle. Some survive for purely practical reasons, the more privileged schools in every country creating social networks that make up for the loss or nonexistence of real friendship.

Zahid and I had attended different schools, but we met up in the mountains each summer. And yet ours was not just a seasonal friendship. We continued to talk when we returned to Lahore. Later we were at the same college, and our shared politics brought us closer still.

For almost ten years we confided all of our political and sexual fantasies to each other. When Zahid developed an obsessive crush on a general's daughter, he insisted that I accompany him on his Vespa to the women's college that she attended. We would wait outside and then follow her car, overtaking it just before it reached her house. She knew. Occasionally she smiled. The memory of a single smile kept him going for weeks. Then she graduated and was soon married off to the scion of some feudal family. Zahid's offer, transmitted via his mother, had been rudely rejected. Zahid's political bent and his father's rejection of honours had made him out of bounds for daughters of army officers and bureaucrats, the two groups that ran Fatherland in those days, presiding over the kind of tyrannies that break a people's heart and their pride. The boy had no future. How could he expect to marry into privilege?

Zahid recovered, though, and shocked his parents by insisting on marrying Jindié, the daughter of a modest but extremely well off Chinese shoemaker in Lahore. It was a Muslim family, but caste prejudices went deep in Fatherland. A cobbler's daughter for the only son of a wealthy Punjabi family? Unacceptable. He might as well marry a Negro woman.

Zahid ignored them. 'What are we?' he would mock. 'Peasants descended from low-caste Hindus whose job it was to grow vegetables for the rulers of this city. Our forebears grew turnips and pumpkins; Jindié's father is a craftsman. Just because he measures your feet for sandals you think he's lower than you.' He married Jindié, the *sunehri titli,* as Zahid's Punjabi friends called her – the Golden Butterfly. Her brother was a member of our political circle. She was a marvel of beauty

Golden Butterfly

and intelligence, a rare combination in Lahore. There was an air of gaiety about her as well as majesty. She had thin lips and profoundly expressive eyes. She had read more books than all of us put together, and in three languages. Her knowledge of Punjabi Sufi poetry went deep, and when she sang her voice resembled a flute. And she did sing sometimes, usually when she thought she was alone with our sisters and female cousins, unaware that we were listening. We all loved her. I more than the others, and I think she loved me. She had married Zahid just before his political treachery was exposed, but I thought she must have known of it and that had angered me greatly. It mattered in those days. Consequently, she, too, had been assigned to the deepest circle of my memory.

Now I found myself looking forward to seeing Jindié again. Our relationship had consisted mainly of letters, lengthy phone calls and attempted rendezvous. The last time we had met on our own, forty-five years before, she had been in a state of unspeakable confusion. Covered with shame, she had fled.

The next time I'd seen her had been at a farewell dinner for a retiring professor. She had come with her brother. It was a very proper occasion, not that she was ever capable of relapsing into coquetry. We did not speak and she appeared to be in fragile shape. Her melancholy glances cut me deeply, but there was nothing to be done. Some months later I received a letter informing me of her engagement to Zahid. It was a very long, self-justifying missive of the sort that women are better at writing than men, at least in my limited experience. I was so enraged at the news of her engagement that I never reached the end. In later years I did wonder whether it had contained any words of affection for me. I tore it up into little pieces and flushed it to the depths of the city. It was better confined to the sewers, I thought, where the rats could read bits of it. She should appreciate that, since she was marrying one. Years later, a mutual woman friend told me she had not detected any awkward corners in Jindié's life. There were two children and they were the centre of her existence. I wondered what had become of them and her life after they left home.

I arrived early and went for a short walk by the river. There was a sudden sinking feeling in the pit of my stomach. Perhaps this was a mistake, after all. Why was I dining with perfidy? The passage of time doesn't always heal wounds incurred in political or emotional conflicts. Tipu's shift from politics to business did not retrospectively justify Zahid's betrayal. As for Jindié, I hadn't thought of her for a very long time and when I did she appeared as a tender ghost. I couldn't help feeling that a restaurant, neutral territory, might have been less stressful. I walked back to my parked car, took out the bottle of wine and inspected their Richmond home carefully before alerting them to my presence. The house, a late Georgian mansion, was certainly well appointed. A mature garden sloped gently to the river and a tiny quay where a boat was moored. But I had been sighted and the French windows were pushed apart as Zahid walked down to greet me. There wasn't a hair on his head. It was polished and smooth like a carrom board. Given our history, a warm embrace or even a perfunctory hug was out of the question. We shook hands. And then Jindié walked out, and the clouds disappeared. Her hair was white, but her face was unaltered and her figure had not coarsened with age. Her smile was enough to flood decaying memory banks. I managed a few banalities as we walked indoors. While Zahid went to get some drinks – just to be difficult, I asked for fresh pomegranate juice and was told it was possible – I looked over the interior of the house.

The large living room was conventional and unsurprising. It could have been lifted straight from *Interiors* or one of the many other consumerist magazines that disgrace a dentist's waiting room. Do they think that their patients are all empty-headed, or are the glossy pictures meant to make up for the dingy décor of their surgeries? The walls were covered with mostly unprepossessing paintings, with every continent unsuitably represented. No Plato, but two gouaches by his dreadfully fashionable rival, I. M. Malik. There were also a few swords and daggers, which had not been dusted for some time.

The only object that made an impression on me was an exquisitely painted Chinese screen depicting three women in earnest conversation with each other. Not a trace here of earthly existence being a mere illusion. Had I been forced to guess, I would have ventured that it was from the late seventeenth century and by someone who either inspired or was inspired by Yongzheng. She saw my appreciative look and smiled.

'Genuine or a copy?'

'It's not a copy. It really is Yongzheng. Early eighteenth century. A gift from my son when he lived in Hong Kong, earning too much money for his own good. I have no idea how he managed to get it out of the country.'

It was a bit early in the evening to start discussing progeny, and I was wondering where the books were kept, when Zahid took me by the arm.

'Jindié knows how fussy you are about food. She's prepared a feast tonight. While she's applying the finishing touches, let me show you my study.'

They seemed happy together, which pleased me. Not that Jindié was the sort who would have accepted being mired in misery for too long. She would have left ages ago.

The large oak-panelled study was certainly impressive; the eclectic collection accurately reflected the different tastes of the household. Zahid said, 'I've bought all your books. Thumbprint them before you leave.' He spoke Punjabi, as we always had when we were alone. He wanted to clear up the past. 'Daraji, what hurt the most was that you rushed to judgement without speaking to me.'

I sat down on his desk and stared at him. His eyes were still the same and looked straight back at me. He then told me what had really happened. His father had simply bribed a senior police officer to get the No Objection

Certificate, and all Zahid had done was sign an affidavit affirming that he was not a member of any clandestine Communist organization.

'We are neither of us young, Zahid. Let's not try to deceive each other or give sweet names to things that were never nice. Who betrayed Tipu?'

'Was I the only one who knew he was working for your aunt?'

'You mean it could have been Jamshed?'

'It was that sisterfucker. He admitted as much to me.'

'When?'

'Forty years ago, when shame was still an emotion he wrestled with. He said he couldn't face you after that and asked me to forgive him for allowing the blame to rest on my shoulders . . .'

'And I thought he couldn't face me because he'd become a corrupt, amoral businessman in bed with every military dictator.'

'Is there any other kind?'

We laughed.

'Zahid. You knew me better than most. Everyone in Lahore was told it was you. If I was in a rage and didn't ring you, why didn't you contact me? Your silence confirmed your guilt in my eyes.'

'It was the cop who took the bribe who spread the vile rumours. My father was scared. If I challenged him and told my friends, my No Objection Certificate might have been withdrawn and I wouldn't have been able to leave the country. I knew that if I told you, you would confront the cop, talk to journalists, tell the whole world and make a big fuss. That would have meant no medical studies at Johns Hopkins and I was desperate to become a doctor. You encouraged me. But this is truth and reconciliation time. There was another reason why I did not contact you.'

'What was it?'

'Jindié. I knew how close you two were. You'd told me everything and I thought . . .'

'Might as well let him think the worst of me as long as I've got Jindié.'

'Something like that.'

'But you never loved her. You would have told me.'

'True, but I liked her a great deal and wanted to marry someone. You loved her but were not prepared to marry her . . .'

'Or anyone else.'

'Yes, but that's not the way she or most girls thought at the time, let alone her parents. You offered her some crazy bohemian alternative, and that, too, in Lahore, where girls learned the art of leaning on window sills to catch sight of their lovers, in such a way as to never be visible from outside. Even logistically your suggestion was crazy.'

'It was a test of our love. Jindié failed. As for bohemian lifestyles and logistics, our poets, professors and artists used them constantly and not just before Partition. Plato had a list in his head of who did it with whom and where . . . boats on the Ravi were regular meeting places. Lawrence Gardens in the moonlight when the wolves in the Zoo were howling. Now the river that so arrogantly and regularly flooded our city has no water left. Were you ever in love with her?'

'No, but I grew to love and respect her, and Dara, please accept this as a fact. We've been happy. Two children and an adorable grandchild.'

'What has the production of children and grandchildren got to do with happiness? I hope you're happy because you like her, because you can talk to her about the world and . . .'

'When I first proposed marriage, she told me there could never be a replacement for you. Her only condition was that if we went abroad she never wanted to be in the same town as you. Never ever. Since you had already found me guilty and executed me for a crime I never committed, I was delighted to agree to her condition. No more was said.'

'Why didn't she ever write and tell me that you were innocent?'

'Now that you're both in the same town, you could ask her.'

'I'm glad Jamshed is dead. I'm glad you've lost all your hair and look really decrepit and aged.'

Zahid burst out laughing. It was spontaneous and unaffected, reminding me of how much we used to laugh when we were young. He looked at me closely.

'Why the hell haven't you changed? Does nothing affect you?'

'I have changed, and in more ways than you think, but some things go far too deep, and however changed the world is, it is criminal to forget what was once possible and will become so again.'

'Always motherfucking politics. What did happen to Tipu?'

'He was arrested, tortured and sent back to Chittagong on the request of his uncle, who was a civil servant. The uncle took full responsibility for him. Tipu stayed in touch. I thought he had died in the civil war of 1971, but he was only wounded. The last time I saw him was at the funeral where he hugged you. He's an arms dealer who uses his Maoist past to pimp for the Chinese. A Parisian wife helps with the French side of the deals.'

A gong, pretentious but effective, was sounded below. We were being summoned for supper. The table was laid out like a work of art. She must have wasted half a day at least.

'I never thought I'd ever cook for you.'

'If it's not good, you never will again.'

But it was good. In fact, it was a convincing repeat of a Yunnanese meal cooked by her mother that I had enjoyed at her family apartment in Lahore all those years ago, the meal that introduced me to proper Chinese cooking, not the muck they served in the two restaurants in town. What a wonderful way Jindié had chosen to revive the most delicious memories from the past, mingling ancient recipes with adolescent love. To start, there were three types of mushrooms, including the most prized: *chi-tʒong*, which when cooked in a particular way tastes like chicken. Then *kan-pa-chun*, or 'dry fungi', stir-fried with red chillies, spring onions and beef fillet, which gave the palate as much pleasure as one's first French kiss. The main course was chicken served in the steam pot in which it cooked, which resembled an espresso coffee pot with a chimney protruding from its middle, seasoned with scented herbs, a great deal of ginger, and more mushrooms. The method produces steamed chicken as soft as marshmallows and the most exquisite chicken soup I have ever tasted. To go with this there were some 'over-the-bridge' rice noodles and *nuo mi*, the sticky rice that is only available in Yunnan and parts of Vietnam. Neither of my hosts could eat the baked green chillies that adorned a single plate put next to me; these, too, I had first tasted at the original banquet in Lahore.

Last, but not least, there was *ru-shan* (dairy fan), another delicacy that sets Yunnan cuisine apart from the cooking of almost all other Han Chinese provinces. This is a cheese-like product, solid, hard, and very thinly sliced into fan-shaped pieces, which are eaten with gooseberry compote and raw mangoes. Since Jindié's stomach, like those of most Han people, is sensitive to all dairy foods, Zahid and I ended up eating too much of it that evening. I declined the *mao tai*, a gruesome spirit whose name when spoken in Punjabi means 'death is near'.

My stomach had been completely won over, but the path to my heart was still blocked by a forest of stinging nettles. In more relaxed mode, I asked after the children and their lives. The son, Suleiman, had tired of making money and turned to Chinese history. He was in love with a Chinese woman and lived in Kunming. No, he was not at all religious and only mildly interested in politics. The daughter, Neelam, was religious, and married to a general in Isloo. Their son would be eleven next year. I smiled, thinking of how desperately Zahid had once been in love with a general's daughter; now his own daughter was wedded to a general.

It was my turn to be questioned, but it was obvious they already knew a great deal, and I sheepishly confirmed much of the information that Jindié had accumulated regarding my life. She even recalled a few episodes that I had totally forgotten. Jindie had kept a strict watch on me even from afar. She asked for details of my life that I had also long forgotten.

'You see', said Zahid, 'we never really lost touch with you even though we could never be in contact for all those years. Jindié's spies reported on your every movement. Once when you came to give a lecture at Georgetown, we sat right at the back in dark glasses and funny hats so you wouldn't recognize us.'

'I wouldn't have recognized you without a hat, you turnip.'

I chattered away in Punjabi, pleased that the thought of Zahid would no longer plunge me into a gloomy reverie tinged with repugnance. The mother tongue encourages imprudence and indiscretions, but both of us were enjoying the reunion. Jindié was silent, even though she was probably more fluent in Punjabi now than Zahid. I thought I detected an anxious look from her at one point, but it soon disappeared. Just as I was about to leave, I realized that we had not yet discussed Plato's plight. Zahid had no idea to whom or why he had got married or whether this, too, was a fantasy. He admitted that he neither liked nor could understand Plato's paintings. Jindié disagreed very strongly and we both united to accuse him of philistinism. I suggested that I. M. Malik's decorative work should be removed to his study or the washroom. He said that he had paid a great deal for the gouaches and asked why I owed Plato a favour in the first place. Jindié could not totally conceal her nervousness at this. I mumbled something about the distant past and fog-bound memory, but promised I would speak with Plato the following day.

The evening had turned out to be surprisingly pleasant. Just before I left, Jindié disappeared briefly, returning with a large packet that obviously contained a manuscript.

'All those years ago you told me I should write the story of my family and the long march that brought us from Yunnan to India. I did, and here it is. At first I thought I was writing it for Neelam, but when she went religious I knew she could never understand her mother. For her, all freedom leads to moral corruption. But I carried on writing. Since it was your idea, I thought I'd give it to you. It's for the grandchildren really. Not to be published, but I would like to know what you think. Sorry it turned out so long.'

I took the manuscript with delight, wondering whether it held up a mirror to the drawing rooms of Lahore. This little butterfly could always sting like a bee. Her waspish descriptions of visits undertaken with her mother to the great houses of the city had always made me laugh.

'Jindié, I'm touched and honoured. If there is anything I can't understand, may I ring you for an explanation?'

Zahid looked at both of us in turn and smiled. 'You're in the same town again. You're always welcome here. And you should know that I was never given a chance to read the manuscript.'

Her eyes flashed. 'You gave up reading a long time ago. Only medical journals and the less demanding airport thrillers. Too wearisome to read proper books. He only bought yours last week.'

'He told me.'

It was time to take my leave. I rose and shook hands with Jindié. The tremor was unmistakable. Zahid walked me to my car.

'Seeing you again was a pleasure.'

This time we embraced warmly, as old friends do. I thought about the evening all the way home and for some days afterwards. It was neither political treachery nor the hard school of misfortune nor my pride and ill humour nor his incessant frivolity that had led to the breach. It was Jindié. Somehow this didn't ring true. I recalled him telling me that he never found her attractive and couldn't understand what I saw in her. He would always insist that my love for her was neither tender nor pure. I'd strongly denied the charge. My love was certainly tender. As for the other, the love that is pure verges on religious ecstasy and worship and that never meant anything to me. It also separates love from passion. The first for the wife, the latter for a courtesan and later a mistress.

True, he had been obsessed with the general's daughter at the time, but how could he have changed his mind about Jindié within a few years? And what had possessed her to marry him? These puzzles remained, but, most importantly, he had not betrayed Tipu. Looking back, it wasn't a surprise that Jamshed was the traitor. His politics and sexuality – ever transient – went in tandem. His charm had once disguised his ambition. He came from a modest Parsi background. All he wanted was to be rich, like the other Parsi businessmen, who had prospered throughout South Asia and especially a great-uncle whose name when pronounced in Punjabi meant testicle. When Jamshed had achieved this aim, the charm disappeared and he became a gangster. His appearance, too, underwent a change. He was bloated and with his awful dark glasses looked like three pimps gone mouldy. Was he paid in cash to betray Tipu? Was that how he had begun his descent to the sewers of big business in Fatherland?

Plato had never trusted him. He would often leave abruptly when Jamshed arrived at the college cafeteria to join our table. The country we grew up in was permanently swathed in cant, and the most tiresome forms of hypocrisy flourished. That was why Plato became so special for us. He urged us to ignore religion, renounce state-sponsored politics, pleasure ourselves in whatever fashion we desired and laugh at officialdom. How in Allah's name had this man become engulfed in an emotional crisis so late in his life?

THREE

Zahid had told him to ring at a decent hour, and when the phone hissed that morning at nine, I knew it must be him.

'Plato?'

'You recognized my voice before I spoke.'

'Are you all right?'

'Never been so happy in my life. I'm not joking.'

'Then why did you swear so much when talking to Zahid?'

'How much time do we have?'

'The morning's free.'

'Then let me start by telling you why I now sometimes use abusive language.'

Slowly, the tale unfolded. Plato was never one for shallow sentimentality and his voice grew harder as he progressed. In brief, Ahmed, a painter friend of his, had abandoned his wife and children for a younger mistress. This was banal and predictable, but he was uneasy and kept returning to the wife and mounting her every Friday afternoon, before having lunch with his boys. One day his wife, Zarina, could take it no longer and lost control. She abused him nonstop: your mother's cunt, sisterfucker, fuck yourself, sodomite, catamite, dogfucker, daughterfucker . . . stay with the camel-cunted bitch you've found and don't come to me again. How long this would have lasted is a matter of speculation. Ahmed covered her face with a pillow and smothered her. Then he wept uncontrollably. The older son rang the police, who took him away.

'I couldn't understand', Plato continued, 'why the use of bad language had led to violence and murder. After all, it was only her way of telling him how angry she was at being abandoned and mistreated. I went to see him a number of times in prison. He was filled with shame and at first did not want to discuss what he had done, but after I pressured him the following explanation emerged. His wife had never used bad language before and had often punished the children when their tongues let slip an obscenity. This is a family that lives in the heart of the old city, where each lane has its own special obscenities. Ahmed told me that the sight of the woman he had chosen to mother his children suddenly transformed by hatred was a blow to his self-esteem, his idea of himself: he had been filled with anger at the thought that he'd married a woman who had turned out to be so vulgar. It was the discovery of this unknown side of her that made him lose control and kill her.'

'Did they hang him?'

'What world do you live in? He was released three months later. His lawyer argued it was an "honour killing", and the judge was paid in advance. Ahmed now lives peacefully with his new wife. The two boys have been sent off to a cadet college and will soon become young army officers. I don't speak to the dog, but occasionally I indulge in obscene language to express my solidarity with his late wife. Do you believe me?'

'No.'

'It's true. Your old friend Zahid loves being abused anyway. Makes him feel he's back home. How was the butterfly?'

'Reserved and dignified as always. More than I can say for you. What do you want of me?'

'Could you write a long essay about me?'

'Your paintings?'

'Yes, but more about my life. She wants it and I can't deny her anything.'

'How old is she?'

'Fifty-two.'

'Not bad. Only twenty-seven years younger than you. I was hoping she might be one of your younger models. When did her husband die?'

'Who told you it was dead? It will never die. It's still alive and present. In fact she keeps it close to her bed.'

'What?'

'Prepare yourself for a surprise, Mr Dara. My Zaynab is married to the Koran.'

'Allah help us.'

'He never does, as we know.'

'So she's the daughter of some Sindhi feudal engaged in sordid calculations about his property.'

Plato was overcome by a fit of bitter laughter. 'Yes, but in her case it was the brother, not the father, who forced her to marry the Holy Book. He must have made a lot of money selling her share of the land. It's not that old age has made him generous. He dropped dead a few years ago. The younger brother adores Zaynab. He bought her an apartment in Clifton overlooking the sea. She wanted to buy one of my paintings. I showed her a selection. She bought them all. Then I did an imagined portrait of her on her wedding night. That made her laugh so much that I fell in love. Can you imagine?'

I could, but Plato still wanted to go through it in great detail and I didn't stop him. I preferred Plato in love to Plato melancholic, filled with whisky-soaked despair and suicidal. He preferred living on the edge and in a way his love for Zaynab fell into that category. For the ignorant she was the equivalent of a Catholic nun, except that she was wed to the Koran, not Jesus. The tradition refused to die out. To become her lover was to defy heaven and become a passionate sinner. I was sure that her marital status was the turn-on. Plato paid no heed to official morality, took great pleasure in defying public opinion and enjoyed startling his conformist contemporaries. His life and his paintings reflected these feelings.

He recounted in some detail how the first meeting had been brief, but profitable. He described her clothes, the colour of her hair underneath the diaphanous *dupatta*. The way her eyes changed colour and so on. She summoned him a week later to explain the allegorical side of his work. Then he asked her to pose for him. She did so fully clothed, but he painted her lying naked in her bed waiting for her Holy Book–husband. He said the picture was inspired by Magritte, but if it were ever shown in public he would be DD'd (disembowelled and decapitated) by some fanatic. I challenged this assertion. Given that the grotesque practice of Koran-marriage was regularly denounced as un-Islamic by every clerical faction in Fatherland and had even united Shia and Wahhabi, surely it was the men in these families who should be DD'd for misusing the Holy Book to safeguard their property.

I thought my logic was impeccable, but Plato ignored me and continued with his story. Zaynab, he said, was not a virgin. I sighed with relief. The advantage of this type of marriage, she had told him, was that there was no need to dissemble. Every pretty woman Zaynab knew in Fatherland had a husband, and quite a few in addition to a husband had a lover as well and, as an extra, another person to keep her from getting too bored during the day. Talk like this had entranced Plato. He was still gripped by madness, torment and joy, the process clinically described by Stendhal in *Love* as 'crystallization'.

'Plato, are you living in her apartment?'

'Why not? She pretends I'm her cook-butler-chauffeur, and whenever her friends or relations visit I act the part, as I once did for you and the Golden Butterfly.'

None of his obsessions with women had ever lasted very long, and I enquired gently how long he gave Zaynab.

'Listen, catamite . . . sorry, that slipped out by mistake. Zaynab will make sure my body is bathed and enshrouded before the burial. I'm too old to move on anywhere now. Will you tell my story and hers?'

'Yes to yours, but I don't know her at all.'

'She's coming to your town next month. You'll meet her.'

'Are you coming, too?'

'How can the cook-chauffeur travel abroad with the lady? Her friends aren't that stupid.'

'That's where you're wrong, Plato. They are stupid. Your photograph has been in *Dawn*. Your paintings have featured on television, and none of them recognized you?'

'Servants are invisible.'

'Till they cut their master's throat.'

We had been speaking for three hours and now at the risk of offending him I said farewell and noted his phone number. Plato's submissive, shy, please-ignore-me-I'm-a-nobody exterior had been carefully cultivated over the years and always worked with those who didn't really know him. It wasn't totally fake, or else he would have promoted his own work more energetically, but when I pushed him on this he would simply reply that if the work was any good it would last and he was not too interested in money. His attempted blackmail of me was crude and ineffective, since Zahid knew the whole story, but it was undoubtedly a sign of Plato's desperation, his fear of dying just as he had met a woman he really liked.

Plato entered our lives almost half a century ago. Zahid and I had left our respective high schools and joined the college in Lahore, where we were blessed with a truly enlightened principal. A biologist by training, he was also a gifted Punjabi scholar and had translated some of our epics into Urdu. They were not quite the same thing in Fatherland's shiny, ornate state language, but he had done them better than anybody else. He had also commissioned a Punjabi translation of Shakespeare. The success of *The Tempest,* staged the previous year, had been helped by the actor playing Caliban, who bore an unnerving resemblance to the military dictator entrusted by Washington to run Fatherland. We had returned to Lahore from the mountains in time for the Punjabi premiere of *Hamlet.* Expectations were high: Ophelia was being played by a very pretty Kashmiri boy called Ashraf Lone, and a number of older students who lusted after him had decided they loved the theatre. *Hamlet* was to be performed in the Open Air Theatre in September, when the heat had abated, the monsoon and accompanying humidity of August had retired for another year and the evenings were pleasant with the scent of jasmine and queen-of-the-night wafted by soft, refreshing breezes across the college lawns to the amphitheatre. The translator was a distinguished Punjabi poet.

A new theatrical production was a big event in the cultural life of the city. The opening night of *Hamlet* was attended by numerous parents and the intellectual elite of Lahore. Those with sensitive posteriors brought their own cushions to place on the circular rows of redbrick seats overlooking the stage. There was a sense of expectation, an evening away from the vulgar interests of everyday life: what could be loftier than Shakespeare translated into the language of our city by one of Fatherland's most respected authors? The latter's arrival at the theatre was greeted with enthusiastic applause.

The play began. All went well till the ghost scene. The actor playing the ghost was a young professor of English, slightly neurotic and very arrogant. He had studied at Edinburgh University and spoke Punjabi with a slight Scottish accent. He had never acted before, but had lobbied force-fully to be part of the play and finally the harassed director had given him the small role of the ghost. When his turn came to speak he was paralyzed with stage fright and forgot his lines. The excessively short senior student playing Hamlet began to panic. The third time he repeated *'Hai, mayray pio da bhooth'* ('Oh, my father's ghost') without eliciting any response from the ghost, an irritated voice from the audience shouted a loud prompt:

'Pidke, bacha apni ma di chooth!' (Runt, save your mother's cunt!)

To say the effect was electric would be an understatement. The actors collapsed before the audience. Hamlet was a giggling wreck. The ghost passed out with shame. The stage lights were turned off and on for at least ten minutes. The sound of laughter drowned all else: as one wave subsided, another rose. The stage management realized the play was over for the night and announced that the critics were welcome on the next day.

Everyone was looking for the Punjabi Freud whose bon mot had made the evening more memorable by wrecking it. The owner of the voice was in his thirties, bespectacled, dressed in *salwar/kurta* and chewing *paan* and had a thick crop of Brylcreemed black hair. He appeared to be on his own. Some members of the audience began to shake his hand and others were pointing appreciatively in his direction, but he seemed determined to get out of the theatre as fast as he could. Zahid and I grabbed him as he was looking for his bicycle in the shed.

'Disappear, boys. I wish I hadn't spoken.'

We invited him to join us the next day for drinks in Respected's juice bar.

'What sort of juice?'

'The most delicious fruit juice in the city.'

He laughed without committing himself. We never expected him to show, but in the meantime news of his witticism had travelled far and wide, from the cafés to the kebab stalls of the city. At college the next day it seemed the only subject of conversation. Students asked each other, 'Were you there?' Zahid and I were much in demand as witnesses, and every time we repeated Plato's words there were gales of admiring laughter. Later the same day, when we repaired to the Coffee House, not far from the college, the poets and critics gathered there had also been discussing the cancelled play and there was an overwhelming curiosity as to the author of the prompt. Why had this young man not been heard of before? Such a natural talent deserved his own special table in the café. Literary veterans racked their brains to think of a precedent as startling as his remarkable intervention. I wondered whether the same discussion was taking place in Cheney's Lunch Home, a five-minute walk away, where aspiring poets mingled with highbrow critics and modernist blank verse was an obsession. At the Coffee House we discussed the poetry of Louis Aragon and Ilya Ehrenburg's novels. The Lunch Home preferred Baudelaire and Gide and regarded Shakespeare as an antique bore, but even they could not avoid a discussion of the Punjabi *Hamlet*.

It was in these cafés that I first began to understand the scale of the trauma that had afflicted Lahore during the Partition of 1947 and transformed this cosmopolitan city into a monocultural metropolis. Names of Sikh and Hindu writers and journalists were recalled with sadness and those present who had witnessed the horrors of what is now referred to as ethnic cleansing would shudder as they remembered those times. Few dwelt on 1947 for long. It was just over a decade ago and the wounds were only too visible. There were more pleasant memories. A club, now sadly defunct, called Metro Fatherland, where in the heady years of the early Fifties young Muslim men and women met, ordered drinks and danced. On his way to this paradise, a writer would suddenly glimpse the veil parting on a burqa-clad woman's face as she bought a piece of fine silk in Anarkali, and describe the vision as celestial light illuminating the Ka'aba. That still happens.

PhD, and, besides, he could educate some of those private school boys in other disciplines, including that of life, with which they were mostly unacquainted.

The same could not be said of Plato. Life had overeducated him and the marks of its lessons were plain to see. He was light-skinned and thick-lipped, with hollow cheeks that gave him an ageless look, and this attractive ugliness was enhanced by thick black hair that he rarely bothered to groom. His Brylcreemed appearance at *Hamlet* had been unusual.

One day he told us how he had escaped from the 1947 pogroms in East Punjab and fled to Lahore. He was in his last year of school when news reached Ludhiana that all of the two hundred or so Muslims in his village, including his parents and three younger sisters, as well as aunts and uncles and cousins, had all been taken to the local mosque and set on fire. There wasn't a single survivor. A kindly Sikh maths teacher who had befriended Plato hugged him and wept. The same man took him to the centre of town where a convoy of buses was being readied to ferry Muslims across to the other side of the partitioned subcontinent. Plato was dazed, unable to register the fact that he had lost everyone. He was put on a bus that contained mainly women and children; his old teacher explained the circumstances and pleaded with a woman to look after his pupil. She did.

'The two buses in front of us were stopped by Sikhs and I saw the men lined up and killed in the most brutal fashion. Some of them were on their knees pleading for mercy, kissing the feet of those about to massacre them. I thought they would kill us too, saving the women to be raped and slaughtered afterwards. But they were interrupted by a military patrol led by British officers. That in itself was rare, but that's how we survived.'

He spoke matter-of-factly, with few traces of outward emotion, but the pain was reflected in his eyes. He went on, 'Then I reached this great city, the Paris of the East, which Punjabis everywhere used to dream of

visiting. He who has not seen Lahore has not seen the world and all that
sentimental nonsense. And here Muslims were hard at work killing Sikhs
and Hindus and looting their property. I was in a refugee camp, and one
of my uniformed protectors, after discovering I had no silver or gold or
any money on me, wanted some kind of reward and decided to rape me.
I was saved by other refugees, who heard my screams and, Allah be praised,
dragged the Muslim policeman off my back. My family had been religious.
I was taken regularly to the mosque, learned the Koran by rote without
understanding a single word, and participated in all the rituals. When I
saw what was being done by all sides in the name of religion I turned my
back on religion forever. '

The table had fallen silent. Respected quietly placed a tray with tumblers
of freshly squeezed orange and pomegranate juice before us. There were
tears in his eyes. In the early Sixties, the trauma of Partition still affected
many in the city, but few wanted to talk about it. The memories were too
recent, and parts of the city still bore the scars. The attempt by the generation before ours to suppress the memory of the killings which they had
participated in or witnessed had left a deep emotional scar, made worse
by never being discussed and dealt with openly. A madness had seized
ordinary people and now they were in denial. When Plato told his story, it
was the first time anyone had discussed Partition at our table. Afterwards
many of us did, and I heard numerous accounts of what had taken place in
the heart of this city during the fateful month of August 1947.

Plato lived in a tiny apartment on the Upper Mall, the main thorough-
fare of the city, past the Government House, the old Nedous hotel and the
canal, in a block of flats known for some reason as Scotch Corner. During
the winter we would often walk up the Mall with him, past the arcades
and the old Gymkhana Club, the school where he taught and the Lahore
Zoo, which housed the most miserable animals I have ever seen. (It was
rumoured that most of the meat rations meant for the lions could be tasted

in the café.) The zoo was a halfway point where we paused to sample that day's *gol gappa* before parting company close to Scotch Corner. Plato never invited us into his quarters, and despite our burning curiosity, we never asked.

Zahid and I talked about him incessantly. A member of our clandestine Marxist cell angered us one day by referring to Plato as a 'petty-bour-geois individualist'. When we told Plato about it he laughed and said the description was accurate. He was never interested in Marxism or the Communist Party and treated them as a form of religion. He had read Marx and admired some of his work, but never admitted it to us, 'because you idiots treat him as if he were a prophet, and if you're going in for that, you might as well stick to the real ones: Moses, Jesus and our very own.'

Discussions became heated when Hanif Ma, a Lahori Chinese studying physics and destined for great things, was accepted at our table as a regular. He was immediately and unimaginatively given the nickname Confucius, which he accepted with good grace but sometimes found irksome. He pretended to be impressed, however: it was sophisticated of us educated Punjabis not to have simply and affectionately addressed him as 'China' as the shopkeepers did in Anarkali bazaar. 'What can we offer you today, China', 'Have some tea, China, while you remember what your mother sent you to buy', etc.

'We are simple rustics, Confucius. Here we wear our arse on our sleeve. And you're a Punjabi just as much as we are, even if you speak a few more languages,' Zahid told him.

Confucius laughed, and we were to discover his stock of bad words had been gleaned on Beadon Road, where gangs of ruffians ruled supreme. I only went there to the sweet shops, to eat *gulab jamuns* and *rasgullas*. Confucius was full of fun, but not unaffected by the great transformation in the country of his forebears, which had also touched many of us. We, too, wanted to make revolution and take the Chinese road. It was difficult to be living in the vicinity and remain unmoved by what was being achieved. Confucius would defend his revolution against all of Plato's taunts. These exchanges gradually weaned us away from Plato, to his great amusement. 'Busy making the revolution, boys?' became one of his more tiresome refrains when Zahid, Confucius and I left the table to attend a cell meeting. Confucius developed a real hatred for him and barely spoke when he was present, even when Plato tried to draw him out on mathematics or physics. Zahid and I could never break with Plato, nor did we want to, even though his cynicism could be extremely corrosive and nerve-racking at times. He had grown so used to being self-reliant that all friendships made him suspicious. It was his intelligence that challenged us all. Even Confucius accepted that this was so.

One year, as the ten-week summer holidays approached, Plato, hearing Zahid and me plotting our exploits, asked casually where we were going. 'The mountains,' I told him, 'Nathiagali for me and Murree for Zahid.' He smiled.

'I might see you there.'

'Wonderful,' said Zahid after a slight hesitation, unsure whether Plato was being ironic. I knew he didn't quite mean it. It was an intrusion. Our summers were very precious. We felt completely free, and even though we were twenty miles apart one of us would often walk over to see the other. We had other friends there too, not part of the table, summer friends whom we met only once a year. These friendships often became intense, since there were few restrictions in the mountains and gender segregation was frowned upon.

The thought of Plato being there did strike me as a bit odd. He was part of our grown-up side. The mountain air had a regressive effect on us. We were children again, but children filled with lustful thoughts. Plato, ultra-sensitive to any slight, intended or real, looked in my direction. He must have caught the ambiguous note in Zahid's response.

'And you, Dara Shikoh. Do you think it's wonderful news as well?'

'Not sure, Plato. Depends on how you behave during picnics. Can you play an instrument? Can you sing or act? This will be your real test. I always know you're slightly tense when you call me Dara Shikoh.'

He immediately relaxed.

'Don't worry. I won't disgrace you boys. And Dara Shikoh is the only Mughal prince I really admire. Akbar was a total fake. Broadminded as far as other faiths were concerned, but a killer of those he regarded as heretics.'

In fact, my nickname was my own fault. I had misinformed many a friend that I was named after Dara Shikoh, a sceptic poet and philosopher who should have succeeded Shah Jehan but was brutally brushed aside by a younger brother, Aurungzab, the devout ruler and ascetic who left us the Badshahi mosque, a ten-minute walk from the college, as his legacy. I was actually named after an old friend of my father's who had tragically drowned while both of them were swimming from one bank of the Ravi to another in the moonlight. Perhaps he had been named after Dara Shikoh.

Before we left for the mountains, Confucius invited Zahid and me to supper at his house. Neither of us knew where he lived, but he had eaten with us at home many a time and his mother must have insisted he invite us in return.

'Please remember not to call me Confucius at home. Won't amuse anyone. They'll just think indigenous Punjabis are stupid.'

'What about Mao?'

'Even worse. My father thinks of him as a bad poet and a philistine.'

All we knew about Confucius's father was that he owned the best shoe shop on the Mall. The family had obviously been there for a long time, as testified by the photographs on the wall in which young Mr Ma posed proudly with long-departed British colonial officers. My father and I went there each year to have our feet measured for summer sandals and winter shoes. Nothing ever substituted for that in later years.

Confucius had agreed to meet us outside the shop, but we waited a while for another guest. He finally arrived. His bike had suffered a puncture and the usual repair stall was not open. This was Tipu, studying physics at F.C. (Forman Christian) College, run by US missionaries on the other side of the city. Tipu had a soft, dark face and large brown eyes. Confucius had met him at a seminar, discovered he was a Marxist from Chittagong in East Fatherland, and wanted him invited to our cell meetings. Our rules were strict. A cell could not include more than six students at a time and none of the members was meant to know about the other cells. We did, of course, since there were only two others, but we pretended it was a huge secret. It added to the glamour. There were no existing cells at Tipu's college. He was contemptuous of his fellow students and his eyes blazed as he informed us that no self-respecting college in East Fatherland was without its Communist cells. I did know of one cell in F.C., but it would have been a terrible breach of confidence to inform him of its existence. I made a mental note to let them know of his.

This conversation was taking place on the Mall, in the middle of a crowd of shoppers. We could have gone on for hours, but were late already. Confucius took us across the road to an old nineteen-twenties apartment block, where he lived and where his mother was patiently waiting to feed us.

'Salaamaleikum, Dara. How's your father?'

I didn't recognize the shoemaker for a minute. Confucius's father was dressed in a Chinese gown and a finely embroidered skullcap. We were introduced to the rest of his family, and that was the first time Zahid and I saw Jindié, the Golden Butterfly. She stood next to her mother, wearing a traditional but stylish Punjabi *salwar/kameez* light blue suit, with the *kameez* just touching her knees. Her silken black hair, covering a head that was an elongated oval, almost touched the floor. The eyebrows formed perfect arches. No makeup disfigured her thin lips. She was a delicate creature, extremely beautiful rather than pretty, but there was not a trace of shyness or affectation as she shook hands, inspecting each of us in turn with a quizzical, semi-humorous look. I never suspected she was a romantic eager for quick results. I found it difficult to concentrate on too much else that evening. What had Confucius said about us? Did she realize I had fallen in love with her? How could she not? It had to be a mandate from heaven.

After greeting Jindié, I bowed politely to Confucius's mother. Like her husband, Mrs Ma was dressed in an antique Chinese gown. Her hair was pinned up in a bun and her face showed a touch of lipstick and powder, but at the same time conveyed an impression of prudence and good sense.

I was so thunderstruck by Jindié that it took me some time to notice that the living room was lined with books, mainly Chinese editions, some of which were undoubtedly very old. Jindié was talking to Tipu, quite deliberately, I think, to punish me for the way I had looked at her. In fact, she ignored me for the rest of the evening, speaking mainly to Tipu and Zahid but occasionally glancing in my direction to see how I was occupying myself. I moved away to look closely at some beautiful ivory objects on the mantelpiece and then the silks that covered the walls, on which hung a plain white plate with blue Kufic calligraphy. Mr Ma sidled up to explain that it was a ninth-century piece made by potters in Yunnan, who produced such ware exclusively for the merchants in Basra, who brought it to Cordoba and Palermo. None of this meant much to me at the time. I smiled politely and asked about the books. He took one out. It looked exquisite, faded gold Chinese calligraphy on even more faded thick leather.

'What is it, Mr Ma?'

'The Han Kitab. You have heard of it?'

'No. I'm sorry. China is a mystery. All we know about is the revolution.'

That annoyed him and he returned the book to its place. Confucius had observed the scene and came up to reassure me. I wasn't bothered at all, but was becoming more and more enraged by the way his sister was flirting with Tipu.

The food, when it was served, was almost as divine as Jindié. The local Chinese restaurants were truly awful, catering to imagined local tastes. Pulp-food is always bad. This was the first time I had tasted proper Chinese food, and I complimented Mrs Ma on the quality of her cooking, the virtual opposite of our Punjabi cuisine. She explained that what we were consuming were Yunnanese delicacies, very different from what was served at banquets in Beijing. I asked if she had received any help from her daughter. The reply was an instantaneous *no* and a glare in Jindié's direction. In a bid to attract the latter's attention, I sympathized loudly, hoping to annoy her and failing miserably. She ignored the bait.

I did discover from her mother, however, that Jindié attended a women's college. This was useful information, since the college in question was packed with seven or eight of my cousins as well as daughters of old family friends. It was presided over by a strict Indian-Christian spinster lady who took her job as principal far too seriously when it came to the social life of her students. To say she kept a watchful eye on her girls would be inaccurate. She had created a spy network of favourites who told her everything. Yes, everything, including the dreams that some of their fellow students recounted over breakfast. The college itself had been set up in 1920 by a prim Scotswoman called Rosamund Nairn and bore her surname. The girls at Nairn were considered to be almost as modern as their counterparts at Primrose in Karachi and Ambleside in Dhaka, and that was saying a great deal at the time.

Apart from my frustration over Jindié, the evening went well. Zahid and I both made sure we called our friend Hanif as often as we could— so often that he began to look annoyed. At this point Jindié addressed us collectively:

'Is it true that you call him Confucius?'

The whole table erupted in laughter. It was only as we were all leaving and farewells were being said that she walked up to me.

'It was really nice talking to you.'

'But you didn't.'

'I know.'

Since my house was not too far from F.C. College, Zahid gave both me and Tipu a lift, dropping Tipu off first so the two of us could have a calm post-mortem. We stopped the car on the unfinished road outside my house. It was a wilderness then, with the only the mausoleum of a Sufi venerable lit in the distance with oil lamps.

I had liked Tipu instinctively and was determined that he should join our cell even if it meant biking six miles to where we were. He was obviously bright, and better read than all of us. Zahid disagreed and thought it would be better if Tipu were recruited to his local cell. But I wanted to keep an eye on him, in case Jindié really did want him and not me. I explained this to Zahid, who wasn't surprised in the least.

'I noticed your gaze', said Zahid, 'and so did she.'

'Are you sure she did?'

'How could she not, catamite? You were staring at her quite obviously. Everyone noticed. That's why she ignored you the whole evening.'

There was little else to discuss, but we did so anyway for almost two hours. Then I went home and searched my father's study for translations of Chinese literature and history. The shelves were packed with Europe and South Asia. Chinese civilization was represented by political and history books written by Americans and Europeans, and a few translations of Mao Zedong and Liu Shaoxi. There was a Foreign Languages Publishing House translation of *Dream of the Red Chamber*, but it was unreadable. Deeply frustrated, I went to bed.

Almost everything lost its importance for me except the memory of

Jindié. In the two weeks before the colleges shut down I made desperate efforts to catch sight of her. Zahid had his own problems on this front, trying to see Anjum, the general's daughter, but was as helpful as he could be, waiting with me outside Nairn to discover how Jindié went home. Many young women biked in those days, and I was hoping she was one of them, but we never saw her leave. I pestered one of the cousins I thought I could trust. She told the others and they would come to stare and giggle at Zahid and me, trying to shame us into leaving. But we had no self-esteem in these matters, and so forfeiting our dignity never posed a problem.

After an hour outside Nairn, we would move on to Gulberg, where the object of Zahid's love went to a ladies' college modelled on European finishing schools, where 'home and social sciences' were so mixed up that cooking counted as a home subject and interior decoration as a social science. Gulberg trained young women to be housewives. *Vogue* was the sacred magazine of this establishment, devoured eagerly by teacher and pupil. Zahid swore that Anjum was not empty-headed but had been forced to go there by her parents in order to prepare for marriage.

Zahid wanted the general's daughter and she wanted him. Letters had been exchanged. They met for coffee in a tiny place run by a kindly old German lady and geared for trysts. It worked like this: Anjum and a girlfriend would be dropped off by the chauffeur; they would get a table. Zahid and I would arrive on his Vespa; we'd get another table. If we recognized anybody, we would maintain the pretence that we were there casually, and move off quickly, but this was rare. I had to entertain Anjum's friend, who was very pretty and very stupid. She would giggle at the slightest provocation, and I got so fed up that I tried to teach her chess so we didn't have to speak to each other. She was flattered and learned the moves, which enhanced her status at the finishing school: 'My, my, you've become such an intellectual.'

Occasionally, vile scoundrels on a motorbike followed the girls and blackmailed them for petty cash, but this stopped when the German lady informed her husband, who turned out to be a senior police officer and put a cop on guard duty in that street. He was merely protecting his wife's business interests, but the gesture was greatly appreciated by her customers.

Mercifully, all this came to an end when Anjum gently broke the news that she was to be engaged to an affected English-public-school-educated feudal idiot from Multan. Zahid's features assumed a deathly pallor as he rose from her table and staggered over to mine. Speech eluded him for a moment and then in a choked voice he said, 'Let's go. Now.'

We left. The soul had been torn out of him. Too many hours were wasted discussing the rejection. The day after, he told me quite seriously that he was having great difficulty in resisting the temptation to blow out his brains. A week later, he was calmer and more reflective.

'She had such a gentle nature, *yaar*,' he would repeat time and time again.

Perhaps that was the problem, I suggested. Her 'gentle nature' prevented her resisting parental pressures as others, we both knew, had done. His heart was sickened by the ease with which her parents had triumphed. I felt a sense of relief. No more playing chess with an aspiring fashion model. I can't remember her name, but she was modelling two outfits, 'Naughty Nymph' and 'Hello, Officer', in the Intercontinental in Rawalpindi when the student insurrection against the military began in 1968. As for my friend, he took to wandering about town, full of emotions but avoiding every location that reminded him of her. It seemed as if the entire city had become a sea of bitterness for him. The memory of Anjum haunted him for a long time. The worst possible passion is the passion for a woman one has never possessed. He recovered slowly.

'There are other sorrows in the world, Zahid,' I said comfortingly, para-phrasing the words of a much-loved poet, then in prison for the third time.

'No, there aren't.'

This should have alerted me. I should have realized that political commitment of any sort was nothing more than a social obligation for him, but it's easy to say this with hindsight. At the time we all thought of ourselves and of university students in general as the backbone of the country. Its future depended on us, but in the words of the real Confucius, 'To lead into battle a people that has not first been instructed is to betray them.' Zahid insisted that the facts proved otherwise and would counter this with the examples of the French and Russian revolutions. He often inclined to more radical solutions than I did and sometimes mocked my caution. Friendship, too, has its illusions, just as strong as those of love.

Three days before we were due to leave for the mountains, our Confucius dropped by for lunch. My mother liked him because he had a pleasing face, was ultra-polite and always made a point of praising the décor of the house and, even more importantly, admiring her rose garden, which was usually ignored by visitors and by us. My father was impressed by his strong support for the Chinese Revolution, not common then in émigré circles. I felt closer to him for obvious reasons. Nevertheless the conversation seemed excessively stilted till my parents left for their siesta. It was late June. The temperature had reached 108 degrees Fahrenheit and the tar on the roads was beginning to melt. I was racking my brains to find a way of asking after Jindié without appearing too eager, but discretion prevailed. He was her brother, after all, and might be offended by an informal display of interest. Then, just before he left, Confucius, trying to sound as casual as possible, said, 'By the way, we might see you in Nathiagali. My mother is desperate to avoid the heat this year, and we've booked a cottage in Pines Hotel for a month.'

I managed to conceal my joy.

'With all of us leaving, the city of culture will be empty.'

We laughed at our own arrogance.

FOUR

In the early days, my father would drive us there, spend a week, and then return to Lahore. The mountain routine in our household was well established. The servants would wake us up at three in the morning, when it was still pitch dark outside. My twin sisters, three years younger, and I would be placed half-asleep in the back of a ramshackle Chevrolet station wagon and by four at the latest my father would be driving northwards on the Grand Trunk Road, which had barely any other traffic at that hour. This was the reason for the pre-dawn departures, which felt like torture at the time. My sisters and I would wake again when the sun rose and wait for the inevitable stop at Wazirabad Junction Railway Station, where they served excellent scrambled eggs on toast, brewed a fine pot of tea and had relatively clean toilets. That was a very long time ago. Soon afterwards we would cross the mighty Jhelum and once again hear the story of how Alexander the Great had found the river too difficult to ford and almost lost his life. We came to know this tale so well that in the years ahead we would repeat it in unison as we approached the bridge, to pre-empt the parental version. The next stop was Rawalpindi, a brief halt to pick up chicken sandwiches and chilled coffee at the Silver Grill before the final stretch, which began on the tarmac road to Murree, the official hill station which my mother loathed because it was not Simla and was overcrowded with the 'wrong sort' of people – not counting Zahid and his family, of course, and the many other friends who spent the summers there. In my mother's imagination Murree was Babylon, to be avoided even as a stopover on the way to our Arcadia.

Beyond Murree lay the rough road to the *galis*, the valleys between the Himalayan foothills, clothed in pines; soon after leaving the hill station the fragrance of these trees became overpowering. More than a hundred years ago, the British had come to the *galis* and built hill-cottages with quaint names like Kirkstone, Moonrising, Retreat, etc., to remind them of home. First we passed Khairagali, then Changlagali, then Doongagali, and on a ridge two miles above that lay Nathia, the queen of them all, with its own club and tennis courts and, most importantly, a library filled with books, mainly by authors one had never heard of before or never would again: the literary equivalent of B-movies and sometimes startlingly good.

Heaven in those days was arriving here, inhaling the scent of wild strawberries, sighting the snow-covered peak of Nanga Parbat in the Himalayan distance and wondering which of our summer friends had arrived.

This year, all I could think about was Jindié. When was she arriving? What day? What hour? I have scant memories of that time now, a time of unrequited passions that seemed to be the fate of our generation. To write the life of Plato I have to work hard to collect myself and remember what else happened that summer. It's easier now, since my memories of Jindié have faded.

When we reached our summer house, the caretaker delivered a number of messages and handed me a scrap of paper. None of the messages were of any significance. Summer friends from Peshawar had already arrived, including two demon tennis players, Pashtun brothers, witty and easy mannered, who usually pulverized their opponents. Zahid and I had beaten them once and that was only because we could see better in the mist that enveloped the court. The note was from Younis, the jolly sub-postmaster who presided over the tiny post office in summer and stayed in the rest house below the bazaar. He wondered when we could meet for a cup of tea. The next day friends from Lahore and Karachi arrived as well. We met and exchanged pleasantries, but my thoughts were elsewhere.

My friends noticed how distracted I had become and assumed that as I was due to leave the country later that year, my mind had already departed and I found their company tiresome. How could I tell them all that I was suffering from love fever? There were also two young women present who were great fun because they never relapsed into coquetry and loathed bourgeois pettinesses and whose company, for those reasons, I enjoyed a great deal. I could only imagine their scathing comments if I admitted to anything that remotely resembled serious passion.

I walked alone to the Pines Hotel and exchanged greetings with the proprietor and staff. Soon after Partition, in 1947, when I was three and my sisters had not yet been born, we began staying at the Pines, and the proprietor, Zaman Khan, a tall, pot-bellied Pashtun with permanently bloodshot grey eyes – the result of an overfondness for the beer produced at the Murree Brewery by one of Jamshed's more prosperous relatives – had become a familiar and friendly figure over the years. There was little that escaped him. He gave me a hug and immediately offered some information.

'That green-eyed girl from Peshawar whom you liked so much last year is arriving next week with her mother.'

I feigned delight and then said in a casual tone, 'A friend of mine,

Hanif Ma, told me he was coming this year. They're a Chinese family from Lahore.'

Zaman grabbed me by the arm and took me to his office. Together we looked at the reservations register. The Mas were due in two days.

'I didn't know you were friends. I'll put them in the cottage where you stayed ten years ago. So I'll be seeing more of you this year. Good. You know you can always eat here.'

'Yes, but not in your dining room where you still serve those disgusting stews the English used to like.'

He pinched me and laughed. Thrilled by the news and on a high I walked down to the bazaar and met old friends, bought an off-white Chitrali hat and warmed my hands on a cup of delicious, if oversweet, mountain tea, a concoction made by boiling tea leaves in milk and sugar till the colour is exactly right. One of the most warming drinks in the world. When I walked into the post office, situated above a sloping ravine leading to the deep-valley villages below, where the local people lived throughout the year, I got a shock. Seated next to Younis the sub-postmaster was Plato. I'd completely forgotten that he was coming here this summer.

'You didn't know that we were old friends, did you?' asked Younis. Younis and his mother had been in the same bus that took the refugees from Ludhiana and it was she who had looked after Plato till they reached the camp. Younis's father, a night watchman working for a Hindu-owned factory in Ludhiana, had never been seen again. They had family in Peshawar, and Younis had matriculated and become a Grade 6 civil servant.

'Grade 6', said Plato, 'is recognition that you will never rise in the service. Sub-postmaster for life.'

Younis roared with laughter. 'Better than a peon. I just hope I can spend all my summers here till I die.'

It was barely noon. Younis offered me some locally fermented apricot liquor in my tea. I declined the pleasure, but both of them poured generous helpings into their own bowls. Some friends arrived to post letters and joined us for a while, till their sisters and mothers waiting outside shouted at them. Once they had left, Younis whispered, 'I hear from Bostaan Khan that the girl from Peshawar will be here next week.'

Bostaan was an old waiter at the Pines, and a cardsharp. Why had they been gossiping about her?

'Because of you.'

The previous summer I had made a fool of myself with Greeneyes and she had enjoyed snubbing me in public. One day I noticed her in a corner of the club avidly devouring a letter, obviously a billet-doux. Her white face turned deep red when she saw me.

'Who is the lucky boy?'

'None of your business.'

But it was. I'd approached Younis, who, as usual, was slightly tipsy. He had become a friend and regaled Zahid and me with stories of ever-so-respectable families being torn asunder by news of constant intrigues and infidelities. How did he know? He read their letters, of course, steaming them open at will and resealing them carefully before delivery. He swore that he only targeted the most snobbish families, the ones who looked down on him and treated him as a serf. I did think of asking him to open the exchange between my parents just to read what they were writing about me, but decided against it on the grounds that there might some embarrassing declarations of love and loyalty. In general it would be accurate to say that what Younis knew, we knew. Today he would be called a hacker and secretly admired, but at the time it was considered quite scandalous and had we spread the word he would have lost his job. Even Zahid, usually immune to ethics, was slightly shocked. We never did betray him. How could we? We were heavily implicated. So Younis was now told what was needed.

There were no photocopiers then. Every time Lailuma, the golden-haired, green-eyed Pashtun beauty – her name meant Moonlit Night – received or posted a letter, a messenger from Younis, usually the local postman, would rush over to wherever I was and drag me to the post office saying there was an urgent phone call from Zahid in Murree. There were few phones in those days and Zahid often rang. Though the telephone engineer at the exchange often let me use his phone in emergencies and took messages, the only public phone was located in the veranda of the post office.

In a small back room, I read Lailuma's letters to her lover regularly and dispassionately. They touched me and were, in any case, far more endearing than her lover's ultra-emotional, overbearing and permanently embittered tone. She was the constant butt of his irony, but for no reason. He was the type who makes me feel that some of us have more in common with apes than with other men. I gave up all hope. She was obviously in love with this stupid beast. The letters revealed how strongly her parents disapproved of the match. I agreed with their instincts if not their reasoning. The young man came from the wrong social class: his father was a shawl-trader with a stall in the Kissakhani bazaar. Despite my strong interest in her, I would have been on the man's side in this whole affair had his character been even marginally more attractive. Either he couldn't express himself properly or he really was obnoxious. After a rambling discussion fuelled by many cups of apricot liquor–laced tea, Younis, Zahid and I agreed that the match should be discouraged.

A few days before Lailuma left Nathiagali, I found her on her own, seated underneath a chestnut tree not far from Pines Hotel. I hinted that a friend of mine in Peshawar had informed me of her dilemma. She was stunned.

'I don't believe you.'

I then revealed her would-be-lover's name and his father's occupation. She nearly fainted.

'Allah help me.'

'He won't, but I will.'

'You!'

I calmed her down first and promised that her secret was safely buried in my heart. However, according to my friend who knew her beloved well, it was obvious that he was prone to fits of uncontrollable ill temper and was boorish in other ways too. Was it true, I asked, that his tenderness alternated with fury? If so, his jealous temperament would create insurmountable problems and for no reason at all. If he even saw her talking to a girlfriend he didn't know, he would lose control. I carried on in this way, describing the worst characteristics of many of my acquaintances. To my astonishment, her startled eyes fixed their gaze on mine and she nodded strongly in agreement.

'Your friend must know him really well. I'm beginning to think exactly the same. I was thinking of breaking off all contact with him, but I delayed writing the letter. I really don't want him to think my parents have anything to do with it. They're just stupid. Just because his father sells shawls and furs.'

'That alone would be reason to wed the boy', I said, 'especially if the father has a treasure trove of old pashminas and shahtoosh.'

For the first time ever, she laughed. My heart missed a few beats. There is an awful Punjabi saying that attaches great importance to laughter as an adjunct of sexual conquest, *'hasi te phasi'* (if she laughs, you've trapped her). It was not true, but for once I did believe I had improved my chances. Younis, too, was convinced that this was the case.

'I know these Pashtun girls. They're much more advanced than your Punjabi beauties. Make your move, my friend. Cement the Punjabi–Pashtun alliance. Give Fatherland something to be proud of.'

But it was too late to make any further moves that summer. She left a few days later, after we'd exchanged English novels. I had suggested she send the break-off letter from here so that she could start a new chapter in her life when she reached Peshawar and not be bothered by him. She thought this was a good idea. Younis and I both agreed that the letter was beautifully written, extremely dignified and far too generous. She went up even more in my estimation.

It would have been disloyal if I had kept Plato and Younis in the dark about Jindié, and in Zahid's absence I needed to talk about her with someone. I told them. Plato was philosophical.

'These things happen. You just need a tiny bit of hope for love to be born. Has she given you cause for hope?'

'Not sure.'

'Then you think she has. Well, we're all here to help.'

Younis was disappointed. 'I was imagining you with the moonlit Lailuma, but Allah decides. There is no reason to seal off that option. Am I to open all the letters addressed to the Chinese lady?'

'No,' I said, mortified by what Jindié might think if she ever found out. 'Let's wait.'

I had sprained my ankle while playing tennis and was incapacitated the day they arrived, but ordered a horse and rode over to the Pines the next day to pay my respects and drag Confucius to the old club. When Jindié saw me being helped down from the horse she burst out laughing, stopping only when she noticed that I was limping with the help of a stick.

'I'm sorry, but I just never imagined you on horseback. You're hurt?' I explained. Confucius had gone in search of me. How we missed each other I don't know, but Mrs Ma ordered some tea and Bostaan duly arrived with a tray and some truly terrible cucumber sandwiches made with stale bread, lightly soaked in water to make it appear fresh. He gave me a knowing smile, which could only mean that Younis had alerted him to my state of mind.

I warned Jindié and her mother against eating too often in the hotel and told Bostaan to offer the sandwiches to my horse, which he promptly did, only to have them rejected by the animal. This caused general merriment and a cheerful Mrs Ma went indoors to unpack.

'It's really beautiful here. You've been here every summer since you were two?'

I nodded, trying not to look at her too openly. She was wearing a blouse over a pair of black trousers and her hair was in a bun held together by ivory clips.

'My foot is on the mend and in a few days I'll be walking again. We're all going up that mountain. Mukshpuri. A path leads to it from the other side of this hotel. The grown-ups usually stop halfway up, at Lalazar, where everyone eats lunch after we kids have returned from the summit.'

'And after lunch?'

'We pick daisies, sing, listen to Zahid play the accordion, tell stories and then come down and light a fire.'

'Where will you light the fire?'

Before I could control myself the words slipped out. 'In your heart.' She became agitated and stood up as if to leave. I was spared the agony of her departure by the appearance of an out-of-breath Confucius.

'One more thing, Jindié,' I said, wanting to make up for my mistake. 'You must walk a lot over the next few days to acclimatize. Otherwise your legs will be stiff after we climb the mountain.'

'I suppose your legs are never stiff.'

'Only because I walk several miles a day.'

'On horseback?' She laughed again and disappeared. I sighed with relief. I took Confucius to the bazaar and introduced him to Younis. Later that day Zahid arrived to stay with me for a few days and prepare for the Mukshpuri climb. In the evening I hobbled with him to the club. While everyone was playing tennis and ping-pong, I retired to the library and relieved the volunteer librarian for a few hours. Jindié came in to look at the books and said, 'Colonial rubbish.'

I had no idea she was that way inclined and was quite delighted, but felt the library had to be defended.

'The best books have been stolen. Only the rubbish is left, but there are a few others. Pearl S. Buck is quite readable.'

'What? Are you mad or just stupid? Every literate Chinese laughs at her.'

'Could that be because she describes the lowest depths of Chinese society and some literate Chinese find that embarrassing? I have to admit I learned a great deal from her books.'

'That's only because you're ignorant and know nothing about China.'

'True. One has to start somewhere. She got the Nobel Prize for no reason?'

'Those idiots in Stockholm were ignorant, just like you. They were taken in by missionary sensitivities. Have you read *The Dream of the Red Chamber*?'

'I tried, but the official translation is unreadable. Is it available in English?'

'How do I know? My father is the expert on all this and will also know the best translation.'

'In Punjabi, I hope. Confucius is a true Punjabi. He has assimilated every Lahori prejudice, including that profound malice against the cultured refugees who crossed the Jumna and found themselves in an illiterate hell.'

She laughed and lit the room, just as a whole gang of kids arrived to borrow books, disturbing our very first conversation. The day we climbed the mountain, Jindié, forgetful of her customary reserve, suddenly took my arm – a *coup de foudre* if ever there was one – and as some of the party looked askance, she pretended she had slipped. The gesture, however, had been noticed, and knowing looks were exchanged. Strange how the exchangers of knowing looks never realize that one can see them.

Lailuma arrived the following day, together with her extended family, and instantly became part of our crowd. She was in remarkably good spirits, understood perfectly that Jindié and I had become close and played the part of chaperone to perfection. She was now engaged to a lawyer she liked and thanked me again in Jindié's presence for all my help last year. Strange, I thought to myself, how my desire for her had disappeared so completely. Love of the sort I felt for the Butterfly had a side effect, in the shape of what can only be the drollest of virtues: chastity.

Once we were alone, Jindié wanted to know the whole truth. Instinctively she had guessed that my motives in helping the Peshawari princess had not been totally pure. I told her the truth, concealing nothing, but made her pledge she would never reveal the sub-postmaster's role. She agreed, but let me know that she thought what we did was despicable.

'The end justifies the means.'

'Have you instructed him to open my mail as well?'

'Not yet.'

'If you do I'll never speak to you again.'

'If I did, you'd never know.'

'I would. I know your type better than you think. Spoilt Punjabi boys who think there are no rules in society. Anyway, most of the letters I get are from friends or my father, and they all write in Mandarin, so neither you nor that creepy postmaster would ever be able to read them.'

'Creepy sub-postmaster, you mean.' Jindié hit me on the arm with a clenched fist. 'Would you like to know what some of our acquaintances are writing home about you and me?'

'What do you mean?'

'What I said.'

'Have you read anything?'

'A detailed letter from that buck-toothed girl you really like because she constantly flatters you. She wrote about us to her best friend in Multan. It's ugly. Guess what. A new romance is brewing in the hills, like mountain chai. You'll never believe it. Dara and Jindié, that Chinese girl who's at college with me. They're so shameless. They can barely keep their hands off each other. They watch each other all the time.'

Jindié laughed. 'You are evil, but I'm warning you . . .'

'Why should I want to read your letters?'

'Curiosity. Jealousy. Possessiveness. Imbecility. All the Punjabi virtues. Your choice as to which applies best to you.'

'I won't read your letters, but get a sense of proportion. What you call Punjabi virtues are really universal. We're just more open. Less subtle, but also less hypocritical.'

She smiled and I wanted to kiss her lips, but was too scared to do so because of the proximity of Mrs Ma, who now called for her daughter to come indoors. Had the old lady been eavesdropping as she watched the sun set from the cottage window?

When I reported this conversation to Plato and Zahid, they both agreed that there was little doubt that she loved me, and we discussed how to move forward. Zahid argued in favour of proposing marriage, but this was foolish since I had promised my parents I'd go study law in Britain. It was too early for any talk of marriage, and I dreaded the thought of saying anything to my mother, in many ways a deeply conservative person with fixed ideas on these matters. Plato advised a long engagement that would signify commitment and, no doubt, Jindié could also go abroad. The final decision could be left till later. A long engagement wasn't appealing, but it made sense. The three of us agreed that this was what should be done once the summer was over. Before proceeding, I had to make sure that Jindié was in favour of this solution.

That last summer in Nathiagali was dominated by a process that I have already referred to earlier in connection with someone else, the process a lovelorn Stendhal described as crystallization in his compendium *Love*:

> At the salt mines of Salzburg, they throw a leafless wintry bough into one of the abandoned workings. Two or three months later they haul it out covered with a shining deposit of crystals. The smallest twig, no bigger than a tomtit's claw, is studded with a galaxy of scintillating diamonds. The original branch is no longer recognizable.
>
> What I have called crystallization is a mental process which draws from everything that happens new proofs of the perfection of the loved one . . . one of your friends goes hunting, and breaks his arm: wouldn't it be wonderful to be looked after by the woman you love! To be with her all the time and to see her loving you . . . a broken arm would be heaven . . .

Admittedly my sprained ankle and ride to her front door had produced different results, but the thought behind it, on my part, had been the same. All of my thoughts that summer were a maturation of the crystallization process. One evening, all of us young people were invited to dinner in Kalabagh, an Air Force recreation centre a few miles away from Nathia. Our hosts were two Pashtun friends, Lailuma's cousins, whose father was a senior Air Force officer. It was an idyllic evening. The sky was beautiful, but it was getting chilly and we draped ourselves in shawls. Lailuma greeted us on arrival and I told her we were wearing the shawls to mark her escape from the shawl merchant's son. She ignored me for the rest of the evening.

We carried torches for the return journey. I have no memory of anything else that happened that evening except the fact that Jindié and I abandoned all pretence. We walked next to each other. We talked only to one another and on the way back we took advantage of the dark and held hands. Lailuma came close to us and whispered, 'Be careful', but we were beyond caution and asked her to walk with us. The full moon was waning, but when we reached the old church in Nathia we could still see its light illuminating Nanga Parbat, the third-highest peak in the Himalayas. There were two or three special places where that peak could be observed, and so our party split up: Jindié, Lailuma and I went to the observation spot behind the lightning-scarred church. The others disappeared elsewhere.

'Jindié.'

'I know.'

We embraced each other, and I stroked her cheeks, but nothing more. We declared our love and I suggested we immediately get engaged to prevent our respective parents from thinking about other alternatives. She held me tight, kissed my eyes. We were surprised by our audacity and laughed about it at the time. Before we could continue the discussion, we heard Lailuma shouting our names as a warning. We walked away and joined her and the rest. Neither of us spoke till we reached the Pines Hotel. Then Zahid and I walked back another mile to my house and I told him. There was another member of our party that evening: Jamshed had arrived to stay with a cousin in Doongagali, but given his weak, cowardly and contemptible character, I'm trying to avoid mention of him as much as I can in this account. Plato despised him and I never told him about Jindié, though he probably found out, since it was hardly a secret anymore.

◖◗

Three days before Jindié was due to leave she agreed to a tryst in the church. I knew where the key was kept, and in the past we had often used it as place to rendezvous. The days when a priest would come from Peshawar for Sunday prayers had ended in the Fifties. The building was in a state of disrepair and often leaked when the rain was heavy. Then Jindié decided that she did not want to meet there. When I asked why, she said it made her feel like a character in a Pearl S. Buck novel. I never let her forget that remark, but her rejection of the church meant a long trek with Lailuma, who was perfectly willing to walk behind us or in front at a suitable distance. She collected Jindié. I met them at the empty Government House. I had gone hunting once with the caretaker and now he let us in with a huge welcome. We walked out the back through its lush gardens and entered a path that led to Miran Jani, the highest mountain in Nathia. We found a beautiful meadow and sat on the grass while Lailuma opened a book and tried to ignore us for the next two hours. Jindié spoke first, and her voice was tremulous with emotion.

'I've decided. I don't want to get engaged to you.'

I seized her hand and kissed it. 'Why? Why?'

'It's wrong for us to behave in such a traditional way. My mother says if we love each other we can do what we want. I could go to Leeds University and enrol in the Chinese department and we could see each other every weekend. And if we wanted to, we could get married. Or not? It's for us to decide. Nobody else.'

I was in heaven. I put my head on her lap and after a while she began to stroke my hair. 'It's done,' I said. 'That's what we'll do. I'm glad you've told your mother. I'll tell mine.'

'No need to if you don't want to,' she replied. 'Confucius said your mother was very beautiful and open-minded in some ways but also very traditional and conservative in others. She may not like her son marrying a Chinese cobbler's daughter.'

I hugged her and kissed her head and hands and cheeks. 'Jindié, my mother is traditional, but she married my father against her own father's wishes. They were from the same family, but my father had become a Communist and . . .'

'The whole of Lahore knows the story, Dara, but that doesn't stop people behaving differently when their own children are involved in something of which they disapprove.'

We carried on talking all the way back. Lailuma told me she agreed with Jindié. No confessions in Lahore whatsoever. In Britain we could do as we wished. Later Plato and Zahid strongly agreed as well.

'You know how headstrong your mother is,' said Zahid. 'Don't say a word. I hope you haven't kept a diary.'

'I have, but it's permanently locked and only I know where it's kept.'

'Don't be foolish. She'll have it opened and resealed or relocked. Don't underestimate Punjabi mothers. They're just as bad as Jewish ones.'

Zahid was also preparing to study abroad, but not till the following year.

✺

Jindié and I would have six more weeks together in Lahore before my departure. When I returned to Lahore, everyone was talking about Tipu's arrest and disappearance, and within a fortnight Zahid had been accused of betraying him. Now that I think back on those days, I can recall that it was Jamshed who conveyed the news to our household. He boasts of his infamies now, flaunts them shamelessly, but on that day his conscience was on parade. He referred to Zahid's base character and how he must be punished. Jamshed was always a lowlife, and his brand of amorality became my supreme aversion.

At first I was devastated and then depressed, but after a few days I was in a rage with Zahid. Who could have guessed that such malignancy was lurking in that heart? Jindié and I would endlessly discuss this event. She was always more careful and warned me not to believe every statement that came from the police. Zahid, meanwhile, had disappeared to Karachi to stay with an uncle, which, as far as I was concerned, was extremely suspicious behaviour. Plato agreed with me, but then he trusted nobody.

'Each of us has the capacity to dissimulate with such profundity that we can often surprise ourselves. Perhaps Zahid thought he was doing you a favour in getting Tipu out of the way. Didn't you tell me that Tipu was stuck on Jindié?'

'There was nothing in that, Plato, just my diseased brain.'

While all this was going on, my mother, as Zahid had predicted, had found my diary with the help of her maids, read it, and discussed it at length with my father, who, to his enormous credit, refused to even glance at it. She worked herself into a terrible state. I knew something was wrong the minute I got home that day. My mother was in a sulk, barely replied to my greeting and pretended she was reading a book. A few minutes later she burst into my room in an elemental rage and announced that she hated weak men who fell in love with women and grovelled at their feet.

I was astonished. 'Then you must hate my father for falling in love with you. In fact now that you mention it, I wish he . . .'

Before I could complete my sentence she rushed forward and slapped my face. Then so much rubbish began to pour out that I decided there and then that if she ever mentioned the word *Chinese* or *cobbler* again I would walk out and seek refuge with Plato at Scotch Corner or flee to the house of a sympathetic aunt. It was almost as if she knew that or, what is more likely, had been warned by my father not to travel down that road, and so she suddenly changed her tack. All her life her feelings about childish trifles had been so violent that in more sane moments she admitted her weakness and reproached herself. Not that day. Now, trembling with rage, she shouted, 'She's the same age as you. She should be at least five or six years younger.'

I was so taken aback that I burst out of laughing, and then pointed out that some of the happiest couples in the family were roughly the same age, including two of her brothers and their wives, whereas Jindié was two years younger than me, not that it mattered in the least. In fact, I told my mother, one of our cousins had married his stepmother's sister, who was ten years older than he was, and they, too, were blissfully happy.

In fact, I said, it was a matter of some regret to me that Jindié wasn't a few years older since I preferred mature women. Unable to respond, she moved forward to assault me once again, but I stepped aside at the last minute and she fell on my bed instead. The next morning she radiated a surface calm, but was still seething. She was sometimes capable of manufacturing the most fantastic untruths, but also specialized in trivial fibs, and was usually caught out because of her inconsistencies. She could never remember what she had said to the same person some weeks previously. As I tucked into my scrambled eggs, I smiled at her to show there was no ill will on my part. She took this as a cue for hypocrisy and a malapropism, another feature of her dialect.

'I know what you're thinking. You think I'm opposed to her because her father has been measuring our feet for donkey's ears.'

I began to laugh. 'No, mother. He has been measuring donkey's feet for my father's and grandfather's ears.'

She hurled a boiled egg at me, which missed. At this point I decided it was best to go out for a long walk. As fate would have it, I found myself walking unconsciously in the direction of Nairn College, and just before I reached the gate a car honked at me. It was a cousin. We exchanged greetings. The chauffeur got out and held open the back door. I got in. We drove into the college car park.

'Dara, have you come to see Jindié?'

'Well, I wasn't planning to, but . . . yes!'

'She may have left. I'll go and see, but if you're caught, Miss Willoughby-Ashleymore will ring all our parents.'

'Nothing she can do to me.'

'Dara, at least cover your head with a shawl so they'll think you're a woman.'

'What about my moustache? Oh, I forgot. Miss Willoughby-Ashleymore sports one as well. I'm happy to put on a disguise. Bring back a bra and some socks.'

She giggled and walked hurriedly to the girl's hostel, a veritable harem where we were denied entry, but where mischief of every sort flourished. Within ten minutes she was back with the required items. I was wearing a *salwar/kurta* and hurriedly assembled a pair of breasts, much to the chauffeur's amusement, covered my head and half my face with a shawl, put on a slight limp and accompanied my ever-so-sporting cousin to a friend's room, where Jindié was waiting. She giggled.

'A bit of eye makeup and you'd be a perfect hermaphrodite!'

The friends scarpered. The minute we were alone I ditched the bra and socks. We fell chastely into each other's arms. I managed to imprint a tiny kiss on her lips. Believe me, dear reader, it was purely token. Our lips barely touched, but it startled her. She sat bolt upright and rapped me on the knuckles with a fly swat.

'Why do you always make me angry? I'll never see you alone unless you promise to behave.'

'Have you read the *Thousand and One Nights*, Jindié?'

She pushed me away. Wanting desperately to amuse her, I described the conversation with my mother. She instantly became melancholic.

'I warned you not to tell her.'

'She ransacked my desk and bookshelves, then forced open the secret drawer in my cupboard and found my diary.'

'Why did you keep a diary? So immature.'

'Fantasies have to be recorded somewhere.'

She wanted to know what I had written. I provided a brief summary. She covered her face with her hands.

'You wrote that we spent all night talking?'

'On the phone! I did. It's true.'

'I know, but it creates a bad impression.'

'Who cares?'

She became silent. Then she said, 'Go. Let me think about all this now. And don't ring me from home. Go to the German café.'

Our guards were outside, waiting patiently and eavesdropping. They entered the room promptly. Slightly depressed, I resumed my disguise and walked out, moving my buttocks suggestively. As we walked past the tree to which was attached the Nairn College bell – that evil tocsin which summoned the women to class and assemblies and signalled that visitors should leave – I took out my penknife and detached the bell from the rope. My escorts, three of them cousins of mine, were horror-struck.

'Hai Allah, Allah. We'll all be expelled. You monster. You're never coming here again. Rude boy. Evil one. Viper!' And so on. I rushed to the car, clutching the bell to my stomach, and was driven away. Miss Willoughby-Ashleymore, I was later told, instituted a full-scale investigation and even summoned a senior police officer whose daughter was at the college, to frighten the students, but the mystery was never solved. The memento, rusty and worn like the college to which it once belonged, still hangs from the mango tree in my mother's old garden, where it was often used by the gardener to frighten away the parrots. The following week Jindié and I met at the German café, and she confessed that the theft of the bell had cheered her a great deal, restoring me to her favour.

But worse was about to happen. As the time neared for my departure, friends organized farewell get-togethers. Those who shared our reserved table at the college café had a special event where fruit juices and *samosas* were provided free of charge. Respected hugged me with emotion.

'You won't forget us, will you?'

How could I forget any of them? With few exceptions they're all dead now, all the friends who were permitted to sit at our table, whose purity and integrity we guarded so fiercely from fakes, frauds and fools. Professor Junaid drank himself to death. Haroon had a heart attack in his late fifties. Respected disappeared with the old canteen, his later whereabouts unknown. And so it went. Plato, Zahid, Confucius and I are probably the sole survivors of our Atlantis. I saw their ghosts when I visited the college after a forty-year absence. I could almost hear their voices. I realized my eyes were moist. My sentimentality surprised me; sentimentality was something that was brutally condemned by us when we were young. How we hated all those at neighbouring tables who talked about nothing else but the glorious Mughal past of the city, Mughal rule in India and Mughal this and Mughal that; Plato would shout, 'Mughal wine, Mughal lechery and opium, Mughal fondness for boys . . .' Another of us would interrupt loudly and sing the praises of Lahore under the Sikhs, deliberately exaggerating the virtues of Maharaja Ranjit Singh, the one-eyed warrior who had held the British at bay and maintained an independent Punjab. His old palace was not so far away from where we sat, close to the Badshahi Mosque and the Diamond Market – cold during the day, a furnace at night – in the old red-light district where some of the gaudiest courtesans' houses had been built by a great-uncle of mine. The old Royal district: mosque, palace and brothel all within easy reach of each other and close to the river that no longer flows.

There were other tables where perfumed young men practised a wit that had been carefully rehearsed, to impress each other and the women students who had their tea and *samosas* separately in an adjoining garden and whose laughter and tinkling voices enhanced the charm of the place.

Rehearsed wit was not permitted at our table. Plato detested the practice as a curse of the age and glared suspiciously at any of us if he thought a bon mot lacked spontaneity. This extempore wit could only be a hit-and-miss affair, but it was preferable to the other sort. Plato's came with an eccentricity that – unlike his wit – appeared to be carefully cultivated. According to some of his own pupils, he had taken to cycling round the school and was often seen precariously balanced as he stood on the seat of a moving bike, arms outstretched, repeatedly shouting, '*Allahu Akbar*'. When we asked if this was true, he nodded. Why? 'Never heard of satire?'

Was it old friends I was mourning or an old city, an old world that had since changed so much and for the worse, a world in which expectations for a better future were always high and in which the ultra-Wahhabi beard, gangster politics and cancerous corruption had yet to appear and drown all hope. The Jamaat-i-Islami boys were present in miniscule numbers then, and would sometimes argue with us, replying parrot-like to all our criticisms with a single phrase, 'Islam is a complete code of life,' and that was how we used to address them. 'Tell me something, Islam-is-a-complete-code-of-life, could it be true that we are descended from apes? Have you ever considered the possibility or studied the evidence?'

As I looked at the faded photographs in the old hall, the scene of so many tumultuous events, I saw a long-forgotten Pashtun face that made me smile. A decent human being but a terrible pedant, he had, to our great surprise, joined the army and risen to become a general. The last I heard of him was a description of his rage at being strip-searched at Dulles Airport while on his way to attend a Pentagon briefing in December 2001. We were all there on that wall, except for Plato, who of course never studied at the college. How strange it seems now, but none of us who congregated at our table each morning were believers. Not a single one. And that was normal. We were not alone.

A few elderly professors wandered over and greeted me warmly, insisting that they had shared the table. Some remembered defying the injunctions against political demonstrations and marching to the US

Consulate to protest the murder of Patrice Lumumba in 1961. Others recounted episodes that had never taken place, an imagined past. I smiled. To each his illusions.

Before I left Lahore for England, I said farewell to all my old haunts except Zahid's house, which his treachery had declared out of bounds. I loved and esteemed this city: its courage, which rivalled its cuisine; its wit and self-deprecatory humour; its energy, male and female; its cafés which, even after 1947, preserved a constancy and a depth of ideas; its softness or hard coarseness, depending on the occasion. The new suburbs that were being built when I left housed an altogether different class of citizens. These were young men born of provincial fathers or nouveau riche traders, who had moved to the city to increase their fortunes.

Plato loathed them as only he could, seeing comedy in what they regarded as virtue. He would insult them to their faces, saying they were the most obtuse and barbaric ruffians he had ever set his eyes on, even though he knew this was a slight exaggeration. He would mock their exaggerated mannerisms and body language, their snobbery and dress codes, their etiolated appearance and abominable egotism, but above all the callousness they displayed towards those they saw as their social inferiors. I knew some of them. In their favour it can be said that they did not yet carry weapons. Their children do.

At home, my mother was convinced that she had won me over, that there was no further cause for anxiety on the 'China front'. She boasted to an older sister that everything had been handled with exquisite grace, the sort of remark a torturer might make after a prisoner he's been working on is found dead. The core of her real world was made up of her sisters, a few younger women who doted on her every word, and her family, which meant my father and, alas, myself. As for my sisters, they were made to look pretty so that they didn't disgrace her at public occasions, but their future was circumscribed by a single deadly institution: marriage.

She possessed many virtues, was amiable and generous most of the time, but prone, as I have said, to fits of uncontrollable rage. Plato accidentally witnessed one of these while visiting me and was impressed by it. She had assumed he was a tradesman.

Her own marriage to my father had not been strictly conventional, to put it mildly. An elopement and secret wedding; a scandal in the family; my grandfather threatening to kill her and himself if the marriage were not annulled; the anger of my paternal grandmother, from a more blue-blooded faction of the family and enraged that her son was not considered suitable simply because of his Communist views. It had all worked out in the end, and an official wedding, attended by the city's notables, had duly taken place. All this should have made my mother more relaxed in her own views, but it was as if, having set an audacious fashion when she was young, she was now surprised by her own boldness, and she often displayed a pseudo-morality that was distressing to all of us. Were there other skeletons in her past of which we had no idea? Her semi-hysterical defence of monogamy, and this in a culture where monogamy is actively discouraged, has left me suspicious to this day. At the time, however, she appeared triumphant. She had wrecked my happiness and was boasting about her success to my father and her circle of intimates.

How wrong she was and how right as well, but not because of my apparent capitulation. It was Jindié who took my mother's stupid strictures to heart. Suddenly we were no longer meant for each other. She was too old anyway. Why didn't I marry one of my delectable cousins, as was the tradition in our family. They were ever so pretty. Surely I could inspect a few fifteen-year-old ones now so that they could be ready in a few years' time. We belonged to different worlds. It was pointless annoying the family. She would not be seeking entry at Leeds University. We must not see or speak to each other again.

I was in a panic. How could this be? Why? She wouldn't tell me. In desperation I went to see her mother, a woman of admirable impulses and rare good sense. Mrs Ma soothed my ego, but offered no advice. Her daughter was the only person who could decide, she told me with quiet pride. Confucius, too, understood my pain, but he was half-scared of Jindié's sharp tongue and would never dream of defying her will. I needed Zahid and cursed him for having destroyed our friendship. Plato was useless in these matters, but said he would do anything to help, and he stressed the *anything*. It was then that a crazy idea began to form in my head, one with which Plato became centrally involved.

FIVE

I had kept nothing secret from Jindié. My self-esteem vanished in her presence. Ever since the summer in Nathiagali, all verbal constraint between us had disappeared. Now I simply couldn't understand the reasons for her emotional retreat. Perhaps she thought that some of my mother's prejudices were genetic and were ingrained in the rest of us as well, but whatever it was I needed to know before I left. I had to lure her to a last, desperate rendezvous, but to reassure her that my intentions were pure, the location had to be simultaneously public and secret. The only place that fitted this description was the marble Mughal terrace in the Shalimar Gardens on the edge of the city.

'How are you going to scale those walls in the moonlight without Satan's help?' Plato asked in despair. It was Thursday. My departure was planned for Sunday.

My plan was simple. I would convince Jindié to meet me one last time. She would tell her parents she was spending the night at the house of one of my female cousins. Plato, dressed as a chauffeur, would borrow a friend's car and pick her up from home on Friday evening. They would meet me outside the Shalimar Gardens. It could work.

'The gardens are locked. There are night watchmen. How will we get in?'

Plato had no idea that I had solved this one. Close family friends were the hereditary guardians of Shalimar, their reward for having tilled the soil and sown the seeds when the gardens – a Mughal passion – were being constructed. Anis, the younger son with languid eyes, a few years older than me, was a dear friend. Sent at a very young age to board at an English public school, he had first become a bit puffed up and then suffered a breakdown, from which he never fully recovered. His forebears had grabbed the adjoining lands when the Mughal Empire collapsed, and had become gentry. We used to laugh a great deal when his father, a radical member of Fatherland's Constituent Assembly, described the rise of his family.

I rang Anis, explaining my dilemma. He offered his car and the key to a private entry gate that had been used for assignations for centuries. And I was not to worry about the guards. They were tenants and would be instructed to protect our privacy. Did I need food and wine? No. A sitar player hidden behind the bushes to enhance the atmosphere? No! He made it sound like a Bollywood movie. Plato and I went to pick up the key and the car. Anis drew us a little map showing exactly where the hidden gate was situated. 'Dara', he said in a loud voice as I was about to leave, 'is this the Chinese beauty your mother has warned us all against?'

I nodded.

'Hmm. Thought so. Whatever it is, I hope you succeed. Don't take no for an answer. Elope with her. Take the car. Allah protect us from our mothers. Did you say you were spending the night here? It's fine. Perfectly fine. I'll alert the servants. Best of luck, dear Dara. Afraid I can't offer you any meaningful advice.'

Everything was now settled, except Jindié's consent. I was twenty. She was eighteen. Neither of us had any real experience of life, which is why we regarded our private conversations, mainly on the telephone, as rare forms of happiness. I had gone through dark imaginings, wondering what existence might be without her. Would my eyes ever light up at a substitute well-curved breast? What would she say when I told her I had secured Shalimar just so that we could talk in peace for the whole night face to face rather than holding a receiver close to our ears? I thought all my persuasive powers would need to be deployed in order to convince her to even speak with me. But our breach had lasted a week, and speaking to each other about everything, as good friends do, had become such a habit for both of us that she, too, must have suffered withdrawal symptoms.

And perhaps it was this that had brought about a complete change in her mood. She agreed readily to the entire plan, oblivious to the surprise in my voice as I expressed my delight. I felt quietly confident. She would be mine. All would be well. We would never part.

Plato played his part to perfection. It was a beautiful October evening. At first we walked to the ramparts above the old wall and gazed at the lights of Lahore. She let me hold her hand and kiss it, which I did repeatedly. She told me, without my asking, all the bad things that were said of me by her friends at Nairn. Since most of them were true I thought it best to sport a lofty air and refrain from responding in kind. The gardens were magical at night, with the city at a distance and the stars above. There was total silence, except for the hoot of a solitary owl. Gradually we got used to the starlight. At first we talked in whispers, till we realized we were the only two people there and could speak in our normal voices.

I remember that we both wore shawls and paced up and down the empty garden as we talked. I wanted to know about her family. When and why had her forebears left China? It was a long story, she said, and would require at least three hundred nights and one. Let's start now, I pleaded, but she didn't want to talk about all that tonight. She had once whispered a song in Punjabi for me and I asked for an encore:

'Then sing some Waris Shah in my ears.'

'There were gleams of Sufi light in China, too, did you know?'

'It's Sufi delights that interest me more tonight.'

She took my arm as we carried on walking and talking in the starlight but keeping well clear of the subject that was agitating us both. Mysteriously, cushions had appeared on the marble benches where we had established our base. Anis, despite my wishes, had organized flasks with tea and a box full of chicken sandwiches. She didn't even notice. If a bloody sitar begins to whine behind a bush, I'll kill you, Anis. Mercifully, nothing else happened.

'Jindié . . .'

'Don't. It's no use.'

I embraced her and kissed her eyes. She lay back in my arms and I stroked her head. 'Why did you decide not to go to Leeds?'

'Why spoil our last evening together by talking about unpleasant facts? Just accept we're not intended for each other, and let's forego lofty thoughts and just be.'

I kissed her lips and she responded. And then I thought if we made love and she became pregnant it would be a fait accompli and she would have to marry me and damn the rest of the world. It sounded, even then, like a bad love drama, but the intensity of the moment drowned all my critical faculties. I was gripped by the passion that combines love and lust.

She was relaxed and kept stroking my face and kissing me. Then as I heard the muezzin calling the faithful to the early morning prayer, I made a fatal error. I put my hand underneath her shawl and then underneath her shirt, searching for the creamy texture of her breasts. I stroked the little orb still concealed underneath the bra. She didn't object, which emboldened me further. I attempted to lift the bra and kiss the flesh. It was a serious tactical error. She jumped up, a look of horror on her face.

'Why did you do that?'

'I want to make love to you. It's our only night together and I thought . . .'

She shouted at me in Chinese, yelling the word *semen* repeatedly as she pointed a finger in my direction.

'Jindié, I'm sorry.'

'You're not. You're semen. You're semen. Do you know that? That's all you are. Semen. I hate you. You don't really love me. There is nothing pure about your love. I want to go home. Now.'

What could I do? I pleaded forgiveness. I wept. I fell on my knees. I kissed her hands. The young are nothing if not melodramatic and the location undoubtedly helped, but it was to no avail. She was in a rage and reproaching herself bitterly for having agreed to the meeting in the first place. She ran towards the gate. I followed her out. Plato saw her tears and understood.

'Please take me home now, Plato. Then you can come back and return Mr Semen to his mother.'

Was it my imagination or did Plato repress a smile? As the car drove off, a familiar voice startled me.

'You should have forced her.'

It was Anis. 'Sorry, D. I was unable to resist bearing witness. Were your tears real? Impressive in any case'

Well aware of his voyeuristic habits, I wasn't totally surprised. In fact, I was now pleased by his presence. It was a welcome distraction and stopped me feeling too distraught. We were both hungry and the sandwiches were rapidly consumed.

'Did you hear everything?'

'Only when you were both seated. Hope the cushions were comfortable. The marble is cold and uncomfortable at night and had you proceeded as you should have the Chinese beauty would have appreciated their warmth, if not yours.'

'I could never have forced her or anyone else, Anis.'

He sighed sadly in agreement. 'Our forebears would weep if they could see how pathetic we have become.'

Though we never raised the subject with him, it was hardly a secret to his friends that Anis's only interest in women was as conversationalists and friends. His mother's attempts to force him in a heterosexual direction failed regularly. City beauties were paraded before his eyes to try and entice him to marry, but he never showed the slightest interest and they never came back. The courtesans hired by his desperate parents to arouse him from his torpor were paid double by him on the condition they lied to all and sundry about his prowess, which they did with verve. I know because I once overheard our mothers discussing the problem and his mother boasting of how good Anis was in bed with a proper woman. My mother happily joined in the barrage of bitchy attacks on 'modern girls'. Anis and I laughed a great deal that day. One of the younger courtesans had ended up a friend of ours and would regale us with stories of city venerables – she always named names – who visited the Diamond Market on a weekly basis. A cousin of mine later fell in love with and married her. 'I know what she was, but so what. That life has made her monogamous and loyal. Rather her than someone from our world.' He was right, of course. And his three children all studied medicine: the girls work in hospitals in Texas; the boy specialized in orthopaedic surgery and became a skilful surgeon and a born-again Muslim. He was head-hunted by the religious guerrillas in Afghanistan and ended up as their in-house doctor, treating the war wounded at the mobile hospitals of the Taliban. According to his mother, he treated Osama Bin Laden shortly before the latter's demise.

I felt much better after Anis and I had finished our tea and sandwiches on the Shalimar terrace, but a puzzle remained. I asked Anis about the word whose use in that evening's unpleasant finale had mystified me.

'Do you think that *semen*, or *tsemen* as she hissed it, is an abusive term in Chinese? That would be a unique coincidence; in English it is the seed that produces life.'

'Or not, as the case may be . . . you didn't have a waking wet dream, did you? Just asking. I did wonder about that usage. I noted that she referred to you as semen at least six times in a sentence and a half, and once again later when referring to you in a conversation with Plato. Impressive. It's a very intimate abuse. She obviously loves you. No doubt about that, but your mother is an effective opponent of all brides-to-be. She's so judge-mental. I'm afraid it's one of her more repulsive features. My mother's exactly the same. Surely they can't have a semen-phobia in the People's Republic? Never been there. We could ask the Chinese ambassador the next time he comes over for supper.'

He relapsed into deep thought and was lost to the world. I was feeling extremely low as well. Suddenly he came back to life.

'I was thinking that the only other place where I once heard a pejora-tive reference to semen was in Venice. The gondoliers, as you know, are extremely competitive and on every level. They often refer to each other as *boron* or *boroni*, which is not local slang for "baron", as assumed by the tourists, but singular and plural for "blob of sperm", or so they told me.'

Despite my broken heart, I couldn't help laughing. 'When were you in Venice?'

'We went in a school party when I was sixteen. Ten years ago. Very enjoyable trip despite the boroni.'

'Surely because of it.'

He laughed. I saw him once again in Edinburgh and later twice in London, and then, like so many other Lahoris, he disappeared from my life completely. Occasionally a letter would arrive asking for my opinion on some book or the other that he was thinking of publishing in Urdu, followed by a long silence. Anis never married, despite his mother's continual pressure, and never left the family house, despite the advice of all his friends. There was no shortage of money or land in the family. He simply couldn't declare his independence. One day I got a phone call from my mother. Anis had invited some friends for dinner. When they left he had prolonged the farewell and waxed ultra-sentimental about friendship, which should have alerted them, since it was out of character, but nobody thought there was anything wrong. Later that night he swallowed a cyanide pill. He had left behind a note explaining why he had committed suicide. When the shaken servants summoned his mother next morning, the old widow remained calm. She looked at his body without a trace of emotion. Then she saw the note and confiscated it before the police arrived. What did you write, Anis? Why didn't you write to any of us? Or was the letter a complaint addressed to your mother?

❦

Playing the chauffeur all those years ago, when he drove Jindié and me to the Shalimar Gardens and both of us breathed only in sighs, was the big favour Plato did for me in return for which I promised him anything that lay within my power. That is why I am immersed in reconstructing his life. What he may not have fully realized was that in writing about him I would, of necessity, have to resuscitate the lives of others, including my own. Whatever he may think now, he did not and could not have then existed on his own.

It was more than thirty years later when I understood what Jindié had meant when she asked me to read Cao Xueqin's *Dream of the Red Chamber*, the great Chinese novel of the late eighteenth century. The author tells his readers that leading a life of poverty and wretchedness has made him realize that the female friends of his youth were morally and intellectually his superiors, and so he wants to record their lives to remind himself of the golden days he carries in his heart. It is a haunting novel of life in an enclosed set of mansions occupied by a wealthy family in the service of the emperor's court. There are five volumes known; apparently the author could not complete the story in his lifetime. The book reminded me a great deal of Jindié, even though she was probably too young when she first encountered it. Had she modelled herself on Dai-yu, the ultra-sensitive beauty whose passions were hidden even from heaven? Reading the novel was an intense experience for me, partly because many of the experiences and emotions of the young people as the author describes them were familiar and made me think not only of Jindié but also of various female cousins I had left behind. The plot is centred on a group of self-absorbed young romantics attempting to ignore the collapsing edifice of the mansion they share with their elders. That, too, was not unfamiliar.

Had I read the book sooner, I might have understood Jindié's preoc-cupations better, but my enlightenment would always have been too late as far as she was concerned. A second novel I read had not been suggested by her but by her brother, Confucius. It was a tale written a hundred years or so before the *Dream*. Hugely diverting, it has to be one of the great erotic masterpieces of world literature. In *Chin Ping Mei*, or *The Plum in the Golden Vase*, every single major character is viperous and there is virtually nobody in all the three volumes that any reader can sympathize or identify with, a polar opposite to the first novels written in English and the works of Miss Austen and the Brontë sisters. Halfway through the first volume I realized that Jindié must have read some extracts from or even the whole book, and an old mystery was solved. What s¹ e had shouted at me on that memorably awful night in the pavilion of the Shalimar Gardens was not *semen* but *Hsi-men*, the name of the anti-hero around whose sexual rampaging and avarice the entire novel revolves. I stopped reading for a while when I realized this and laughed. I was slightly shocked as I thought of her yet again. She had been eighteen at the time and must have read the book in secret. Perhaps Dai-yu was not her role model after all. And then memories stirred of some of the things Confucius had said when we were discussing erotic literature. 'Nothing equals what we had in China,' he'd told me, so there must have been an old edition of it on her father's shelves. And, leaving aside Hsi-men himself, this is how one of the minor personages in the novel is described in the list of characters: 'Wen Pi-ku, Warm-Buttocks Wen, Pedant Wen, Licentiate Wen, a pederast recommended to Hsi-men Ch'ing by his fellow licentiate Ni P'eng to be his social secretary; housed across the street from Hsi-men Ch'ing's residence . . . divulges His-men Ch'ing's private correspondence to Ni P'eng, who shares it with Hsia Yen-Ling; sodomizes Hua-t'ung against his will and is expelled from the Hsi-men household when his indiscretions are exposed.'

Even in retrospect, I was mortified at being compared to the amoral libertine who inserted his plum in every golden vase that he could lay hands on and from every possible position. All I had done was to try and feel the curve of her left breast.

Clearly I had to discuss Chinese literature with Jindié at our next meeting and hopefully in Zahid's absence. If I was Hsi-men, surely Zahid must be Wen Pi-ku. I e-mailed her to that effect and she replied instantly, suggesting a time, a date and a location. She also wondered whether I had been able to read her letter, essay and diaries. I hadn't, but I am now about to do so.

SIX

Dear D:

You asked far too many questions before you left Lahore. One that irritated me the most was whether I saw myself as a Punjabi or as a Chinese girl. Instead of replying that I was a Chinese Punjabi, which I think is what you wanted to hear, I remained silent because it is more complicated. Did you ever notice how often I remained silent when you questioned me? Did you? It would have been impolite to tell you that they were usually stupid questions that irritated me greatly. You always asked about my family history. In this case the reason I did not reply was not because your query was foolish, but somehow I felt the timing was wrong, and, to be truthful, I didn't want the information passed on to your mother, which you would have done and with a look of triumph.

The enclosed manuscript is really for you. Perhaps it's too lengthy and dull. If you feel that, don't even try and be diplomatic. That was never your style. It was such a sad and difficult subject that I was often inclined to stop. But it became a habit and was my way of conducting a one-sided conversation with you, in which you just had to listen and not question me every few sentences. The early section is typewritten! I had a great deal of spare time at Georgetown before the children arrived, while Zahid was saving lives. He's good at his job but sometimes goes too far. A few years back he saved a life that the entire family, except for him, felt did not deserve to be saved.

I did not much care for the company of other medical wives and was never into shopping as a habit, let alone acquiring jewellery; these objects slip by me unperceived. So I spent many hours in the university library reading Chinese history, something that was impossible to do at dear old Nairn College, where the history we were taught was too, too farcical. So what you have is in three parts. Tales that my paternal great-grandmother told us when we were very small and that were regularly repeated by her grandson and his mother. It is oral history of the kind familiar to most families, though if I remember well your family stories always had alternative versions that were probably closer to what must have happened. The bulk of what I have sent you is oral history, but where I can I have confirmed it during my labours at the library. I have added a map to help you situate Yunnan. Punjabis are genetically provincial and need all the help they can get.

There are my incomplete diaries about what happened to me after your attempted rape failed (I'm teasing; I never thought that for a moment) and you left Lahore never to return. I think I know why. Zahid did return for a while and we began to see each other, first to talk about you and then ourselves, and when he suggested marriage, neither of us pretended it was love or passion. It was friendship and convenience. And, just so that you know, he is a very sweet and kind man and my life has not been unhappy at all. Of course he has become very wealthy now, but this has not made him miserly or disagreeable. In many ways, though not politically, he remains the same. I can't pretend that all is well. My life has lacked something, but then whose life is perfect? Yours?

One question I will answer now. I always thought of myself as a Lahori Punjabi. If pushed further, I would have said I was a Yunnanese Punjabi. Never a Chinese Fatherlandi. Those two identities were not mine. At the time you would not have understood this, because, like my brother, you were infected with the revolution, and talk of Han domination would have been brushed aside by all of you with contempt as it still is by Zahid. Perhaps the reason for this is that the Punjabis have become the Han equivalents of Fatherland, crushing other nationalities at will, but that's your story. Better write it before the Baluch and the Pashtuns and the Sindhis produce their own.

Sometimes I wondered whether you ever took me seriously. I suppose I should have written ages ago and told you that Zahid had had nothing to do with Tipu's arrest, but knowing you I also knew what would happen. You would have established contact with Zahid, apologized, made friends and, being Punjabis, wallowed in a lot of emotion, male camaraderie and self-pity. Had that happened, with you coming in and out of our house on whatever continent, it would have been unbearable for me, since in the shadow of that brotherhood I would have become a cipher. So it was pure selfishness that stopped me from telling you. I prevented him from doing so as well, by employing underhanded arguments. When the children arrived and became the centre of my life, then I could have told you, but we inhabited such different worlds that I thought you'd probably forgotten our very existence. Nothing in your novels that I have read indicated otherwise. Enough. I hope the manuscript answers all the questions you asked when you still loved me, and if there are others I'll answer them as well, since we're in the same city again after forty-five years.

—Jindié.

PS: You asked me about the Chinese equivalents for Arab names; here are some of them:

* Ma for Muhammad
* Ha for Hassan
* Hu for Hussain
* Sai for Said
* Sha for Shah
* Zheng for Shams
* Koay for Kamaruddin
* Chuah for Osman

SEVEN

My great-grandmother Qin-shi, whom we knew as Elder Granny, was a niece of Dù Wénxiù. The name will not mean anything to you or to most people, but it's inscribed in the annals of the Han as a byword for rebellion, Islam and 'petty-bourgeois nationalist deviations'. Elder Granny would talk about the rebellions in Yunnan as if they had happened in the previous week. Hui, or sometimes Hui Hui, was the Chinese name for Muslims or people of Muslim origin, but I suppose you know that by now. Or was China only Mao and Lin Biao for you as well? Nothing else mattered. I can't help these asides because I can still get very angry with you sometimes.

❧

Every evening just before we went to bed, Father would send us to Elder Granny's tiny little room near the kitchen. She must have been in her nineties at the time, and we all knew she would die soon. My father worshipped her. She was his last link with Yunnan except for Old Liu, a cobbler from Dali who really was an antique – one hundred years old in 1954. He had taught Grandfather and Father the art of measuring feet and cutting leather to make shoes. Father would tell us that Old Liu always made a shoe from just one piece of leather. That was the test. If you used more than a single piece you would never be a master shoemaker. Sandals were different, of course, but Liu never took them seriously.

Elder Granny had no teeth at all and could eat only soup and barley rice. Her toothlessness made us laugh, because we were children and even though veneration of our elders had been instilled into us at every opportunity, a Punjabi cynicism had crept into our lives as well, infecting us with the Lahori sense of humour. Often stupid, sometimes surprisingly subtle, but usually very funny.

At story-time we would sit at her feet, not looking at her when she talked, so as not to giggle when she became really excited and a shower of spit descended on us and it became really hard to keep a straight face. Despite all this we understood every word. She spoke Mandarin with a strong Yunnanese accent. When she used strange words, Hanif would shout, 'We don't know what that means, Elder Granny,' even though it was considered rude to interrupt elders and he always pretended that he didn't really care about our past. She didn't mind at all. She would stop in mid-sentence and patiently explain what each word meant. Hanif wasn't really interested in the stories, but he loved her presence, so mostly he sat quietly, thinking about cricket and his school friends. Elder Granny would begin each story the same way, so that her introduction became embedded in our heads. I used to tell the same stories to my children, but in Punjabi because they never learnt Mandarin, to their great regret. 'Please start now, Elder Granny,' I would say, and she would begin:

'And there was once a city, a beautiful city, much more beautiful than Beijing, and it was called Dali. It was built on the edge of a lake, surrounded by mountains, and in the spring when the blossoms were out we could be forgiven for thinking that this was a replica of heaven. Kunming may have been the capital, but Dali was the heart of Yunnan, which, as you know, is itself the most beautiful country in China. In this beautiful city, there lived a family. Our family. We had been here for such a long time that nobody remembered how long, and in China that can only mean a very, very, long time ago. Some of us lived on the land, but most of us were traders, including Dù Wénxiù's father. He was a salt merchant, but that did not satisfy him because it was not aesthetically pleasing, and so he set up a shop with the finest textiles and pottery.

'The textiles were beautiful, but designed only for the nobility. They were made of pure silk. The pottery was simple. He had discovered that our potters were making thousands of plates with the blue that had become so popular in all of the Muslim world. From Yunnan these plates with Arabic calligraphy would be transported to Baghdad and Palermo and, later, to the Ottoman lands of the great Sultan, and from there to Cordoba in al-Andalus and to Africa and even the barbarian world. When trade with the Arabs ceased, your great forebears made sure that the potteries never closed down. Skills handed down from father to son are too precious to lose. Once lost, they never return.

'Those plates became the pride of every family in Dali, even those who were not Hui. At the Third Month Fair, which was the largest in the world, I think, because traders came from every province in China, but there were also Lamas from Tibet and tribal peoples and others from Siam and Bengal-India and Burma and Cochin China. They used to say that in the very early years of the fair there were traders from as far away as Mesopotamia in the world of the Arab peoples, and that it took them six months to make the journey, so they were all a year older when they returned to Basra.

'My grandfather, Wénxiù's father, always used to throw a big banquet for the most important visitors, whose families had been trading with ours for many generations. Dù Wénxiù had always thought that he would continue in the trade of his father and forebears. My grandfather said that our ancestors had first come here with the armies of Qubilai Khan. It was said in our family that our great forebear, who finally settled in Dali and built the house where we all lived afterwards, had been responsible for supplying the Great Khan's armies with food and women. I have no idea whether that is a fact or not. I hope it was just food he supplied. So we had been in the city for many centuries.

'Some Hui, especially those who live in Khanfu [Canton] and Beijing, would never be happy tracing their lineage to the time of the Great Khan. They insist they are the direct descendants of the Arab traders and ambassadors who came to these shores while the Prophet, honour his name, was still alive. The Prophet had once said, "Seek knowledge where you find it, even as far as China," and the Hui in Khanfu claim that is why their ancestors arrived in the first place: to seek knowledge, not profit. People are so ridiculous sometimes. Sultan Suleiman used to smile and say that every Believer wants to believe that he has a tiny drop of Arab blood in him, because he wants to be blessed with the same blood as the Prophet.

'However we came, we intermarried so much that were it not for the taboo on pork and circumcision we would be no different from the Han. But we would never be the same as the Manchu. [At this point, D, she would pause, not to regain her breath, but to offer a short prayer to Allah asking him to punish the Manchu for their crimes. Hanif would always interrupt, 'Mao Zedong is not a Manchu, Elder Granny,' but she would brush him aside with a gesture. Then she would continue.]

'Dù Wénxiù was happy helping my father organize our trading activities. He would have done that for the rest of his life and remained happy, but Fate had other plans for him.

'I think it was springtime in 1856, when the worst killings of our people took place in Kunming. The Manchu governor hated the Hui people in any case, but prices fell and the newly settled Han became resentful of those who could still work. The Manchu governor, Shuxing'a, hated us Hui because when he had been in the northwest he had been defeated by some Muslim rebels. They were not Hui. They spoke their own language and had their own customs, but of course they shared our faith and prayed as we do, facing west, and, naturally, they never ate pork. Shuxing'a's soldiers had been defeated by them and he was running away disguised as a woman. The rebels captured him. Let's see if you are a woman, they said, and then they stripped him and threw pebbles at his testicles. He hated them forever after that and suffered from pebble-sickness for the rest of his life. He did not think how lucky he was to be alive. Then he was sent by the Manchu to Yunnan, and once in Kunming he began to plot his revenge, but against us Hui. He thought we were all the same as the people in the northwest. It was he who organized the massacre in Kunming. And once these things start there's no knowing how they will end. Even before he came, the Han were killing us in the villages, burning our homes and mosques. By the time this monster started in Kunming, we had lost nearly forty thousand men, women and children. So our young men took up arms to defend themselves. What else could they do?

'Wénxiù suddenly adopted an Arab name, Suleiman, to stress his faith, to unite our people and defy the Manchu. They killed so many of us that year. Thousands and thousands perished. It made our young men very angry. We are not goats to be led to slaughter so easily, Wénxiù told his father, and he and other young men went into the mountains to teach themselves how to fight.

'My father was a Han, but he fought on our side because he wanted Yunnan to be free of the Manchu. All we Yunnanese are very proud people. The Manchu called us bandits, but they were the real bandits. Do you know what bandits are, Hanif Ma?'

'I like bandits, Elder Granny. I want to be a bandit.'

Her cackle was infectious and made everyone laugh, including Father.

'There are good bandits and evil bandits, little Hanif Ma. Good bandits help the poor. Evil bandits work for the Han rulers, never the poor. Wénxiù was only nineteen years old, but my mother told me that he never lost his temper, not even when he was a little boy. So after they went to the mountains and changed their names, all his friends would call him Suleiman Dù Wénxiù, till he became the Sultan. Did you know that, little Jindié and Hanif? Your ancestor was the Sultan of Yunnan. I may have been only eight years old, but I can still remember when all the people came out on the streets of Dali to greet him: "Sultan Suleiman *wan sui*, Sultan Suleiman *wan sui*." It was the first slogan I ever learned. When we went with my mother to see him in his small palace, she made us repeat the slogan. He lifted me up and kissed my cheeks. His beard was very soft, very different from the beards in Xinjiang.

'There were many different people of every sort who lived in Yunnan during his time. Han, Hui and non-Han, many of whom were tribal people and others who were Buddhist. Suleiman Dù Wénxiù fought the Manchu armies and defeated them, but he never permitted any discrimination against the Han people in Yunnan. There was so much intermarriage. My mother, Wénxiù's favourite younger sister, was married to a Han Yunnanese, who was my father. It was like that all over our country. We were all interrelated, and if the Manchu had not interfered with us and sent in more and more of their people to steal our work, our mines, our trade and our property, and this at a time when things were bad for everyone, there would have been no rebellion.

'And it was all the people, not just the Hui, who fought against the Manchu. Had it only been us, we would have been defeated much, much sooner. Always remember this, children. Your great ancestor was a Muslim, a Hui, but he ruled for all the people. Not just the Hui. That made my father so happy, because after the killings in Kunming and the villages everybody expected the Hui to go in for revenge killings. Sultan Suleiman knew that well and it made him angry. "We are not such poor-spirited people that we seek revenge on innocents. The best revenge is to make the whole of Yunnan strong and free from the rule of the Manchu, who steal, oppress and kill all Yunnanese who refuse to wear the queue." The day after he said that, many of the Han who had lived in Yunnan for many generations came out and publicly had their queues removed. That was the way they showed their support for your great ancestor. You must always be proud of him and respect his memory. Are you listening, Hanif Ma and little Jindié?'

She rarely said more than that, but soon after she died my father began spending a few hours each Sunday telling us more stories and sometimes reading from manuscripts he had in his possession and showing us where these places were on the map. Your friend Hanif/Confucius became really alienated from these stories and would plead with my father to be allowed to go and play with his friends on the neighbouring streets.

'You can play with whomever and whenever you like, Hanif,' my father would say. 'But I sometimes worry that they will warp your mind and drag you down to the gutter. You must never lose your self-esteem.'

Hanif would surrender abjectly. He hated seeing our father upset and he would sit through our family history lessons, but his mind was usually elsewhere. Once when he was fifteen or sixteen and my father was not in the house, he told me angrily, 'China is being transformed by Mao Zedong and the Communists. Everything will be different. What's the use of blind ancestor-worship, which was the curse of the old society and kept the peasants enslaved? If I had been alive at that time in Yunnan, I would have fought with our forebear. What's the point of all this now?'

I never could see it that way myself. For me it was an accretion of knowledge. Even if our forebears had not been involved in the rebellion I would have wanted to know who we were and why we had been forced to flee Yunnan. We did not leave voluntarily to seek work elsewhere. We were frightened. We thought they would kill us all. Young girls were being kidnapped every day and sold as slaves. We had kind neighbours in the other regions and they helped us because over centuries we had traded and intermarried with them as well. Many of our people were given refuge in Guangzhou and Tibet and also in Burma. What made Hanif really angry was a tendency, I don't think it was stronger than that, on the part of my parents and Younger Granny to portray life in Yunnan before the Manchu went on their killing spree as a golden age. I know these rarely exist in history, but we always preserve memories of some good things and call them a 'golden age' to keep our hopes alive. For if it was possible once, it could be again. [Utopian thoughts are not necessarily bad, or are they, D? I once read something by you many years ago either in praise of or predicting a world revolution in your lifetime. Perhaps I misunderstood what you wrote, but even though the thinking behind it struck me as crude and schematic, I liked the utopian strain. Have I got it completely wrong? If so, apologies.]

There were some good things that happened in Yunnan when Suleiman declared himself the Sultan. He put a stop to the ceaseless raids authorized by the Qing court, which had affected most Yunnanese, who regarded the Han marauders as odious. I once compared the Yunnanese Sultanate to Yenan and the Maoist attempt to unite the people against foreign (in their case, Japanese) aggression. Suleiman tried to unify Yunnan as a single state to stave off the imperial masters in Beijing. Just because the Chinese empire was coterminous with the people it conquered did not make the Manchu better than the Japanese.

Of course I developed this line of thinking to argue against Hanif's uncritical and crude Maoism. [And yours? Or did your brand of Marxism impose a ban on blind worship? Can't remember now.] Of course he was enraged at any comparison of the revolutionary government to the reactionary Manchu, but that was not what I was arguing. I was simply comparing it to a mid-nineteenth-century uprising that succeeded for a while in creating a state that was not theocratic like the Taiping Heavenly Kingdom in Nanjing, where reading the Bible was made compulsory.

Hanif got so angry with me one day that he sat in the living room and read a few books and manuscripts. He had a typical Elder Brother look on his face when I came home from Nairn one day, a mixture of contempt and triumph. 'Let me tell you a few things, Jindié', he said, 'before you take ancestor worship in this household to such heights that it becomes difficult to find a way down.' I was pleased at being taken seriously and sat down obediently to listen to Elder Brother.

He picked up the late-nineteenth-century book he had found on Father's bookshelves and read out the following passage:

'Dù Wénxiù set into action a series of building programs based on Qing imperial institutions in Beijing, including an imperial Forbidden City. At both the upper and lower passes, he had Great Walls built, with only one entrance, which ran from high in the Cangshan Mountains deep into Erhai Lake, making the valley impenetrable.'

I shrugged my shoulders. 'So what?'

'That is far too childish, Jindié. So what? So this great forebear was engaged in pure mimicry. Qing buildings and Ming robes.'

'I don't think that was so stupid. He wore Ming robes to stress that it was the Manchu who were the interlopers.'

'But Jindié, don't you understand what I'm saying? There was nothing progressive about Sultan Suleiman. The Taiping were better. They nationalized the land and gave women equal rights.'

That drove me mad: 'And imposed a Christian theocracy! They were much more irrational. The crazy guy who led the revolt believed he was the younger brother of Jesus. You prefer them only because the Maoists refuse to recognize the Yunnan rebellion as progressive for fear of encouraging something similar. But I accept that Sultan Suleiman was not a progressive. How could he be? Your beloved Marx hadn't yet been translated into Chinese.'

'I know, but the French Revolution had taken place. In this part of the world, Sultan Tipu, who was fighting the British fifty years before Suleiman's victory, exchanged friendly letters with Napoleon in which he signed himself "Citoyen Tipu". At least he tried.'

'But his enemy was Napoleon's enemy, and anyway Napoleon made himself a Sultan. Suleiman did not appeal for outside help. He knew he could win only with the support of his own people.'

'Then why did one of his generals appeal for support to Queen Victoria?'

'That was after the defeat, and he appealed for refuge, which is how we came to Lahore.'

Later when I asked Father about why Suleiman had tried to build a Forbidden City in Dali, he smiled.

'Very simple. He wanted to show that his government was for all the Yunnanese, including the Han. The architecture was designed to reassure people that they could have their own state, just like the Manchu in Beijing. His enemies were spreading the rumour that everybody would be forcibly converted to Islam. He knew it was an attempt to divide the Yunnanese and did everything possible to counter that suggestion. Large banners were painted and hung over the city walls: *Make Peace with Han Chinese, Down with Qing Court: Unite Hui and Han people as one, to erect the flag of rebellion, to get rid of Manchu barbarians, to resurrect Zhonghua, to cut away corruptions, to save the people from water and fire.*

'Sometimes he deliberately refrained from praying in the Grand Mosque on Friday, spending the afternoon with non-Hui leaders drinking rice wine. Of course he never touched pork. That would have been going too far. The seal Suleiman used was in Chinese as well as Arabic, but the calligraphy was in our own style. Go and look at it. It's there, just above the mantelpiece, one of the few mementos Elder Granny managed to keep, apart from one robe.'

The more Hanif became disaffected from our Yunnanese past, the more it became a refuge for me. How could one fail to be moved by the glorious resistance of the Yunnanese and our ancestors? The impact of the victory in Dali was beginning to spread. It's always like that isn't it, D? A big wave creates ripples. Then and now.

Imperial agents in Guangzhou were extremely worried by how much support there was for the long-haired rebels in Yunnan. They described how even in Guangzhou people had stopped shaving their foreheads and were growing their hair to demonstrate solidarity with the government in Dali. Similar reports were coming from border towns near Tibet. Everyone assumed that the long-haired people were all Hui, but this was not the case. The Taiping rebels had also grown their hair to show contempt for the Manchu.

Father often used to say that if the Sultanate had survived another five years, the British and perhaps even the French would have recognized Yunnan as an independent state. Beijing, aware of the developing trade links between Dali and the Europeans, was determined to move swiftly and crush the Sultan's armies.

Someone intelligent must have been advising the Qing emperor, who was told to ignore the insults – Suleiman had let it be known that his grasp of Mandarin and Chinese culture was on a much higher level than that of the Manchu barbarians in Beijing, and it is said that when the emperor was informed of this remark by his son, he became so angry that he had a seizure, and six eunuchs were required to lift him and place him on his bed. The emperor wanted to assault Dali immediately but was told the provocation was a trap and the Hui generals would wipe out the imperial army. An old palace eunuch reminded him that the European powers had won the Opium War just over a decade ago. They were waiting and watching, and if Beijing became isolated the foreigners might decide to help the Hui in Yunnan. If you attack Kunming and Dali, he told the emperor, there will be a prolonged conflict that will undermine the court, and what if some new rebellion erupts in the lower Yangtze, cutting off the supply of grain and rice? If our supply routes are cut we are finished. The long-haired rebels might even move on to Beijing reinforced by Britain and France. The Hui have been accumulating muskets and building gun-towers all over Yunnan. That is what the emperor was told, and for once he listened to his advisers and asked them to prepare an alternative method of destroying the independence of Yunnan.

That decision turned out to be our undoing. The Qing court bought some Muslim generals and made overtures to the Hui in Kunming, who were meant to be our allies, and by dividing our ranks they defeated us. That, D, is the verdict of history and the overriding weakness of Islam. Since the very beginning the followers of the Prophet have been unable to live in a single mansion. This has led to many defeats, but I fear you might be getting bored with this history lesson from an untrained historian, and so I've translated this document from our family's archive that my father guarded so devotedly and which I inherited. I have now sent many of the documents and books to the museum in Yunnan, where they are displayed quite proudly.

But this one document I kept, because it was very personal. It was written by Elder Granny's mother a few weeks before she died. She was Sultan Suleiman's youngest sister. He had appointed her Yunnan's trade commissioner in Burma. That's how she survived, and later the British gave her permission to shift her operations to Calcutta. We moved to Lahore soon after her death in 1882, and only because some of the Hui who were descendants of the collaborators had established themselves in

Calcutta and began to make our commercial existence difficult. My great-grandfather refused to pay them protection money and, as a consequence, we had to leave the city.

That history is without any intrinsic value to anyone outside our family. It's like immigrant life everywhere, and I observed similar divisions among the subcontinental Hui in the United States. Always divided by clans and political affiliations. What always amused me greatly was the facial expressions of Punjabi taxi drivers in New York and Chicago and now London when they realized I was more fluent in their language than some of them – they tend to use too many English words – and that I had understood every word uttered on the cell phones to which they are permanently attached. It was as if they had received an electric shock. I suppose it would be the same in Yunnan if a healthy, moustachioed Punjabi boy suddenly broke into our dialect. Forgive the digression.

I have translated the old document from Chinese as accurately as I could, but I could not have it double-checked by anyone in the family. Everyone is dead and your old friend Confucius has disappeared. We haven't seen my brother for more than twenty years. Outside help I considered inappropriate. For one thing, the document is still private, and for another, I am not convinced that it is an accurate account. Also there are elements in it that are cinematic, and I would hate a tart like Zhang Yimou to be tempted. He's wrecked enough Chinese history. Some swear words I have left in Chinese with my translation in brackets. Very mild compared to Punjabi, but more hurtful, said without a trace of affection.

I think Elder Granny's mother was searching for other explanations. She could not quite bring herself to believe that the great betrayal was due solely to money, jealousy and an unhealthy power addiction. Many centuries ago, as you keep writing, al-Andalus and Siqqiliya had already experienced what happened in Yunnan a hundred and sixty years ago. A case of those who never learn from past mistakes being destined to repeat them?

EIGHT

Qin-shi, my dearest child, I am writing this memorandum for you and your children and whoever comes after them. It is the story of your uncle's last days, but also about a great deal more, as you shall read. I am not used to writing anything except trading reports and balance sheets and, rarely and only when my brother Sultan Suleiman instructed me, detailed dossiers on the rulers of Burma and India and what we might expect from them in the future. As you know, I loved my brother dearly. He never treated women as mere bearers of children and he permitted me to marry a Han, outside our family and community, but a pure Yunnanese boy. Your father refused to leave Dali with me in 1872, even when ordered to do so by the Sultan, who was worried about his pregnant sister travelling on her own. I was three months pregnant with you and had returned to give a report on our trading situation. My brother had ruled for sixteen years, but he knew we were about to be defeated and he wanted us all to leave. Your father refused. He was killed defending the Sultan. A Han fighting the Hui traitors. His memory has never left me, which is why I never remarried, though there were more than a few offers. Together with your uncle, your father was truly the kind of man of whom our great scholar Liu Chih wrote in older times:

> *Only those who are the most sincere, authentic, true and real can fully realize their own nature;*
> *Able to fully realize their own nature, they can fully realize the nature of humanity;*
> *Able to fully realize the nature of humanity, they can fully realize the nature of things;*
> *Able to fully recognize the nature of things, they can take part in the transforming and nourishing process of Heaven and Earth;*
> *Once this is achieved they can form a trinity with Heaven and Earth.*

Before I tell you what happened in those last months, I want you to remember that the Hui in southeastern China were never fully trusted by the Muslim people in the northwest, who were far more rigid than we were in the application of their beliefs and the observance of rituals. The Han mistrusted us because all that divided them from us was ritual. They simply could not understand how pork could be forbidden, since, unlike some Buddhists, we were not vegetarians. When they started burning our villages near Kunming before the big massacre, they would first address us impolitely as *Hou didi* [monkey's brother], *Gou nainai* [grandmother's a dog] and always *Zhu shi ta de Zuxian pai* [your ancestral tablet is a pig]. One of my great-uncles used to say that the Hui are descended from the good son of Adam who did not eat pork and the Han from the bad son who ate pork all the time. It is strange that this meat became such a big issue, but the Han regarded eating it as healthful, and many Hui noble families, ordered by the emperor to desert their faith or incur his displeasure, used to prove their loyalty by ostentatiously eating pork at court banquets. At my brother's banquets in Dali, since there were many non-Hui Yunnanese present, pork was always served, but the polluted dishes were never kept in the palace kitchens. Our northwestern cousins would regard serving pork even to non-Hui as a heresy.

I sometimes wondered what the emperors would have demanded had the Arabs not observed the pork taboo and had the meat not been forbidden by the Honoured Classic. It would have been difficult to sew the foreskins back onto the men. But enough of this nonsense.

Six months before the Sultan was captured, a young soldier arrived at the court from Kunming. He was unarmed, but hurt. His arm was bleeding profusely through makeshift bandages. He was offered food and water, but insisted on seeing the Sultan personally. Suleiman saw the young man and immediately ordered that a surgeon be sent for, but the soldier insisted that it was a flesh wound and had been wrapped in a salt bandage. He would be fine soon. He asked to speak to the Sultan in private.

Very few people knew that my brother had a network of spies throughout Yunnan, mainly to report on Manchu activities in our country and the neighbouring regions. The soldier said he was one of them. The code to help identify the network was Wang Tai-yu's 'True Answers'. Each region in Yunnan had been given a separate set of them.

'What is your password?'

'A question.'

'Ask.'

'The language of the Lord – what is its sound and script?'

Suleiman gazed at the young man's face and smiled. 'The real word of the Lord belongs to neither sound nor script. Ask the second question.'

'How did the Honoured Classic come to be?'

'It descended from heaven.'

The soldier was from Kunming. Suleiman gave him some water and insisted on tending to the wound himself. He gently removed the soldier's shirt and blouse and drew back in surprise. It was a woman. She covered her breasts, leaving the hurt arm hanging by her side. Suleiman washed it and dried it tenderly, then tore a bit of his own silk tunic and bandaged her arm.

'How were you hurt, Li Wan?'

She looked scared. How could he know her name?

'It's inscribed on this amulet. It is your name?'

She nodded in relief. 'One of Ma Rulong's men tried to stop me as I was leaving the city, since I had no identification. I brushed him aside. He drew out a dagger, which grazed me. I broke his neck and left the city.'

'How old are you, Li Wan?'

'Eighteen. Ma Rulong is my uncle.'

'What?'

'Our family despises him. That is why I agreed to join your network.'

'Who recruited you?'

'We are forbidden to say.'

'I am the Sultan. I can find out easily.'

'Please do. I am forbidden to say.'

And nor did she, but the inevitable happened. Your uncle avoided the four vices. He was not addicted to wine, lust, avarice or anger, but he was a human being with all the strengths and weaknesses of one and we Yunnanese are a passionate people. My brother was overcome by emotion. The young woman must have been flattered, but she resisted. Then he asked her another question from the master's work.

'Which is prior, heaven or earth?'

She smiled, but refused to reply and insisted, very correctly, that the question had nothing to do with her recruitment to the network.

'You are talking statecraft and I am speaking passion', said the Sultan, 'and I order you to reply.'

She answered: 'If you know the sequence of men and women, you

will naturally know the priority and posteriority of heaven and earth.'
He roared with laughter, and she added: 'The Master Wang Tai-yu was a
brilliant sage, but not always correct. That was a wrong answer, since in
our country and especially in the more remote regions, the sequence of
men and women is not always the same.'

You can tell from this conversation, Qin-shi, that your uncle was developing a passion for Li Wan, and despite her pretence, it was obvious that
she was not indifferent to his attention, but she was a very disciplined girl
and would not let him touch her till she had given him a detailed account
of what the Qing court had asked of Ma Rulong in return for the promised
governorship of all Yunnan.

His fever of passion cooled as he heard the story. He became firm and
fierce, but first he wanted to be sure that Li Wan's sources were trust-
worthy. She hesitated, but only for a moment.

'He told me so himself.'

'Explain.'

'The network teaches us that we must utilize every possible method
to gain information without arousing suspicion. Ma Rulong sometimes
visited our household. I saw him looking at me in the way old men do.
Then he asked my mother whether I would come and keep his daughter
company. She resisted, but I stood up with a smile and said I would like
that very much.'

'Enough. I don't want to hear any more.'

'You should. It concerns you. After he had his way with me, and I
should report that he had the violent and rough manner of a shepherd
locked in a mountain hut with only his sheep for the winter, and believe
me, it filled me with revulsion, but afterwards he spoke openly in my presence. He spoke of having you killed and your head sent to Beijing in a
diamond-encrusted silver basket as a gift to the emperor. He spoke of
becoming an ally of the Manchu and ruling Yunnan from the Forbidden

City in Dali. His allies tell the people that Dù Wénxiù is not a proper Hui, that he eats pork, does not say his prayers and has no concubines, that they alone are the real defenders of the Honoured Classic. All this is being said even now.'

She provided the Sultan with a complete picture of what the traitors were planning. For days Suleiman was busy and did not see her, but he could not forget her features nor the soft skin that he had bandaged. Together with her obvious intelligence, they weighed on him a great deal. Since this is not a story of personal passion but a history of political defeat I will not dwell on every detail except to say that she became his favourite lover. They were inseparable, and since she knew the enemy so well she was often present at meetings of the Grand Council that organized the defence of the city.

When this news reached Ma Rulong he panicked and is reported to have considered suicide, since he thought that Suleiman would send assassins to kill him. Men who plot murder always believe that it is being plotted against them. Suleiman was generous. He sent a messenger to plead with Ma Rulong not to commit treachery but to share power in Dali. Suleiman suggested that their children should marry each other to cement the alliance, but Ma Rulong was too far gone in his intrigues and was afraid that this offer was a trap, that Suleiman meant to ensnare and kill him.

Suleiman was dominated by one idea, and that was to never let the Manchu retake Dali and Kunming and to remain free of the Qing court. For a while it seemed he would succeed. Of the governors-general despatched by Beijing to Yunnan, one was assassinated, another committed suicide, one lost his mind completely, several were fired for incompetence and one refused to take up his position in the rebel region. Even their policy of using Hui to fight Hui had failed, and Ma Rulong was becoming increasingly isolated as more and more of his Hui soldiers deserted him. But fate was against us. There were too few of us and just too many Qing soldiers, and they were now all united to crush Dali. Incapable of defeating the Europeans, they wanted to prove they were still capable of some victories against us.

The rest you know. Our council met and the Sultan told them that further resistance was impossible. The Manchu would kill every person and every animal in the city unless he, Dù Wénxiù, gave himself up. He had decided to go to the Qing encampment early the next morning and surrender. Your father wept, Qin-shi, and begged to go with him, but he refused. He would go alone. The next morning he put on his sultan's robes for the last time and seated himself in his sedan chair. Thousands of people rushed out of their homes to say farewell. Many were weeping. At the Southern Gate he got out and thanked the people for the way they had supported him for eighteen whole years. Once inside his chair he swallowed a fatal dose of opium and was dead by the time he reached the enemy camp. His corpse was dragged in front of the Qing army and he was decapitated.

His surrender was a mistake, because the Manchu were determined on revenge. They persuaded our generals to disarm, and three days later they assaulted the city. Your father died defending his people. Thousands of innocent Hui were slaughtered. Women and children still alive were given as war booty to the Qing soldiers.

And Li Wan, with her heavenly beauty? Several months before the surrender, she had given birth to a daughter and was pregnant again. She was greatly vexed and even offended when Suleiman insisted she had to leave the city and seek safety elsewhere. She did not want to go, but he insisted and became angry, reminding her of her duty to the higher cause, to their lofty principles and the questions and answers. He said, 'One day you or your daughter or the child inside you now might be needed to continue the fight for Yunnan.' Then for the last time he asked her a question from the great work.

'Why is this place of worship called Clean and Aware?'

She sobbed. 'When water is clean, fish appear.'

'What is water? What are fish?'

Tears poured down her cheeks. 'The True Teaching and Real People.'

'Never forget that, my dearest woman whom I have loved more than anything in this world.'

Still she resisted the idea of leaving him, and then, finally, much against her own will, she agreed to accompany her parents in a heavily guarded caravan ordered by the Sultan to take them to Cochin China. He promised he would join her there; she knew it would never happen. Fifty soldiers escorted the family to their safe haven, where some of our people were already living. The soldiers, too, had orders not to return.

I made some inquiries in Burma and offered money for any information, but never heard anything about them. Perhaps one day Li Wan's daughter, or, who knows, her son, will find you, and then you two cousins will have much to discuss.

Qin-shi, memory is the preserve of the victors, but wherever you go, I never want you or your children to forget who we were and what they did to us. They say that the grass grows stronger on plains enriched with blood, but sometimes nothing will grow on that soil.

NINE

A quarter of a century had elapsed since I had left Lahore, and then fate placed a painter in my way. Plato re-entered my life in 1988, but in such a unique fashion that at first I didn't recognize him. A London newspaper rang to ask if I would write about an unusual exhibition of paintings by an unknown Fatherland artist in an obscure East End gallery. The gallery was housed in a former medieval nunnery and only exhibited new work. From first-time sinners to first-time artists, said the woman on the phone to amuse me. The painter's name, Shah Pervaiz Shah, meant nothing to me, and that in itself was intriguing, since I thought I knew every serious painter in Fatherland. He must be a new young thing, and I wasn't in the mood. The woman persisted. It was his first exhibition. It would mean a great deal to him if I went, and the painter had wanted me to know that it didn't matter if I hated the paintings. He never painted to please, and if I chose to ridicule his follies in print that was fine by him. This injunction had the desired effect. I decided to go the following morning, and it was agreed that I would write a piece only if I liked the work. They rang me back and told me that the caretaker would let me in and turn on the lights.

It was a beautiful November morning, cold, crisp and cloudless. I got off at Mile End and walked to the old nunnery. The Bengali caretaker was waiting patiently. He was dressed in a slightly eccentric fashion: a bright red beret covered his head and huge dark glasses concealed most of his face. Perhaps he, too, wanted to be an artist. Neither of us spoke as he unlocked the door and turned on the lights. The place was horribly lit, perhaps in homage to its past, but extremely unfair to the poor painter. To my great irritation, the caretaker hung around in the background, watching me closely as I began to look at the works. They were black and white etchings and they depicted pure agony, which was what the exhibition should have been titled. It took me some time to study each frame. The figures depicted were in different stages of despair. Munch's *Scream* multiplied by a hundred.

Some years ago, after giving a lecture in Oslo I dragged a group of newly arrived Punjabi migrants who attended my talk to the Munch museum to show them their new country's greatest artist. Some were reluctant to waste precious time but came anyway. All of them were stunned, and one, Salah, who became a dear friend, had moist eyes as he whispered in Punjabi, 'This is an artist who knew inner pain. Our Sufi poets say that the cure for that lies in oneself. Neither Allah nor a psychiatrist can help.'

I was reminded of that remark now as I studied each etching closely. This painter had experienced more than inner pain. He was bearing witness to a terrible tragedy. Men, women and children stood dying, together in three of the pictures, separately in the others. One showed a child stuck to its mother's breast. Their eyes were gazing in different directions. Both were dead. After an hour I slumped on a bench. It was not what one expects so soon after breakfast. I looked for a catalogue or the sheet of paper detailing the work and the painter. There was nothing.

The caretaker, whose presence I had by now completely forgotten, muttered in broken Urdu, 'Upstairs, more. No rush. There are no limits on time.'

Upstairs? I was not sure I could take any more, but as he turned on the lights I staggered up the winding stairs to another space. What had the nuns done here? It was obvious. This had been a primitive chapel, with a tiny confessional in a corner for the mother superior to console her charges in whatever way she considered fit. Nunneries always make me think of the *Decameron*.

Then I looked at the pictures. Colour! These were not etchings but vibrant paintings: watercolours and a few oils, though miniature in size. As for the subject matter, we had gone from Munch to Grosz, though in reality this artist was like neither. Shah Pervaiz Shah, or SPS, as he signed himself, was an original. I had no doubt on this score. My mood changed and I began to laugh loudly. These were the most savage caricatures of mullahs that I had ever seen. The literary tradition in the Punjab and else-where in the Islamic world had, of course, never spared the rod when it came to the mullahs, but this was something new and refreshing. Virtually every painting made me laugh. Here was a mullah walking with his veiled wife, but in his mind's eye he was seeing naked *houris* with huge breasts. Another bearded venerable was holding an erect friend in his hand as he enviously watched two young men pleasuring each other. I roared with delight. I wanted to meet SPS or whatever his real name might be, since it was obvious now that he painted under a pseudonym, and who could blame him? I would do more than just write about it. I would get his work filmed and shown on television.

The caretaker had been following me as I studied each of these master-pieces, but I hadn't noticed him. As he saw me laughing at a sketch of a mullah absentmindedly stroking his penis while he gazed longingly at the forbidden apple on the celestial tree, he addressed me in Punjabi.

'Like them?'

'They're brilliant. Do you know the artist?'

'I am the artist. Don't you recognize me?'

He took off his stupid beret and dark glasses. Even then I had some difficulty, since he was bald as a turnip. Then I realized.

'Plato? Can it be?'

'So now you don't recognize me.'

We embraced each other. My failure to recognize him was an even bigger shock than his actual presence. It worried me. The only explanation was that I had not looked too closely at the caretaker unlocking the gallery and later it was the paintings that had demanded all my attention. I apologized profusely but he was triumphant.

'How long have you been in Britain, Plato?'

'I came some years after you, but I had to find work and so I had no time to look for you or Zahid Mian or anyone else.'

'Zahid was here?'

'Yes, and the Butterfly, but not for long. He's a heart surgeon in Satan's city now. Washington, DS, District of Satan.'

I managed a weak smile, wondering, as usual, how Jindié's heart had survived the marriage. Plato had returned with unwelcome memories.

'This is amazing work, Plato. In Lahore you never spoke about painting. A leap from mathematics.'

'You really like it?'

'I do.'

'Then I'll paint more. I had decided that if you thought it wasn't worthwhile I would stop.'

'I'm not an art critic.'

'If it was one of those I wanted, I would never have pushed them to invite you. You understand. By the way. That woman from the magazine wants me to paint her.'

It wasn't 'by the way'. Something was up and it was Plato. He smiled at me.

'Now you understand the etchings.'

'Partition?'

'What else?'

'The pain expressed is universal. War. Famine.'

'Partitions. Always partitions. Whenever they divide, we suffer. Have you time? Should we find a teahouse?'

'Yes, but not here. Let's go to Drummond Street.'

I inspected his bald head and told him that would have been a better disguise than the beret, but irritatingly, now that we were in a public space, he insisted we only speak English. His aversion to mixing languages was as strong as ever, and he reacted angrily when I pointed out that every language was a mixture. Had he counted the number of Sanskrit words in Punjabi, or Persian and Arabic derivatives in Urdu or Arabic in Spanish? He brushed Urdu aside with a rude gesture.

'What else do you expect from a courtier's language?'

'Ghalib, Iqbal and Faiz . . . all courtiers?'

'Iqbal and Faiz were born in Sialkot. They should have written in Punjabi.'

'But Plato, Faiz explained why he didn't write in Punjabi. Baba Bulleh Shah had said all there was to say in Punjabi. There could be no other.'

'Nonsense,' said Plato. 'He could have equally said that Ghalib and Mir had said everything in Urdu.'

'But they hadn't, don't you see? Faiz used the model, refined it with political imagery. Politics as love. Love as politics.'

'Please speak in English.'

'Can't discuss our poets in English, Plato.'

'Then save talk till later.'

He had shrunk a little and walked with a slight stoop. And there was something else. Perhaps it was because I was so much older now that I noticed, but Plato appeared lost in a way he had never done in Lahore. Would he have prompted Hamlet's ghost at the RSC? Since I was going to review his work, I needed to know why and how he had become a painter. That was the surprise. Mathematician, literary critic, cycling acrobat, conversationalist, bon vivant and now a painter and a very unusual one, too. But he had to tell the story in Punjabi, and so had to wait till we reached Punjabi space in Drummond Street.

I said in English, 'Is there anything you want to do here that for some reason you haven't yet done?'

'Yes. I want to see Cambridge and the mathematics section of their library. So I can see a world that offered me attention, but that I rejected. No hurry, understand? When you have a free day, take me there.'

By the time we reached the Indus café in Drummond Street it was almost time for lunch. I asked for a corner table in the recess near the back, close to the 'family tables' where women were accommodated and where we wouldn't be disturbed, and ordered kebabs and tikkas and the *haleem* for which the place was famous. It was cheap food infinitely superior to the trendy Indo-Pak eateries that catered to indigenous tastes and would do anything for a Michelin star.

It was here that Plato reverted to Punjabi and described his life since he had left Lahore, two years or so after me.

'We were lucky in those days. We didn't need visas. I borrowed money and left. Why? Because things were changing. Life at our table died soon after you left. They were planning to demolish Babuji's café and Respected's fruit juice parlour and replace them with something modern and ugly. The college centenary was approaching, and they thought they should tart up. They put on too much lipstick and face powder, like the girls in the Diamond Market. Also I was no longer happy with just teaching rich kids. The quality of my pupils was not improving. If anything, the opposite. I don't know. Many reasons. I got fed up. Some of our friends were cuddling up to the military dictator, just like all the newspapers. I was disgusted. I reminded myself that, after all, this wasn't my country. Lahore wasn't my town. I was a refugee from another Punjab. The only friend I had left from those days was Younis the sub-postmaster. Remember? Of course you do. You had your own relationship with him. But he lived in Peshawar and loved the place. He was married. Children. Very different from me. I left.

'When I arrived in London I had the name of one contact, a cousin of Younis who was married to a Mirpuri girl, and worked on a building site carrying bricks for the bricklayers all day long. He lived in Ealing, in a house filled with others like him. He greeted me warmly but said I would have to find a night job, so I could sleep in his bed during the day. Later I could find a room. I got a job within a week, working as a waiter in an all-night place where trucks stopped regularly for petrol and I made tea or coffee. I lived on baked beans and white bread every day and for many months. The body suffered. Not interesting.

'Then Fate dealt me a slightly better hand. A cousin of the petrol pump's owner fell ill. He had a franchise selling newspapers outside a tube station in North London. They asked me whether I would work there till he recovered. So I became a newsagent. It was better work, even though I had to start at five in the morning and finish at six-thirty in the evening. Morning papers till last editions of the evening papers for final rush hour. I now had a room of my own in a boarding house near Kilburn High Road. I earned enough to eat two meals a day and go to the cinema. Also, I must be honest, to strip joints, which were very expensive for me, but I had to make those visits, otherwise I'd have gone mad. Ten shillings entry it was, but I needed the images to comfort my *seekh* kebab at home. I was paid ten pounds a week, which was a lot in the early Sixties in London. One pound on strip shows twice a week, but still I saved three pounds each week.

'The life of a newsagent was very dull, and between twelve noon and six I had a lot of spare time. I read all the papers and did the *Times* crossword puzzle. Still I had too much time. One day I bought a hardcover exercise book and in my spare hours I started drawing, but just to occupy myself. There was nothing else to do. Strange people with wounded bodies began to pour out of my wounded heart. It was just like that, and I had no idea what was happening. In my youth, as you know, I was good at equations, and sometimes I played with the figures in algebra, adding a few testicles here and some nipples there, but stopped after being caned by the teacher for my sins.

'One day an English customer saw one of my sketches and said, "These are good. You should show them. Want to sell one to me? How much?" I asked for ten shillings. He gave me a pound. I hoped he would return, but I never saw him again. It was a fluke, but it encouraged me. I carried on drawing. All those sketches you saw today I did in black ink as I waited for people to buy newspapers. I bought larger and better pads from artists' shops and better ink and did not stop till I had nothing more to say. Sometimes at home I would look at the drawings and think they were rubbish and many times I thought of destroying them, but something stopped me. I know it sounds stupid, but once I thought I heard your voice in my head telling me not to do anything till you had seen them.

'One day a Punjabi boy, a Sikh who used to leave early for work and buy a *Mirror* from me every morning suggested he could find me a better job as a bus conductor. So I thanked my employer and handed in my notice. After a week of learning I became a bus conductor. That's when I really got to see this city. No time for sketching, but much better wages and a strong trade union. The Sikh boy was a driver, and we became good friends. He would tell me not to get too worked up by racist abuse unless it was a passenger. Then I should stop the bus and we would throw him off. We did this sometimes, but got no support from any other passengers. They looked out of the window, pretending not to notice.

'I began to look out of the window as well and ignore the abuse. I noticed there was always a long queue in one place on Charing Cross Road, and that some very beautiful young girls and handsome boys always got off the bus to join it. One day I asked one of the boys, and he explained they were art students queuing to paint nudes every Thursday, which is when the queue was longest. I asked if it was free. He looked at me strangely and nodded. This was a real discovery. In Soho they charged ten shillings to see nude women. On Charing Cross Road, just next door, it was free.

'I was owed my holiday, so I took two weeks. On Thursday of the first week I bought a pair of denims and a nice jumper and joined the queue. Nobody questioned me. I walked behind a cute girl with a ponytail and sat at a desk just behind her. In front of me there stood an easel and a small tray full of pastels. As the naked model walked in, my heart started beating so fast I thought the others must be able to hear it. The model came to the front of the room and stood there, taking up different poses. Finally she lay down with her arms outstretched and the beard between her legs glistening. That was how she stayed, stark naked and in that pose for most of the two hours, with small breaks to stretch and drink tea that aroused me even more. I was the only person who appeared excited by the sight of her. She seemed so natural, unlike the naked women I'd seen in Soho. The others started painting. The teacher was looking at me looking at the model and I hurriedly picked up the pastels and began to sketch without thinking. After ten minutes there was a tap on my shoulder. It was the teacher.

'"You have a very good eye for colour."

'This surprised me since the only colour I had used till then was grey, but I smiled and thanked her and hurriedly added other colours. That finished work is still at home. My first real piece of work. The teacher praised it. The other students congratulated me. That is how I became an artist. I forgot to say that the first time I saw that model's body hair I imagined a mullah's beard. And I saw the mullah's face, but that is what I painted at home. My tiny bedroom was now also a studio. I carried on working on the buses for a few more years, but worked overtime at weekends and took Thursdays off till the teacher told me to go home and paint. I did not need a teacher anymore. One of the girls in my class had become a critic. We became lovers for a short time and some of the women in the mullah paintings are based on her. Another friend of hers is some big editor on the magazine that rang you. What are you going to write? Whatever you do, please don't blow it up too much. No embroidery on the cloth. Just pure and simple; that's usually more effective if you have something to say. If they need advertising copy they'll hire someone.'

'I'm useless at all that, Plato. I'll just write what I feel. I hope it works for you. But there are some good critics here and I hope one of them likes it.'

He shrugged his shoulders. 'Believe me, Dara. I don't care. There are five other people whose judgement I value. If they like my work, that's enough for me.'

'You have to make a living, Plato.'

'That is a disgusting sentence. At our table in Lahore you would have been asked to leave for a few days. Please withdraw it immediately.'

I did, but I was worried about him. At the time he was working as a security guard for a warehouse, and that meant a night shift and wearing a uniform, but all this amused him. When I asked why he had changed his name, he smiled.

'I was told by the girls that Plato sounded ridiculous and pretentious in the West.'

I disagreed. Why not Aflatun in that case? But he had made up his mind, and it was as Shah Pervaiz Shah that I wrote of him and introduced him to a documentary filmmaker. She wanted to take him back to Lahore and Ludhiana, whence he had made the bus journey etched in his psyche, but Plato wasn't agreeable to returning anywhere. He refused. Flummoxed by his obstinacy, she ended up making a twenty-minute documentary based on a brief interview and his paintings. A serious art critic reviewed them for the film and it was shown on a well-established arts programme. Plato may have bound himself by the strongest possible vows to resist the passions of the marketplace, but I think even he was pleased by the impact of his first exhibition. The etchings and the mullah paintings all went quickly, and Plato, for the first time in his life, found himself with a healthy bank balance.

With the help of his new friends and admirers, he found an artist's apartment near Hogarth's roundabout on the busy road to the airport in West London. Now he felt oppressed by too much space. It was too grand for him. He paced up and down all the time, watching the traffic go by, but he couldn't work. He moved back to North London and bought a ground-floor three-room flat in Kilburn. One of the rooms was huge and had French windows that opened into a garden with a crumbling wall and a few apple trees. All this became precious to Plato. He seemed happy whenever I saw him but far from any illusions of being successful in the traditional sense and still prone to fits of a melancholy that went so deep that it frightened me. He really had been carefree in Lahore. The past had been repressed in those early years. He never talked about it, but it had returned to haunt him in middle age. Or had there been something back then, too, that I had completely missed? He was surrounded by women these days, and that was certainly a step forward. In Lahore he had always been lonely and had rebuffed all questions referring to his sexuality, unusual in a city where different parts of one's anatomy were proudly worn on one's sleeve.

He had three more exhibitions over the next few years. I went and bought some of his work. His style had changed. The mullah with exposed genitals and a nude on either arm had given way to imagined landscapes with surreal beasts and mermaids. Always mermaids. I didn't like them at all. What was going on his head? I might never have known had I not received a phone call from Alice Stepford, a feminist art critic and painter who loathed being referred to as a feminist painter. There is no such thing, she would say. I had met her with Plato and assumed they were together in the way people were without actually sharing the same accommodations. I never questioned him about her. It was obvious he adored her. What she said about his work mattered a great deal to him, and even when she was scathing he tended to agree with her and dump the work. I warned him once, gently, against becoming too dependent on her whims. That she didn't like all of his paintings was no reason to destroy any of them.

In return for this unwanted and unwelcome advice he gifted me with one of his old exercise books containing a slightly boring sex story set in ancient Egypt that he had written himself and illustrated with paintings of ancient males with multiple penises engaged in endeavours of various kinds. It did make me smile, but Alice Stepford hated it, and, to be fair, I could understand her reasoning. He could not bring himself to destroy the book, which is why it remains in my possession. On hearing that I was slightly mystified by the present, he said.

'Look at the painting of the priest with three penises. Look at them closely.'

I did so and realized that all three organs were depictions in various sizes of the Egyptian president, Hosni Mubarak. Somehow, that made them really disgusting. I managed a weak laugh.

Alice Stepford had rung to invite me to her studio for lunch, saying, 'Today, please, if possible.' It was possible and I motored over to the address in SW3, assuming that Plato would be present. Her Chelsea studio was a revelation, a bit too tasteful for a bohemian pad. Lunch was served soon after I arrived, and Alice wasted no time in sharing her concerns with me. Our conversation turned out to be extremely serious and I was touched by her intensity. Not that it prevented me from wondering what her breasts might be like underneath her sweater, and that was before she uncorked a bottle of Château Lafite and decanted it with an apologetic smile.

'My only weakness apart from painting. Stolen from Daddy's cellar last weekend.'

Daddy was Lord Stepford, whose forebears had fought on the wrong side during the Civil War – and he had three beautiful daughters, two of whom were married to their milieu. Alice was the family bohemian, and when she informed her parents that her boyfriend was an Indian bus conductor who was trying to paint she had received a terrible missive from Stepford, who was old-fashioned on the subject of mixed marriages. The letter made it clear that while he did not care who she saw in her own time, he absolutely forbade her to soil the family name by marrying a Hottentot, an Eskimo, a Negro, a Chinaman, a Nip or a Wop and certainly never a jumped-up Indian, let alone a Paki. Plato saw the letter and laughed. He had no thought of marriage and suggested she tell Daddy that she was safe, but Alice was livid. She wrote back asking whether her father was aware that she had been invited to exhibit her work in Sydney and Wellington. And if he was, why had the Maoris and aboriginals been excluded from his otherwise comprehensive ban? He wrote back immediately. When he compiled the list he had assumed that even she would exclude cannibals as potential husbands. Her mother tried to make up by suggesting Alice bring 'your Indian' home one weekend. Alice impolitely declined the offer.

All this I knew, but why were we having lunch? She described her affection for Plato, which was no surprise, but there was clearly a problem.

'Can I rely on your eternal discretion, Dara? Please don't tell him about this, but I thought you might be able to help.'

Till now, nobody in my whole life had ever asked me, leave alone with such soft eyes and pouting lips, whether they could rely on my discretion. I was so touched by her trust that I pledged total secrecy and help whenever and however it was needed. The wine, too, was delicious. The hours were gliding by.

What emerged was that she had been seeing Plato for more than two years. They had painted each other naked. They had sported with each other, but not too seriously, and he had, she now told me, always kept his penis safe from her touch and she had only seen it flaccid. I was seriously taken aback.

'And there I was, so glad that everything had turned out so well for both of you. Work, love and sex in the same space. Purest joy.'

'No. Definitely not.'

Not once had Plato wanted or attempted to make love to her. All her attempts had been rebuffed. This worried her. It worried me too.

'What is it with him, Dara? Am I that unattractive? It can't be a religious inhibition, can it? Or is he gay? If so, I wish to bloody God he would just tell me and we could all relax.'

I was desperate to relax, but the news had stunned me. What the hell was wrong with Plato? Was there someone else?

'You don't think he's gone religious?'

'Can't be religion, Ally. That would be good for you. Islam is truly sensuous. Men who let women down by staying down themselves are considered worse than heretics and unbelievers like me. No, definitely not religion. Could he be gay? It would have been impossible to keep that a secret in Lahore. We would have known. Let me make a few ultra-discreet inquiries and get back to you.'

'Will you, Dara? I'd be so grateful. This is so bad for one's self-esteem.'

We finished the bottle, and while she made coffee I inspected her books and paintings and peeped into her bedroom, where Plato had let the side down very badly.

'Would you like some cognac with your coffee?'

'I like your paintings very much. Surprised me. I thought they would be . . .'

'More didactic.'

'Something like that.'

'Glad you like them. I always feel that financial considerations sometimes necessitate bad art. Never found that tempting and nor does your friend. Affinities.'

'True. But it's always worth remembering that fine sentiments do not automatically produce good work, either.'

'Do you think melancholy can be contagious? Is it possible that if a friend is depressed you can feel depressed too, even at a distance?'

'Only if the friendship is so deep that a part of it is repressed.'

She agreed strongly. We looked at each other and it was obvious to both of us what the next step would be. Nor did we let each other down. As the enjoyable afternoon was coming to an end and I was putting my clothes back on, I asked whether she still wanted me to head an unofficial inquiry to uncover Plato's secret.

'Yes, please. I mean I should know, don't you think?'

I was hoping she had moved on already, but hurt egos require nursing. I promised to have a report ready soon. She said she sorely needed my advice as to how she should proceed with Plato. I suggested that given the failure to establish physical contact, a close working friendship might be more appropriate. She nodded eagerly.

'And can we have lots of lunches together, Dara?'

'That is a much simpler request and easy to fulfil.'

But this is Plato's story, not mine, and all temptation to describe the idyllic year I spent with Ally Stepford must be resisted. I thought Plato might be more inclined to share confidences in our mother tongue, so I rang him a few weeks later, and we repaired, as usual, to Drummond Street. It was he who began the inquisition.

'Are you fucking Ally Stepford?'

This straightforward question sounds so crude in Punjabi that even my well-conditioned ears rebelled. I reprimanded him without answering his question. He rephrased it.

'Did her eyes bewitch you? Was it lust at first sight? Was it her paintings or her apartment? Tell me, dear friend. What really attracted you?'

I decided to answer in the affirmative. It was pointless to lie, but I twisted my response so as to force him on to the defensive.

'Yes, I am seeing her and for none of those foolish reasons, but there were no divided loyalties, Plato. She told me you weren't lovers at all, not even on a spiritual level. I wasn't sure whether to believe her or not. Was she lying just to reassure me, or is it true?'

An embarrassingly long silence followed, and a remorseful look replacing the earlier anger on his face.

'What is it, Plato? Is there someone else?'

'What she said is true. I've never told anyone else this before, but I think you should know.'

I thought this would be a declaration of his coming out and breathed a sigh of relief.

'I'm impotent, Dara. Always have been. My *alif* won't stand to attention. It won't take the *meem*. It's never erect. Unlike the sun, I never rise. Understand?'

How could I not, but I was nonetheless stunned since this contradicted so many earlier stories. I recalled some of the ingénue's tales we had heard in Lahore. Were they all duplicitous? Or had the fantasy trapped him to such an extent that he found it difficult to back out?

'But Plato, you described your visits to the strip joints and how this was all because you needed a memory enhancer when you masturbated.'

'I did tell you that, and it was true, except that I could never jerk off. I have never had an erection.'

'Why didn't you tell Ally?'

'I was embarrassed. I thought it would disturb her tranquillity.'

'Not telling her disturbed her tranquillity a great deal more. Have I your permission to tell her?'

He became thoughtful. 'Okay, but please stick to the facts. Don't make the story more salty or spicy.'

'I won't. She'll feel reassured and will be very sympathetic. She's a good person. Have you ever thought of seeing an analyst?'

'Greedy charlatans all of them and with very dirty, one-track minds.'

'Plato, be reasonable. You sound like a Punjabi rustic. Not all of them are like that. Let me find a good one for you. If it works, your life could change. If it doesn't, you certainly won't be worse off than you are now. The impotence may be psychological, and if so it can be cured. It may well be linked to the horrors of Partition. You were fifteen at the time. So those memories stayed. You saw women being raped and killed. You owe it to yourself to see a good analyst. Tell me something. Before Partition, did you have any experiences in the village?'

He cheered up. 'There was a village girl. She was so beautiful. I really wanted her. In the summer months, I'd follow her to the stream where she washed and spy on her, but she never took off all her clothes. Only her top to hurriedly soap her armpits, wipe her neck and breasts clean. And it's true that at the time I did feel a rise below and had wet dreams as a result and was slapped by my mother, who had to wash the sheets more often.'

'Did anything happen or was it a romance from afar?'

'One evening I walked up while she was washing herself and asked if I could put my hand on her breast and kiss her lips.'

'And?'

'She slapped my face.'

I kept a straight face. 'I doubt whether that was a real trauma, Plato. Did it never occur to you to just do what you asked permission to do? Then the slap would have been worth its weight in old silver. But this is very promising. Let me find you a good person. We'll figure out something.'

He agreed. A few weeks later, I approached a highly regarded analyst on his behalf. She knew his paintings and was quite keen to see him after I had explained the problem. But Plato had disappeared. His phone had been disconnected. The apartment was being let by an estate agent and there was no forwarding address. The rent, I was told, was being deposited in his London bank account.

I found it odd and slightly upsetting that he had decided to flee without a single word of farewell. Perhaps he resented the fact that he had been forced to reveal his ailment to me. On previous occasions and in relation to other subjects when he found himself trapped he would mutter that he was an unsophisticated provincial at heart and leave the room. But he was always impassioned and slinking away was out of character.

Ally and I talked about him often. She was quite upset when I told her of the malady that afflicted him. Soon she gave up painting. One day she rang to say that she had realized her real vocation was to study music. She had done so as a teenager and had played the piano reasonably well, but life had intervened and she had changed disciplines and gone to the Slade. Of late the music embedded in her had returned to the fore and she was returning to her first love. She couldn't see me because she was making hasty preparations to leave for New York and she hated farewells. Years later she was acknowledged a distinguished art and music critic, and one day I received an invitation to her wedding along with a cryptic note:

'Even though the parents wanted a white wedding they're not coming. Hope you are. Could you give me away? I would like that and it will be wickedly funny.'

I saw the joke when I reached the church on the Upper West Side. The groom was an African-American violinist. He certainly was on the Lord Stepford banned list, and so I had to give her away, much to the puzzlement of many present, though not of her sisters, who found the whole business hugely diverting. Poor Lord Stepford became unwell soon after this event was widely reported in the English tabloids. Ally's husband behaved exquisitely when her father passed away the following year. He attended the funeral and played a Beethoven violin solo at the wake that followed in Stepfordshire House, and was, unsurprisingly, a big hit with the Stepford clan and their friends. Then the couple returned to New York and we lost touch.

As for Plato, after a year I was told that he had resurfaced in Karachi. He refused to live in the Punjab. Too many memories lay buried in that world. Since he had become known in Britain, his work had been exhibited in all the top galleries in Fatherland – all six of them. He returned to the mullah paintings and added a few local politicians to improve the texture of the satire. These were never exhibited, but remained in his private collection, rumours regarding which swept the small world of the native elite. The begums of high society would invite him and his collection to their homes, mostly when their husbands were at work. He became the equivalent of a high-grade dealer in Kashmiri shawls with his illegal *shatoosh* much in demand. Plato charged a surprisingly high price for these paintings. I suppose he was justified in doing so, since a number of them could have cost him his life. The bearded subjects of his clandestine caricatures had established a strong base in Karachi, and getting rid of Plato would have been part of a day's work. So Plato bribed the secular gangsters who ran the town, who found him a large house on the outskirts of Karachi where he grew old comfortably and was regularly visited by aspiring painters. Naturally, the gangsters wanted a cut on each painting he sold, but then everyone does that to someone or other in Fatherland. That was the last I heard of Plato till his startling phone call to Zahid.

TEN

The call was unexpected. A voice I hadn't heard for almost fifteen years. The accent was now transatlantic, but it was definitely Alice Stepford. What did she want, why me and why now?

'Greetings, Dara.'

'Where are you?'

'In London. We moved here after the Iraq war, though heaven knows why. It was a mistake. England's dead. Dead politics, dead culture, servility the norm, even the old *Guardian* looking more and more like a marketing artefact. The BBC trying hard not to be like Fox TV, but in some ways worse with its hand-wringing conformism. Fake objectivity is the real killer. Anyway, you must have seen that Ell played at the Obama inauguration? Time to return.'

I hadn't seen the live broadcast of the inauguration and had missed Eliot Lincoln Little Jr. playing the fiddle. She wasn't pleased.

'Ridiculous. Where were you? In some remote corner of the Amazon Basin? I thought television was everywhere. A new Roman emperor is chosen and anointed, the world is watching, but not you. You really didn't see it live? Amazing. Ell was so good. His violin wept with joy. Not a cliché, not a cliché . . . anyway I didn't ring to quarrel. Free for supper tomorrow? Still a bachelor or would you like to bring someone? There's a lady over from your parts extremely keen to meet you. A friend of old Plato.'

'His latest flame, I hope. I need to speak with her.'

'Cruel choice of words, my dear. No flame without fire, and as we know . . .'

'Mean, mean Ally. It may not be physical, but appears to be a very intense affair, according to our old friend. I'm suffering as a result and have to meet her. It will also be good to see both of you again.'

'Ell left last week. And Jezebel, our teenager, went back to Brooklyn a few years ago. Jez is now the lead guitarist in a crazy neo-punk outfit in Brooklyn. She's only eighteen. You'll love the band's name. The Seventeenth of Brumaire, the French revolutionary equivalent of the seventh of November. It's because they had all just turned seventeen when the band was set up and were flicking through my books and found a reference to the 18th Brumaire and delved deeper. Cool, they all thought. Real hoot. I've closed the house. Come to the studio. Eightish? Promise supper will be served promptly. It'll just be us three.'

Her artistic energy was now channelled into her husband's and daughter's work. As I drove to Chelsea later that day, I made a mental note to ask whether she was painting again. Unlike its owner, the studio had changed little. Ally was elegantly attired as always, but the dyed hair was noticeable, which surely defeated the whole exercise, and she was much bulkier, but then so we were we all. But the continuities outweighed the changes. Ally's throaty laugh revived old memories, as did the wine.

'George got the buildings; my other siblings got money and pieces of furniture. I inherited the cellar. It was in the will. Naturally, I share it with the siblings, except for pre-1986 wines. Ell doesn't drink at all.'

'Is he a Muslim?'

'But darling, you know full well he is . . . surely I told you.'

'Ally, I gave you away in church.'

'So you did. So you did. Of course, it was some years later that Ell shifted faiths and did the Hajj. I didn't much care that he found Islam was more congenial than Presbyterianism. All I said was that if he as much as looked at another woman lustfully, I wouldn't hire a Blackwater mercenary to castrate him, I'd do it myself. Otherwise it didn't bother me too much. Most Americans love religion, and it's part of the package if you marry one of them. What did annoy me was that he chose such an unbelievably pompous name. It was only when his agent warned him very firmly that his fame as a violinist had been built wearing the old identity, and that concerts by al-Hajj Sheikh Mohammed Aroma might not appeal as much to the box office, that he decided to carry on under a "false" name. He is so very weak and in so many ways, otherwise he'd have discarded the old name like a pair of soiled underpants. After awful 9/11 he panicked yet further and simply stopped using his Muslim name at all. This, I've always thought, was utterly pathetic and pandering to Islamophobia. It's as if Muhammad Ali had reverted to Cassius Clay. But at least he remained a Muslim. I dislike all religions, Dara. I hope you're not thinking of a late-life conversion.'

'Don't be silly. And speaking of Islamophobia, why should Ell need a change of religion to be unfaithful?'

'I'm going to make a salad dressing.'

She could not explain the reasoning behind Eliot's conversion. It was surprising, since it wasn't the result of a lengthy stay in prison, where the Honoured Classic has had a magical impact on many young African-Americans and especially on their diet. I made a mental note to delve deeper, but all gloomy thoughts vanished with the appearance of Ally's other guest.

Zaynab Shah's appearance startled me. Her deep brown eyes were not languorous but filled with mischief. Her aquiline nose gave her a haughty expression, but the minute she smiled her entire face relaxed. She spoke in a lively and deep voice, her mind was clear-sighted and, instinctively, I felt that she scorned the mask of hypocrisy. Many women from the same social class are layered in duplicity, a price they pay for living and functioning in Fatherland.

Whatever the basis of their relationship, Plato had struck gold. Of this I had no doubt. I had done some homework and realized that I knew one of her brothers, the decent one, as she later informed me. The other had laid the abominable trap that wrecked her life.

I had not been prepared for this combination of intelligence and beauty. Zaynab was dressed in a colourful Sindhi *cholo* and maroon *suthan*, or loose cotton trousers. She crossed her legs as she sat down, the Sindhi colours blending well with Ally's decrepit, faded olive-green velvet sofa. There was not the slightest trace of starchiness in her, of the variety often displayed by society begums in Fatherland when first encountering strangers. Zaynab was informal, and her darting, smiling eyes suggested a free-and-easy approach to life. Outside, I remember, the sky was overcast.

A writer with no other concerns or preoccupations would have produced a masterwork based exclusively on the tragedy that befell this amazing woman. My version, alas, can only offer a prosaic account as per the strict instructions given me by the progenitor of this book and currently an intimate of the lady. The last thing I feel like doing is questioning her about him, but promises must be kept. I will only provide a basic outline, and here, too, as is my weakness, explain the history and social conditions that produced someone like her and explain why she fell in love with my friend Plato. Or did she? What lay hidden in so lovely a body, or behind so many backward tosses of the head? Did she have an angelic or a devilish soul, or was it a mixture of the two that had affected

Plato so deeply? She had not yet looked at me seriously, but concentrated her attention on Ally. An old tormentor, vanity, made a sudden appearance and began to mock at me, at the same time alerting me that any false steps could only lead to the abyss. And the warning irritated me, for I was far from green and hardly devoid of experience, unlike Plato.

Zaynab looked younger than fifty-two – as if she were in her late forties at most. It was difficult to tell. She'd been born to an extremely wealthy family of Sindhi landowners. These men were the most primitive lords in Fatherland, where competition in the field remains high. To add to the woes of their serfs, for that is what the peasants were, some of the landowners were hereditary saints or *pirs*, which meant that their word was not simply the law but came directly from the special relationship they enjoyed with God. Challenge this status and they would fight like devils possessed. When the British annoyed a distant cousin of Zaynab's grandfather, he had replied with a rebellion that had lasted a whole year and forced the empire to deploy troops in the interior of Sind, and this in 1942 when British troops had just suffered a crushing defeat in Singapore.

Unable to resist the Japanese, they turned with a vengeance on the Hur peasants and crushed them. An English district officer involved in the conflict had written a pretended novel, *The Terrorist*, really based on his interrogations of Sindhi prisoners, some of them informers. The rebels were depicted as unthinking but courageous men who had blindly followed the *pir*, their religious leader. This was, of course, an incomplete view, since the colonial officer found it difficult to acknowledge that there was genuine hatred of the occupying power and that this had merely been used by the *pir* – in this case, Zaynab's great-uncle, who was quietly hanged with only a few people watching, probably including the novelist. Unlike the French and Italians, the British rarely showed off in India: they hanged their enemies without fanfare for fear of inspiring new martyrs.

The event left a mark on the whole family. Zaynab's eldest paternal uncle, the community's new leader, spiritual and temporal, decided to follow the fashion of the times and become ultra-loyal to the British. He had never thought much of the various nationalist leaders who were fighting for India's independence. All the Sindhi primitives – as they were called by peasant activists who escaped to a city – felt threatened by the departure of the British. The only question that worried them was whether their enclosed world of property and serfdom would survive. History has recorded that these institutions survived well, as did such sacred privileges as the droit du seigneur, which is not exactly the same as the Rights of Man, though Ally in her more militant feminist days would strongly dispute this assertion.

Zaynab was born in one of the many large houses built amid the dozen villages and thousands of acres that made up her family's estate. This one was not far from the small town of Jamsadiq and a four-hour drive to the satanic city Karachi, so all modern conveniences were available, and some of the primitives affected an ultra-cosmopolitan personality when they appeared at the Sind Club.

When she was eight or nine, Zaynab's extraordinary beauty began singling her out for special attention. Her father, who adored her, died when she was twelve. Her older brother, who inherited his father's share of the estate, was a dour and reactionary primitive. He saw how all who came into contact with her worshipped his young sister. She was singularly devoid of artifice. Her private tutors, all of them female, had educated her well. In addition to Sindhi and Urdu, she could read Arabic and Persian and speak English and French. She possessed a natural grace that was obvious at first glance. Word of her beauty had spread throughout the province. The primitives discussed it often, and many young bloods were determined to win her hand. Which primitive would her family bless? Bets were laid and, unbeknown to Zaynab, a fierce rivalry had already commenced. There were demands from primitives with even more land than Zaynab's family. They all wanted an immediate engagement, so that as soon as she was seventeen they could pretend she was eighteen and celebrate the nuptials.

Zaynab's mother had died giving birth to her, and her father's second wife was a coldly calculating society woman from Karachi, not in the slightest bit interested in little Zaynab or her older brothers. In fact, she was rarely on the estate. Her main interest was accumulating enough jewellery and money so that she could scarper to a European city after the old man died. This she achieved successfully, if not gracefully, and when last heard of was living in Knightsbridge, close to an Egyptian grocery.

Sámir Shah, the small-minded, bigoted oldest brother, was smitten with jealousy of his sister. He knew that had Zaynab been born a man, she would have displaced him completely. She was still only twelve years of age, and already tales of her small kindnesses to the families of serfs who served in the household had spread throughout the villages, and there were many expressions of regret that she had been born a woman.

Sámir Shah called a conference of male elders to decide his sister's fate. These primitives met and agreed that the only bridegroom worthy of her, clearly, was the Koran. Her favourite brother, Sikandar, fought valiantly on her behalf, but he was only sixteen himself at the time. The poor boy was brutally mocked for his immaturity and even more for his disregard for property. He stormed out in tears.

This was as much as I'd known of Zaynab's story before she arrived.

We exchanged pleasantries while Ally laid the table and offered us wine. Zaynab did not refuse. She asked how my life of Plato was proceeding. I muttered a noncommittal reply.

'Tell me honestly', she asked, 'is there much to write about? Might it not be simpler for you to just write an essay to go with his paintings?'

'He told me to write everything, and much of that would be unsuitable as an introduction to his paintings.'

'I don't see why. They're explicit enough.'

'In a way they are, but they still require a great deal of interpretation. Wait till you see the collection that our hostess wanted him to destroy because it was a complete "male fantasy and totally sexist". Rather than do that he gave it to me, and I thought you might like to see his earlier work so I've brought it along. Ally was unfair. I just think he had seen too many erotic Japanese works, where they draw these things very large. This was Plato's version of all that and it isn't without a certain charm. Not that Ally agrees.'

'Dara', said Ally, 'I've been meaning to say this: Do you mind not addressing me as Ally anymore? Everyone I know calls me Alice.'

'But why?'

'Because Eliot hates "Ally".'

'Why? It sounds like Ali as it's pronounced here, and given his own faith it should make him feel closer to you. How pathetic of Plato to call you Alice. And you, Ms Stepford, agreeing to let a male decide how you should be addressed. Shame.'

Zaynab, clearly feeling that the discussion of nicknames had become tedious, successfully diverted the conversation.

'I love the way you call him Plato so naturally. For me he's Pervaiz, sometimes Payjee, but I might try Plato. Sounds nice the way you say it.'

Alice announced supper just as Zaynab was leafing through the Plato penises. She smiled at some of the drawings but lingered on none. I knew then that the book would stay with me. Ally had been looking over her shoulder.

'Zay-Nab, don't you think I was right? I may have mellowed somewhat, but I still think that these paintings offer nothing to the world or to anyone.'

'Not to me,' said Zaynab in a reflective tone. 'But they obviously meant something to him or he wouldn't have done them. I think Dara as his biographer should retain custody, as we often say in our country. Perhaps one of them could be the cover of your book on Plato.'

'Perhaps not. Perhaps they could replace Fatherland flag, more representative of the people who run the country.'

Zaynab laughed. 'I'll suggest it to my brother, who's now a senior minister for something.'

'Corruption?'

'Suppertime, children.'

Zaynab seemed so self-assured and at ease in the world that I wondered whether her life had been as much of a tragedy as it had been painted by Plato and others. I knew that Alice would broach the subject before too long, and she did not disappoint me.

'Zay-Nab, er, we've been wondering. Plato said he had fallen in love with a married woman. Is your husband alive or are you divorced?'

'Neither, really, Alice.'

Alice, slight puzzled, looked at both of us in turn. 'I give up. What's the mystery?'

'Surprised Plato hasn't told you. I'm married to our Holy Book.'

'What? Is this real? Are you kidding? Dara, did you know?'

'Yes. These things happen in Fatherland.'

Zaynab explained her plight to an astonished Alice, who had thought she knew everything on matters related to gender. It was wonderful watching her face register an escalating scale of incredulity as Zaynab's story proceeded. The effect was enhanced by the deep calm voice in which Zaynab told it.

'In my part of the country the big landlords are so desperate to preserve their estates that anything that threatens the size of their holdings has to be fought. As a female I was entitled to my share of the property – under Islamic law that's a half of what the men inherit. Were it not for sharia I would get nothing at all. Makes one think. In the absence of laws that insist on a totally equal share, it's better to get something. Don't you agree, Alice?'

Would Alice agree? She would. I snorted with delight, only to be silenced by a gesture from Zaynab.

'Even a quarter of a man's share of our estate amounted to thousands of acres, and in the natural course of events all that land would have gone out of the family. If I married and had children, my share of the estate would be divided among them, diminishing the family holdings. Even if I married a cousin, my brothers would lose my share. There was one remedy, a scheme devised many moons ago: a female whose right of inheritance threatened her family's estate could be married to the Koran. So a ceremony took place when I was twelve in which the local pir, a retarded pockmarked primitive – a male cousin of mine – declared my marriage to the Koran legal and holy. For a month I was locked up with our Holy Book and nothing else. Food would be left outside, and none of the maids was allowed to speak to me. How I wished my mother were still alive.

'The purpose of this confinement was to acclimatize me to my future. A year later, when I began to menstruate, the book would be removed while I was unclean. They thought that under this treatment I would either adjust to my new reality or take my own life. There were stories of women in my position who had done so. And, to be honest, there were times I thought it might be easier to die than to live like this, and I spoke of my thoughts with women friends who would start weeping at the idea. But one woman did promise that if I really wanted it, she would obtain a cyanide capsule from her husband, a senior officer in some intelligence agency. I promised I would never swallow it without talking to her first, but I needed a couple for emergencies. She obtained two. I wanted to make sure that they worked, so I fed one to my brother's frightening hound, a dog that had cost him a fortune and was as large as one of your Shetland ponies. It worked.'

Alice was horrified.

'Oh, Zay-Nab. Tell me it isn't so. You poisoned a pedigree greyhound. Why not your brother?'

'It was the Hound of the Shahskervilles, my dear. It terrified the peasants. There was much rejoicing when news of the animal's death spread. Some of the serfs called the dog Pir Sahib, and at first people thought it was the pock-marked pir who had met with an accident, which also pleased them, but the dog's death came as a relief, since he had already killed a child. Don't tell me hounds are gentle creatures, Alice. Depends on their masters. Sámir Shah had encouraged the hound to be what it was. Do you want to see the other capsule? I keep it in this little *naswar* container that once belonged to my mother.'

She reached for her bag and took out a tiny old silver snuffbox. Inside it lay the beautifully disguised killer, a capsule the size and shape of a pearl. She told us how on hearing of the hound's death her brother had become totally distraught, cancelled an important political tour and immediately returned home in his official helicopter. The country's top veterinary surgeon was sent for and an autopsy performed. The poison had left no trace. The vet, who smuggled heroin as a night job, declared with an air of total confidence that the Shah hound had suffered a fatal heart attack. Sámir Shah screamed at him.

'I never knew that hounds had heart attacks, you pimp.'

'I'm afraid they do in Fatherland, sir, and especially in this region. Must be the heat. They are used to cold weather, you see. German shepherds are immune, but not hounds. General Farooqi's hound had a fatal heart attack only three months ago. If I had known your beast had a weak heart I might have attempted a dual bypass or organized a transplant. Too late now and I'm truly sorry, sir. To which honourable person should I send my invoice?'

Even Alice managed a smile as Zaynab continued her story.

'The dog was mummified, and that is how I first saw Plato, though from a distance. My brother had asked for the best painter in the country to be hired to paint the beast. I. M. Malik was away at a biennale somewhere in Europe, so your Plato was given the commission. He heard the official story, and, being Plato, found out a great deal more by talking to the villagers. As we know, he can never paint a realist portrait. What he did instead was brilliant. He portrayed a strange beast with angel's wings and, alas, too large a private part, but it was the face that was remarkable. At first glance you would realize it was my brother. The expression on the hound's face replicated the permanent frown that disfigured his master's. I thought my brother would be furious, but no. This is a wonderful painter, he told us later, who has captured the affinity between hound and master so beautifully. The painting hangs in the hall where you enter his house.

'When I asked for permission to congratulate the painter in person, to my astonishment, Sámir Shah agreed. Strange man he was, my brother. He was amoral, without scruples of any sort, ready to trample on anything and everything that stood in his way, as I know only too well. Yet the death of the hound undoubtedly affected him, and quite deeply. Plato was very handsomely rewarded for his work and I had my first conversation with him. It lasted exactly fifteen minutes, and then the Pajero drove him back to Karachi. Of course, he knew immediately that I had guessed his real intention and did not attempt to dissimulate. All he said was that every landlord and politician in the country should be painted as a mongrel. The mischief in his eyes was appealing, and also, I suppose, the fact that he was the first man outside my immediate family, excluding our serfs, with whom I had ever spoken, and I was fast approaching forty. That made an impact, though even at first sight he did not seem very developed from a sexual point of view. A woman in my position is more alert in these matters than someone like Alice, for instance. I felt that physical pleasures were not a Plato priority. There are some people I know, male and female, who can never accept any feelings they themselves are incapable of experiencing as authentic. Plato was the opposite. I could read that in his eyes, and it was confirmed in the months that followed.

'Are you wondering why I didn't escape from my prison, especially as I had the key to the door in my pocket? Simple. I had no money in my name. No bank account. No nothing. I didn't really exist. There was another factor. Had I met a man and married him it would have been a suicide wedding. The primitives would have met and decreed that I had dishonoured the Koran, and pirs would have been found to pronounce the death sentence. It wasn't till Sámir and the brother next in age to him, whom I hated so much that I prefer not to mention his name, died in a plane crash and Sikandar came home to take charge of the estates that my life began to improve.

'Sikandar and his wife took me out everywhere, and for the first time I began to experience everyday life in the big city. Sikandar bought my share of the land, and gave me the money and a great deal more, including the large apartment in Karachi. He had a sorrowful expression when he told me that though he wanted my happiness, it would be best if I didn't marry. He was not powerful enough to prevent the pirs from issuing a death sentence. By this time I did not have any desires in that direction, and then Plato entered my life, bringing happiness and intellectual comforts that I had not thought possible. Everyone believes he's my cook-chauffeur. You know his face. With a tiny disguise and a change in body language he can play any part. He told me that he had taken you in, Dara, by pretending to be a Bengali caretaker.' She threw back her head and laughed. Alice looked shell-shocked. None of us spoke.

'Tell me, Zay-Nab, is marriage to the Koran permitted by Islam? Never heard of it before.'

'Of course not. The clerics attack the practice every day, denouncing the landlords, but they do nothing. A few suicide bombers in the haunts of these guys might work wonders. Instead, they punish the poor.'

'A primitive device to destroy primitives,' said I. 'The idea is not without merit, but it's their economic power that needs to be destroyed. No point killing individuals if the institution survives.'

'Which government in Fatherland will ever do that, Dara? It's been going on for too long.'

'So medieval,' said Alice. 'So bloody medieval.'

'Medieval Europe perhaps, Ally, but not the medieval Islamic world. They were spared feudalism. Zaynab's misery can't be blamed on Islam. Didn't you once say in public that patriarchy plus property equals murder?'

'Spare me my juvenilia, Dara. Please. There are more important issues at stake. Zaynab, may I ask you a very personal question? We can tell this male monster to leave if you want.'

'The monster can stay. Ask whatever you wish.'

'Are you a virgin?'

For the first time that evening, her face clouded over, and for a moment it seemed that Alice had crossed a heavily protected frontier. Zaynab sighed, then said, 'I don't mind the question at all. Plato asked me exactly the same one and became quite upset when I replied truthfully, and it was the memory of his sadness that I was thinking about when you repeated the question. No, I'm not a virgin. Technically, if I can put it like that, I deflowered myself with a candle when I was seventeen. That was also the year I was beginning to read Balzac, not that the two events are linked in any fashion. It's just that when I started rereading him many years later, memories of the candle I had burnt at my altar always reappeared. The maids had replaced the sheets very quickly. They were my only confidantes and friends. I told them everything and they never, ever betrayed me. It was the only girl talk that was possible and I enjoyed it greatly. There were no affectations, no melodrama, no feeling that we were entering uncharted or perilous waters. None of that. They were all married and would describe their experiences in great detail. Two of them had husbands who performed like animals. They made the comparison well, because their sex education had consisted of watching stray dogs and donkeys and horses copulating at various times. One of them had a more thoughtful husband who would give her a great deal of pleasure and she was not shy about describing the foreplay. The others would giggle and ask to share him. I actually did.'

Even I jumped up at this point.

'You did what?'

'When I first put this proposition to her, she thought that I was teasing and giggled at my joke. I said I was serious and her face went pale as the sand. At first I imagined it might be jealousy on her part. That I would have understood, even though I had not at that time felt the emotion myself, but had read about it a great deal in French novels. If she had been jealous, I would have immediately withdrawn the request. When I made this obvious she was mortified. It wasn't that at all, she told me. She then admitted she had talked about me to him, told him about the candle and the stained sheet. He had expressed sorrow at my fate and abused the men who had reduced me to these straits.

'She was sure he would oblige, and for her part she was happy to share him. Had I not after all, she asked, shared much with her and the other maids? Her only fear was that we'd be found out, and there, too, she was not afraid on her own behalf. If he and I were caught we would both be put to death. Him first. They would disembowel and burn him. She could not bear the thought of losing him or me. I reassured her: it was merely an idea and between the idea and the deed there is often a long interval. In any case, everything would have to be very carefully planned.

'When she informed him of my proposition and her concerns, he immediately calmed her fears. Over the next months we devised a plan. Its details are of no significance. In my situation, melodrama was never far from the surface, and with some reason. And so one day it happened, and everything his wife had confessed regarding their most intimate moments turned out to be true. From that day on, whenever I was menstruating, he would come and pleasure me, except when unforeseen circumstances made the operation risky. That is how I came to experience the delights of being a woman. And you know something, after my first year in Karachi, where I observed the unhappiness of so many women from my class who had been married for some time, and heard their tales of woe about philandering husbands and being abandoned by their children, I did begin to wonder whether being married to the Koran and being pleasured by a man I shared with a dear friend had in some ways been a less cumbersome experience.'

Alice applauded loudly, which grated on me. 'It's truly wonderful,' she crowed. 'It restores my faith in humanity. When we were young we used to say that marriage was akin to prostitution, since cash dependency made many women prisoners. May I ask how long this business of sharing went on?'

'It still does, but extremely irregularly. Once or twice a year I send for him. I once tried a very clever journalist, but his cleverness, alas, was confined to his newspaper columns. He was very stupid and crude in bed and I had to ask him to leave before it went any further. Afterwards when we met on social occasions I think he was more embarrassed than I was.

'My friendly maid moved to Karachi with me, and so did her children. He would come here once or twice a fortnight to see them. So we've never lost contact. He's also a very sharp-witted observer of what goes on in that world. Often I pass on the things he tells me to Sikandar, who is always amazed by my "spy network". I wrote a poem about him in Sindhi but it doesn't sound so good in English. It was in praise of the soil, rich in ardour, that produced such men, compelled to seek the sun inside themselves; their secret passions, concentrated energies that kept their muscles taut and produced a voluptuousness without a trace of languor. Enough. I'm very fond of him, even though our conversations are often limited to issues relating to the land. That is what upset Plato. He found it all quite disconcerting. I told him I would be delighted if he could replace my aging peasant, but he simply couldn't. We did try.'

'So did we,' said Alice, unable to resist the competition. 'That's when Dara walked in and served my needs so well. I can recommend him.'

'All that is over now, praise Allah. My life has changed its course. I'm on a grand tour, first Europe, then China.'

I left to visit the washroom with their mocking laughter in the background. I could see how Plato had fallen so badly for her. She was an amazing creature. Could she be the inspiration for all the mermaids that he now painted? When I returned I asked whether she was his latest muse and model.

'I am. I sit for him, but he can't explain why I must always be depicted as a mermaid.'

'Surely it's disgustingly obvious,' said Alice. 'He doesn't want to imagine you with private parts. What other possible reason could there be? The role of the mermaid in ancient mythology is essentially that of a prick-teaser.'

The remark irritated me. She was trying to show off. 'Don't be ridiculous, Ally . . . er, Alice. Mermaids have a totally different function in different . . .'

'Please, let's not argue abut mermaids. I've had a really nice evening, but we haven't yet discussed your Plato, and I'm worried.'

'Why?' we asked in unison.

'His depressions are getting worse, not better. You can see all of this in his latest work. There are days when he is completely suicidal, which is why I never leave this capsule at home. I carry it wherever I go. In a melancholic fit he could grab and swallow it, and where would that leave me? I see less and less of him. He spends more and more time in his studio. Drinking and painting, day and night, as if he were racing against death. The humour in his work has almost disappeared.'

'But why?'

'I'm not sure. There is this absurd and foolish rivalry promoted by the press. Is Pervaiz Shah as good as I. M. Malik? Numerous articles, and people who know nothing about art writing long and dull essays on both painters. Even those who praise Plato haven't a clue as to what he's about and where his art stems from. Has either of you seen I. M. Malik's work?'

Alice had never heard of him. I knew him slightly from the past and had seen his paintings at various exhibitions.

'He's decorative, shallow, pretentious and this was my opinion long before Plato entered the field. I. M. Malik paints to please and sell. Fair enough, but I can see why it drives Plato crazy. But I can't totally accept that IMM's success is the whole cause. Plato knows IMM's artistic worth perfectly. If you can bear to download images of his latest piece of conceptual art, you'll see that even old IMM realizes that shit produces money. He has used horse manure, dried cow-dung cakes and pigeon droppings to create a huge birthday cake for his own ninetieth. There is an additional problem. I. M. Malik looks like a shrunken, constipated accountant, which can be slightly off-putting.'

Alice disagreed with my assessment. She thought it was perfectly possible that Plato had gone into a decline because of the state of global culture. 'It's the same everywhere. As a music critic I sit through countless operas and concerts here and at the Met in New York. Tickets are so overpriced that not many music lovers can afford seats. It's corporate entertainment now and the audiences are very philistine. Directors know this and play to their weaknesses. They laugh at some stupid slapstick in a Mozart opera, they applaud a badly sung aria simply because the star stops and waits for the applause, etc. It is depressing. The ability to discriminate is disappearing fast in Western culture. People like what they're told to like, and since they've paid a high price for it they convince themselves that what they've seen and heard was good. The theatre's no different. Any serious criticism is regarded as disloyal. After a week at work I often feel suicidal.'

I knew Plato better than either of them did and knew that his depression had little to do with lack of appreciation. That had never bothered him at all. I feared it was his past, and his impotence and his love and desire for Zaynab that he could only partially fulfil. He had refused to see an analyst. Might a chemical do the trick? It seemed cruel, but I wondered whether Zaynab had tried Viagra or one of its equivalents.

'He'd be horrified. He's always making vicious jokes about the sixty-somethings who cruise nonstop in the Viagra triangle in Clifton. The thought of him . . .'

'I wasn't suggesting you hand him a tablet. But you poisoned the hound, didn't you? Give it to Plato mixed with what the Bangladeshis refer to as *shag gosht*. Who knows, both of you may get lucky.'

Alice backed up this suggestion. 'No harm in trying it once. If it works and the depression disappears, do it regularly. If it doesn't, you lose nothing. Why did you never suggest it to me, Dara?'

'We were much younger then and you were still Ally.'

Zaynab was worried. What if it gave him a heart attack? She'd read that a former president of Nigeria had died of an overdose while on the job. We advised caution the first time. Perhaps just half the recommended dose. She promised she would try when she returned. Before that she planned a trip to Paris. It was her first time and she wanted to see with her own eyes the Latin Quarter where Balzac had lived, worked and staved off his creditors. French novelists had kept her company during the early years of her marriage to the Honoured Classic, and she still returned to them from time to time. Her life had become a never-ending rush. She could never stay in one place for too long. Even when at home she travelled a great deal, seeing parts of the country that were new to her.

Her sister-in-law belonged to the old ruling family in Swat, and she would often go and stay there in the summer, using it as a base to visit Gilgit. She told me this as I was dropping her off at her hotel.

'Have you ever been to Swat? Strange to think that there's a war going on now, a war in which Plato and I find it difficult to support either side. One of Plato's paintings shows both sides as one. A hydra-headed beast.'

'No mermaids on the landscape?'

'None. You haven't answered my question.'

I described a trip I'd taken to Swat over forty years before, with a small group of students travelling by a GTS bus from Mardan, where I had been staying with close family friends. Our bus wound its way along tiny roads where one had to pull to the side and stop when a car or lorry approached from the opposite direction. Suddenly an old Rolls Royce pulled up behind us, its driver honking aggressively and gesturing that he wanted the bus to move out of the way. Overtaking was not permitted, and our driver, correctly, refused. Ten miles on there was a broader stretch of the road. The car passed us then and screeched to a halt in front of us. We stopped. The owner of the Rolls was the Wali of Swat, a traditional tribal chief, ennobled and placed in power by the British and mercilessly lampooned by Edward Lear. He walked out of the car. The Swatis sitting in the bus cowered. Men and women covered their heads and tried to hide. The Pashtun driver, now trembling with fear, was asked to step outside. He pleaded for forgiveness. He'd had no idea it was the Wali's car. His pleas were ignored. The Wali took a rifle from one of his bodyguards and shot our driver dead. Then he drove away. We were stranded for three hours before another driver arrived.

'Allah save us,' said Zaynab. 'That was my sister-in-law's grandfather.'

I let her out of the car.

'Perhaps we can continue this conversation in Paris? I'll be staying at the Crillon for two weeks.'

'Enjoy, it was the SS headquarters during the war.'

'Does that mean no?'

'No. But it doesn't mean yes either.'

'Why? I have much more to tell you, things I didn't want to mention in front of Alice Stepford.'

'And it has to be in Paris?'

'You must admit it would be more congenial. Where else can I practice that French that Mlle Verbizier taught me in my youth? *Vous comprenez?*'

I made neither comment nor commitment, but waved a friendly farewell as she let herself out of the car.

ELEVEN

The news was on the front page of the *International Herald Tribune*. A former general and two of his guards had been shot dead in the heart of Isloo, the heavily-policed Fatherland capital. From the tone of the report it was clear that he had been genuinely supportive of the West's efforts in Afghanistan and the killers were assumed to be al-Qaeda or the Taliban, or both, or an offshoot of either. In other words, there were no clues at all. It had not been a suicide terrorist. On the contrary, the report stressed, it had been a well-planned execution by a killer or killers who had escaped and left no traces. Yet another casualty of the Afghan war, I thought, and turned the page to read the rest of the international news, no longer to be found in most British papers.

Then my cell phone, a little-used object, began to buzz. Jindié was ringing from Isloo. She had to cancel our dinner engagement scheduled for that night. The dead general, she informed me, was her son-in-law. She sounded calm, a bit too calm, I thought, as I offered my condolences.

She would ring on her return, which should be within a fortnight. Zahid could stay the forty days if he wished. Not her.

Paris beckoned. Zaynab would be there for three more days. I rang. She was surprised and, I think, pleased. I reserved a room at my favourite dive in the Quarter and booked a seat on an early afternoon train to France.

I had been looking forward to seeing Jindié on her own and discussing the events in Yunnan that had transformed her family's life. The letter describing the last days of the Dali sultanate affected me more than I had realized. At least they hadn't decapitated his dead body before the eyes of his women and children. Why bother, they must have thought, when we are going to rape and kill them all. What had happened to the beautiful spy and her child? Did they survive in Cochin China? How delicious if one of the descendants had fought against the Americans in Vietnam. I had recurring thoughts about imperial rulers since ancient times who never paid heed to the rest of humanity.

Jindié had supplied me with knowledge usually available only to specialist scholars. The Taiping and Boxer rebellions feature in virtually every book on modern Chinese history. Why not Yunnan and Dali? Weighed on any scale, eighteen years of semi-independence defended against repeated Manchu assaults was no mean achievement. I could not fully fathom the reason for disappearing this rebellion from history.

Deprived of Jindié's company for another two weeks, I had time to read her diary at leisure and began it as the train moved out of London. She had provided me with photocopied extracts. They were handwritten, but in the neat scrawl that she and others had been taught by the nuns at a Jesus and Mary convent school in Fatherland and that never got better, usually worse, when the luckier girls finished their education at Nairn College. The extracts I was given began on her wedding day. This irritated me greatly, even though the event was given a three-line entry, dated January 1970. Why was she censoring the earlier years? I wanted to compare her version of events with mine. Instead I got a detailed account of the children, the joys of breastfeeding, teething problems, choice of nursery, speaking Mandarin to them as well as Punjabi, the novels she was reading, described without any sustained reflection. Her father had died in 1974. Her mother had sold the shop and the beautiful old colonial apartment in Elphinstone Buildings and joined them in Washington, enabling Jindié to spend more time away from her family chores, in the university library. The entry on Confucius detained me longer than the others. Even though he had become a blowhard Maoist and severed all connections with his counterrevolutionary revisionist friends, I still had a soft spot for him. He was a brilliant physicist and there is little doubt that had he remained in Fatherland he would have been dragooned to work on the Fatherlandi nuclear bomb. The leaders had been desperate for nuclear physicists. But Confucius, like Maoism, had long disappeared. All attempts in DC and Isloo to get the Chinese embassy to help locate him had ended in failure. He was fluent in written and spoken Chinese. Had he taken on a new identity, changed his name, broken with his recent past and gone in search of other roots, or had he been killed in a factional battle with a rival group? Nobody knew. I couldn't believe he was dead.

❦

June 1979, DC

Mother very agitated on seeing the scenes from Tien An Mien Square on the evening network news. She's sure she sighted my brother. I try to explain that Hanif would have little sympathy with most of these students. He would regard them as 'capitalist-roaders' and 'revisionists'. But she won't listen. Her eyes are glued to the television nonstop these days. We all worry. No letter from Hanif for nearly four years. Before he used to write at least once every three months. I wish he hadn't gone to China. 'I must participate in the Great Proletarian Cultural Revolution, Jindié. It's happening now. History is being made. I can't stand on one side.' He pleaded with the Chinese embassy in Isloo for a one-year study visa in 1969 and then disappeared. Did they find him and lock him up for having no legal papers? The Red Guard group he joined was disbanded. He wrote that he was teaching English at a school in Kunming. Then a postcard from Dali. Three letters from Beijing and then silence. I'm sure he would write to our mother if he could. Is he still alive?

24 January 1984, DC

Mother died peacefully today. I got a shock when I took her some tea and saw her lying there stiff with her mouth and eyes wide open. I screamed. Zahid felt her pulse. He examined her and thought she must have died a few hours previously. Her heart stopped beating, but no noise, no attempt to shout my name. It was in her sleep and that was nice to hear. I kept thinking of all the things I should have done for her. I don't think I ever told her how deeply I loved her and how much I had depended on her in my youth. Even in those days she said things only if she had to. It was Father who talked to us a lot and punished us. She would watch, a wry smile on her face.

It was different with my children. They later told me how she laughed and played with them when Zahid and I were absent. She would talk endlessly about Yunnan and the last days of Dali, telling them the same stories that I had heard from Elder and Younger Grannies, stories that I had put aside, not wishing to burden the children with memories that meant nothing to them. It was after my mother died that Neelam started praying and wearing a hijab.

Hanif's disappearance weighed heavily on my mother and not talking about it must have made it worse. Whenever I mentioned him she would ask me to be silent. She simply did not wish to talk about it.

We've all been weeping. The children, who adored her, insisted on staying *at home today. We buried her late in the afternoon in the Muslim cemetery. Zahid angrily brushed aside the Imam who said that Neelam and I shouldn't be present.*

She never said much after Father died, always felt she was a burden on us. How many times did I reassure her that we couldn't do without her. It was true. She loved the children and cooked for them, went out with them when Zahid and I were out of town. Her only regret was that she had never visited Yunnan to pay tribute to her ancestors.

I went to the children's bedrooms in turn to kiss them goodnight. Suleiman was too upset to talk. Neelam asked: 'Who is Dara?' I answered quickly. 'An old, old friend of your father.' She persisted. 'And a friend of yours?' I wondered if my mother had said something, but that seemed so unlikely. 'Why don't you answer, Mom? I've read your diary.' I slapped her and then started weeping and hugged her. That night I destroyed the old diary. 'What difference does it make if she knows?' was Zahid's tired response. It made a difference to me. Neelam never raised the matter again. Didn't sleep all night. I went to the kitchen, made tea the way mother used to and kept bursting into tears as different memories of her queued up in my head. She never lamented the loss of her past, but the children had confirmed that it never left her. I wandered into the attic and opened the suitcase full of old photographs. I was still there when the children woke up the next morning.

But what had she written in the now destroyed diaries? It was not like her to burn anything related to the past. Her father had impressed on his children that archives were an important part of a family's history. A family without archives was one that was ashamed of or trying to conceal its past for whatever reason. He said that in my presence on one occasion. This was a sore subject in our household, where the servants without thinking had sold my father's entire archive to the recycling merchant who came to collect old newspapers every month. It was my father's fault for not filing them properly, but he blamed my mother for having kept them in sacks that were deposited next to the discarded newspapers. I hoped it wasn't the trauma of reading the now destroyed diaries that had turned young Neelam towards religion. More likely it was the identity politics that is the curse of American campus life. I carried on browsing, skipping descriptions of holidays till I saw the word Nathiagali on the page. I hoped this might be a more reflective entry.

✑

5 July 1986, Nathiagali

It's changed. Overcrowded, each new ugly house intruding on another. No planning at all. Depressing being here and this is our first week. The place is full of eyesores. Too much logging has denuded the pine forests. From a distance the mountains look like shorn sheep. The children have heard so many stories about the magic of this place that they're wondering what it was that Zahid liked so much about it. He was amazed, too; 'It's become like Murree and compared to that this was heaven.' The old club no longer in use. Peeped through the broken window of the Library. The leaking roof was never repaired. Books wrecked. Zahid insisted we walk to the Post Office. Still there but no Younis. The old postman recognized Zahid. Said Younis died a few years ago. Cirrhosis of the liver. There's a new sub-postmaster. A young man with a flowing beard introduces himself. Tea offered but declined. This young man would never have let D and Z read letters not intended for them. Yesterday I walked to the Church. Still there as the spot where D and I first felt close. What he would make of this place now? Did he ever return? When? Can't help thinking about him here . . . we all walked across the path to Mokshpuri and came down in Doongagali which was less crowded and seemed much nicer. Would D think that too now? He used to be scathing about Doongagali even though two of his friends lived here. He was always teasing them. The children, too, preferred this gali and Zahid asked the locals about land availability. They clammed up.

The days creep by and my spirits are low. I want to leave here and go to Lahore.

I had felt the same about the place when I returned in 1984, even though at the Green's Hotel end of Nathia the eyesores were some distance away, but even then there was much talk of Afghan refugees and nearby training camps for the jihadis fighting the Russians in Afghanistan. Many locals had complained that the Afghans were wrecking the environment. The region is much worse now. I try not to think about it too much. I was hoping to encounter an arresting penned portrait of Zahid in her diary, something that gave some account of his professional and personal trajectory. Jindié was never overtly political like her brother or like the rest of us, but her sympathies lay on what used to be our side. She would listen carefully, occasionally interject a remark or two and sometimes denounce poor Confucius as a mindless fanatic. The adjective was misplaced. I certainly wasn't prepared for what I was about to read.

4 December 1986, DC

In a few hours today much of what I had built up in my life over the past nine and a half years has collapsed. All that remains are the children. This is much, much worse than the affair with the nurse. That never bothered me. In fact I was relieved, since I could never provide him with the passion that he needed so desperately. But this is unacceptable. He came home at the usual time. Halfway through dinner he tells me in as casual a voice as he can manage that he has decided to join the Republican Party. The Fatherlandi doctors in the United States are divided. The new arrivals gravitate towards the Democrats or are apolitical. The older settler doctors, now earning small fortunes, go in the direction their investments take them. Reagan is better for business so they go with the Republicans. Zahid used to denounce them as tarts. He's become one himself. It marks a real degeneration and a big shift in sensibilities. How long can I live with him? Till the children have left home? Five more years.

On a personal level I have no complaints. Our marriage was one of convenience. Neither of us pretended we were in love. We knew each other reasonably well and that helped. Better than marrying a complete stranger. There were no hidden corners in our lives. We both had our ghosts. He knew everything about D and me. I knew a few things about him and Anjum. Her loss had hurt him more than he would ever acknowledge. In the early days of our marriage I would try and draw him out, but the pain was too strong. He told me: 'Talking about her to you or anyone else won't help. If it did I would.' I never mentioned her name again.

After he announced his new political affiliation, I left the room. He didn't follow me to try and explain the philosophical leap that he had made. There was only one explanation. Opportunism born of greed. He is a doctor. He can turn the microscope on himself. I avoid him now. The children know that something's wrong.

Today he tried to confront me. Pure bluster. He didn't believe in it, but others had insisted. It would help the community of doctors from Fatherland. What did it matter to me, since I had never shown the slightest interest in politics. I let him wallow in self-pity for a while, before replying.

'I was never political like you were, but the reason I liked you and married you was because I thought you had some integrity. Some principles in which you believed. That meant a lot to me. Now I find you loathsome. I can never respect you again. You're no different from your colleagues who still organize gender-segregated dinners to show their affection for the old country. You've become one of them. If it weren't for the children I would leave you now and make sure I hired a really good divorce lawyer.'

He didn't reply and I couldn't resist a final kick.

'Dara was so right when he told me once that it wasn't institutions like marriage

that mattered. The only unions that work have to be based on genuine passions. Love and politics.'

He was silent.

I told the children. They didn't reply, either.

Poor Zahid. He must have been as stunned by this response as I was now. Did I say that to her? Slowly it came back. It must have been that night in the Shalimar Gardens. It had been a response to something she had said linking love to marriage. Eighteen at the time, she was limited in her experiences and had a fixed notion of the perfect lover-husband. She may well have identified with Dai-yu, the ethereal heroine in Cao Xueqin's masterpiece, but surely her ideal lover couldn't possibly be Bao-yu – or had the fiction become so real that it had impinged on reality? Even so, not Bao-yu. No. He was far too flaky. She had certainly changed since those days. Experience is often the best teacher, but what on earth had impelled her to stay on, and especially after the children left home? Habit? Convenience? I wanted answers. She had to come back soon. A fortnight was too far away.

The train had reached the Gare du Nord.

TWELVE

I wasn't completely sure why I was in Paris. Zaynab was a pretext, since she was returning to London. I was too old to brush up my French. The time for *J'aime, tu aimes, il aime, nous aimons* was long gone. And an old and close friend here, Mathurin, a gifted composer, was no longer alive. Usually Matho was the first person I rang. We would meet within hours, debrief each other on the state of the world and the world of our personal lives, retire to a café near St-Germain, and there he would detail the latest atrocities of certain Parisian intellectuals, far gone in vanity and conceit, that we had both come to loathe. They were the 'ultras' of the new order: social, economic, political liberals, they hated their own radical pasts and now even opposed traditional conservative Gaullism and republicanism for being too *gauchiste* and *étatiste*. Their carpings, far from costing the intended targets any sleepless nights, simply provoked mirth.

Matho would provide me with rich gossip, complete accounts of what was really going on underneath the surface. Political and sexual affairs were effortlessly combined in his narrative. What angered him greatly was that even some of the French extreme left had become partially infected with the neoliberal ideology; *Liberation* acted as the principal conduit of these ideas and was often less interesting than the traditional conservative journals. The paladins of the financial markets were seen as bold crusaders, opening new paths for the subalterns of consumerist excess. It was not envy that had soured Mathurin. It was a mixture of contempt and anger with the new order. He would speak of some colleagues in the world of music as having become so tense that they stifled the music they were being paid to play. He would name names from the past, friends we had in common, women we both knew, and describe their current activities. He often spoke of one woman in particular, a particularly dogmatic *ouvrieriste* for whom he had kept a permanent space in his heart, a bit like the irritating reserved signs in public car-parks, who was now an enormously successful arms dealer and had bought herself a farm where she reared pedigreed horses and rode them as a leisure activity. We laughed. He was firmly convinced it would end badly for the turncoats.

'And yet', Matho would say in his gravelly voice, 'I still miss her sometimes. There was something beautiful and soft underneath the hard exterior that she wore both then and now. Sadness can sometimes last for years. I composed a symphony to bid her farewell. She came to the premiere with one of her clients from the Gulf. They left after fifteen minutes. None of the critics liked the work. I think they were right. It was too sentimental, but it sold well. Too well in Paris and not at all well elsewhere. Later I discovered that a PR firm she used was buying the CDs in bulk from all the shops here. Strange gesture, but my bank was happy.'

On one occasion, as we were sitting at his table in the Café de Flore, a former acquaintance sauntered over towards us. Matho warned me: 'He's completely gone over to the ultras but for some unknown reason likes to pretend he's still on our side, wallows in rubbishy nostalgia and has nothing to say. Please don't encourage him to stay. I can't stand his spindly legs walking in our direction.'

As long as Matho was alive, I would come often to Paris. I was stuck in deepest Fatherland without access to a computer or cell phone when he died fifteen years ago, and as a consequence I could not attend his funeral. After that I virtually stopped coming to this city. I missed him. I missed his sharp tongue, his energy, his vicious sense of humour and his refusal to surrender to the world in which we all lived.

Once, after an overlong New Year's Eve supper – waiting for 1976 – at his lover's apartment, where too many bottles of red wine had already been consumed before the bubbles that greeted the New Year, I thought Matho was fast asleep and not listening to our conversation, knowing that he had the capacity to drop off whenever he felt intellectually exhausted. I'd forgotten that it was foolish to put too much faith in these naps, because as soon as he disagreed, which he did on hearing me discussing the events in Lisbon with his mistress, he would immediately wake up and resume the thread of the discourse taking place around him. That same evening, Matho opened his eyes and became genuinely irate when I confessed to the assembled party that I had never read any Stendhal. To make up for the *faux pas* I named the French novelists I had read and enjoyed, only to be brushed aside by him.

'No need to flaunt your ignorance, my dear. Read him and I guarantee that you will love him. I don't know the best English translations, but in French he's without an equal. Zola is essentially a journalist; Proust is a self-indulgent genius; Balzac is, of course, brilliantly predictable; but Stendhal, he is something else. The way he unveils a struggle of ideas and the resulting emotions is masterful. An unwitting reader not fully able to grasp the writer's mind suddenly begins to sympathize with a character whose radical beliefs are far removed from his own. Before he knows it he's trapped. Happiness and misery are often related to the rise and fall of revolutionary politics. Read him, Dara. This is an instruction from the Committee of Public Safety.'

Thanks to Matho, I did exactly that and have never stopped. His books became the equivalent of an indispensable lover. They accompany me on all my travels. What is so wonderful about them is the way in which he breaks the rules, political and literary. He writes at an enviable pace and explains somewhere in one of his novels that 'I write much better as soon as I begin a sentence without knowing how I should end it.'

Once I had read him he became regular fodder in my discussions with Matho, and new questions arose. Had Stendhal ever lain with a woman outside a brothel? I did not think so. His biographers failed to convince me of the opposite, but Matho became indignant at such a thought, even though he had no proof whatsoever. I was quite pleased to discover that the great novelist shared this lack of facility with my painter friend Plato.

As I dragged my suitcase in the direction of the taxi queue, I wondered what Stendhal's refined intellect would have made of contemporary France, where the ultras he hated so much had recaptured official politics. The unrequited love that dominated his life and fictions was twined to memories of political passions and betrayed hopes. The sight of Paris, if you don't live there, brings back all these memories.

Stendhal and Balzac had strolled along these streets, the latter puzzled as to how there could be not a single reference to money in *La Chartreuse de Parme*. Before them others had walked here, too, Voltaire and Diderot, Saint Just, Robespierre, and later Blanqui and the Communards, followed by Nizan, Sartre and de Beauvoir. It was the intellectual workshop of the world. Here the individual enterprises of philosophers and revolutionaries became part of a continuum that was certainly one side of the intellectual history of France. That is what makes the city precious for outsiders and exiles, even when times are bad. Those who love history must love Paris. Wander the streets late at night in the Quarter and linger over their nameplates; it's a refreshing antidote to prevalent fashions.

Matho is no more, but his circle of friends still exists, a valiant minority of dissident publishers, intellectuals and workers who regularly and courageously challenge the established order and its mediacracy – men and women who live in a huge bubble, who are unable to account for themselves, and do not regard this in any way as a problem, who rarely question the sociohistorical realities that have produced them, not even when those realities erupt and threaten to bury their future in the lava.

I have maintained contact with many of the dissidents, all good people, but none of them can ever replace Matho. The question 'Why fight back if nobody else does?' always remained alien to him. Had he been alive I would have attempted to explain the reasons for this trip and he would have asked why I was going to dine with such an unusual lady from Fatherland and why she was staying at the Crillon, and I can read many other questions as if in your living eyes, Matho, old friend. Your absence has made you even more vivid and I can hear your music and your indignation very clearly.

To my surprise, she was waiting for me at the station, slightly over-dressed and a bit tense. I didn't immediately recognize her. It can't be the woman I saw in London. She's transformed. A haute couture trouser suit, makeup, immaculately cut and dressed hair and too much jewellery.

'Dara!'

'You should have warned me. Is it a fancy-dress dinner?'

'Don't be mean. Why should I spend the rest of my life mourning my past? I have a reasonable income because my only decent brother has a conscience. I'm free here to do as I wish. Don't I have the right?'

'That's not a good question and never will be and you know that perfectly well. You look lovely.'

'But you're disappointed.'

'Paris is always best after it's rained a bit, the city is cleansed and the sky reverts to blue.'

'You seemed preoccupied when I rang you. Who were you thinking of?'

'Stendhal.'

My response triggered a memory and I laughed at myself. She insisted on sharing the joke, and realizing that her sparkling eyes and red lips would give me no rest, I told her. Once in Berlin, researching a novel soon after the Wall fell, I returned to my hotel and picked up a message to call Vera Fuch-Coady, an East Coast academic then in town working on Walter Benjamin's radio broadcasts for children at the Wissenschaft College. I rang. She was obviously distracted. I asked whether I had disturbed her. I could ring back later. 'No. Not at all. I'm not doing anything. Should we have dinner tonight?' I agreed. She rang back a few minutes later.

'Dara, you know when you rang a minute ago, I said I was doing nothing. This wasn't exactly accurate. In fact I was thinking of Adorno. See you later.'

I was speechless, muttered something to the effect that I looked forward to seeing her soon and hoped she liked oysters, put the phone down and collapsed into laughter.

Zaynab smiled politely. 'Who is Adorno?'

Mercifully a taxi became available at that moment. She seemed nervous, inwardly exasperated or scared. When I asked if anything was weighing on her spirits she described an episode that had taken place earlier that day. While walking in the Quarter and savouring the sunshine she was startled by the sight of a gang of policeman, who poured out of a van, surrounded an African, spread-eagled him against a wall, searched him, demanded papers that were not forthcoming and then bundled him into the van and drove away.

'It happens in Fatherland all the time, but here, too, Dara? I was really shocked. People watched in silence and turned away.'

'Just like Fatherland,' I told her. 'It happens all over Europe. In Italy they love burning gypsies and taunting Muslims. Repression and cowardice in the face of it have become everyday occurrences. Africans from the colonies, kids from the *banlieus*, are often treated like shrivelled leaves. Kicked into the dirt. You'll get used to it.'

'Have you?'

I didn't reply.

Later that evening as our meal was being served I tried to discuss her life and Plato's, which was after all, the supposed purpose of my trip. She was determined to discuss literature. We compromised. My reference to Stendhal had intrigued her.

'I must confess I'm still besotted with Balzac. I can match many of his stories with real-life equivalents in Fatherland. Money and power, corruption feeding on corruption, and the origins of every rich family usually uncover a crime.'

The only Stendhal she had ever read was his compendium *Love*.

'I could never identify with the crystallizing bough in the Salzburg mines. So European. Not his fault, of course. I tried to transfer his method to Sind. Here, I would say, it is the sand that is supreme. The dust storms, the hot winds that sear the skin and the mind, leaving us numb and temporarily paralyzed and distraught. That, too, is like love. Have you never read Ibn Hazm's treatise on love? He wrote it in Cordoba, eight centuries before Stendhal. Very brilliant. I've surprised you. You prefer thinking of me as a martyred provincial from an Asian backwater.'

I had not been sure till then, but now I knew I wanted to spend the night with her. She read my face.

'Did you know that my lush room with a four-poster was once a torture chamber, or so the maid told me.'

'Are you still in love with Plato?'

'No. I was for the first few weeks, but it was pure fantasy. He was very honest with me regarding his condition and we became very close friends. I could discuss anything with him.'

'He's always loved martyred provincials. Why the hell did you insist I write a book about him?'

'Just to see if you could and would, and if you did we had to meet.'

'I'm flattered, but did it never occur to your provincial mind that we could have met without the book?'

'Had you been a composer I would have insisted on a Plato sonata. If you had been a painter I would have asked for a portrait, just to see how you saw him. Try to understand, Dara. I was bored.'

'Hmmm.'

'He told me you were once in love with a Chinese girl. Where on earth did you meet her?'

'In Lahore. She was a Chinese Punjabi.'

'How sweet. Tell me more.'

'No. Provincials trying to patronize their superiors always make themselves look foolish. She'll be in the Plato book. It's all about milieu these days, not just the individual and his ideas.'

'I need some advice from you.'

'How could I dare to advise such a strong-minded and singular woman as yourself? You've managed pretty well on your own till now.'

'I'm touched. Does this mean you'll spend the night in my torture chamber?'

'Would you like me to?'

'Yes, but only after we've had dessert. It's too delicious here.'

'Are you sure it isn't an ill-considered subterfuge?'

She laughed as she placed the order, and after an espresso each, I suggested some fresh air before retiring. She took my arm and we walked the Paris streets, which were slowly emptying of people as the city went to sleep, discussing its history and the ways of the world. I spoke of the country where I could not live, where people were spewed out and forced to seek refuge abroad, where human dignity had become a wreckage. Her own life was a living-death example of a human being putrefying in the filth that was our Fatherland.

'You hate it so much?'

'Not it, but its rulers. Scum of the earth. Blind, uncaring monsters. Fatherland needs a tsunami to drown them and their ill-gotten gains.'

She became quiet.

After we made love, she returned to the question of Jindié and I told her the story.

'Another strong-minded and singular woman. You seem to specialize in them. How could she bear to walk off with Zahid? You were such close friends.'

'Perhaps that's why Plato, unlike Zahid, remains a very good friend.'

'Don't worry about him. He knew we were destined for each other. He told me that every woman he really loves but can't satisfy ends up in bed with you.'

'Surely there've been more than two.'

She laughed without restraint, highlighting another attractive feature of her personality.

The next morning over breakfast she asked whether she should move to London permanently. There was no way she was going back to Fatherland. She was fearful that Karachi was going to explode and there would be a civil war between the North and the South, Pashtuns versus Urdu speakers with Sindhis applauding from the side, hoping each would destroy the other but fearful that the Punjabi army would ride to the rescue.

'And Plato?'

'Plato is dying. I didn't want to tell you last night, Dara, and for purely selfish reasons. I did not want you to think of anything else.'

This came as a complete shock and was deeply unsettling. For some time neither of us spoke. Another old friend was about to die and with him a large part of my own past and shared memories of catamites that we had collectively cursed. I felt a single, salty tear creep down my face and Zaynab brushing it away.

'I did wonder when I heard his voice on the phone. It was hoarse, but he could sound like that after a bad night. What is it?'

'Lung cancer that has spread. It was diagnosed a few months ago. I pleaded with him but he refused to come abroad. He refused chemotherapy. He lives on painkillers. All he does is paint. He said you would like his last paintings because they are from inside him, like the very first etchings. Except these are huge canvases. There is a ladder in the studio. Before I left he said, "Look at this one. My last work. This huge cat is me and I'm watching Fatherland. Look, here are Fatherland's four cancers: America, the military, mullahs and corruption. For the cat there's just a single one, but the cat will die first. Fatherland is on intensive chemotherapy. All sorts of new drugs are being used, but they might end up producing new cancers." It's a horrific painting, Dara. The inner circle of Hell. He wants you to write about it.'

'I will after I've seen it, but why didn't he tell me?'

'He didn't want you or Alice Stepford to know. I have no idea why this is so. And that is the real reason he was so desperate that you write about him. It had nothing to do with any request from me.'

◖◗

When Plato died, Zahid and I would be virtually the sole survivors of the table around which we had all become friends. Of all of us, Plato had had the most extraordinary qualities, and while some of these were visible in his art, one always felt that he had never allowed himself to reach full bloom. He was at once the most honourable and the most unforgiving of men.

I think he felt that loss when I drove him to Cambridge all those years ago; I observed his concentrated gaze as he looked at the latest books in the field that never became his own. He had smiled in a strange way that I interpreted as regret but was probably not.

'Do you still understand this stuff, Plato?'

'A little, but it has moved so far ahead. Way beyond me now. The cold would have killed me. Like poor Ramanujan, incapable of tolerating the cohabitation of extremes.'

'I thought it was repressed homosexuality that sent him scurrying back to India.'

'Another way of putting it could be that it was the unrepressed homo-sexuality of the great mathematician who invited him here that frightened the poor catamite.'

'Both of us could be right.'

'Let's avoid Punjabi melodrama. I think he died of tuberculosis that he contracted here, but I'm not sure.'

It was a crisp November day, but bitterly cold. We had walked for an hour by the river and a friendly poet at Kings gave us lunch. Plato never spoke much in company and when he did there was no artifice. That is why I was puzzled by his failure to tell me he was dying. It would have been in character for him to joke about it and regret that he wasn't a Believer, otherwise he could have looked forward to at least one houri and his ailment instantaneously cured. Ours was a heaven for old men. When we were driving back from Cambridge, he expressed no regrets. All he would say is that one can never completely determine the path that one's life takes. Other factors always intervene to shape our biographies. I asked if he was thinking of anything specific.

'If there had been no Partition I might have come here.'

'But you would never have had time to paint.'

'I would not have needed to paint.'

✺

Zaynab ordered more coffee.

'Perhaps you should have left him the poison capsule.'

'He would be dead by now, and he is desperate to finish the painting.'

'He never will. He can't. He knows that and all he'll do is to carry on enriching the colours.'

'Listen to me, Dara. I hired two nurses to be with him at all times. There is a doctor on call who has promised me to make his last hours easy. I just could not bear to be there when he died. He knew that, which is why he asked me to leave the country.'

I believed her. Suddenly I had a desperate urge to speak to him one last time. To say a few things I had never said to him. About how important he'd been for all of us. Of how the pleasure he took in defying public opinion had infected us, who were a generation younger, and how his unceasing attacks on time-servers and opportunists during a military dictatorship had given us courage.

'Zaynab, ring the nurse, please. I want to speak with him.'

She dialled the number. There was no reply.

'Keep trying, keep trying.'

Finally the nurse answered. She was in an ambulance. Plato had collapsed some hours ago and was unconscious. They were taking him to the hospital. Zaynab and I embraced each other and wept. We spent most of that day in the Louvre, walking in a daze, sitting for a long time in front of a Poussin, thinking of Plato all the time and wondering whether he was already dead. When we returned to her hotel there were dozens of messages. We did not eat, but went straight up. We wept first and then laughed as we sat on the bed and talked about him. We paused to drink some cognac and went to bed, but sleep came fitfully. Images of Plato at different stages of his life kept me half awake, and when I trembled, Zaynab's soothing hands would massage my head.

◗

Plato had left firm instructions regarding his burial. No protection money was to be paid to secure a place in any graveyard. He was quite happy to be eaten by dogs. Zaynab had suggested that since his painting of the dead hound for her dead brother had enhanced the value of the Shah estates, he should be buried close to where she had first sighted him. Pir Sikandar Shah accordingly arranged for Plato's body to be transported to his lands and he was buried in the Shah family graveyard, but without any headstone, as is the custom in that region.

'I can talk to him when I next visit the prison of my youth. May I ask you something?'

It was obvious that we were going to spend this day doing nothing, but I needed a brisk walk and Zaynab showed no inclination to get dressed.

'What?'

'If you were asked to describe me to someone who had no idea of me, what would you say?'

'A Sindhi matron whose natural beauty is inextricably linked to her pride.'

'Why matron? Am I really getting plump, you unfeeling hound? Apart from "matron" I liked that description.'

'"Matron" stays. It denotes maturity and authority more than plumpness.'

'When the Stepford lady was questioning me about intimate matters you did not speak at all. Does that mean you had no thoughts, or were they repressed?'

'I did think that, for your peasant paramour, making love to you must be like having a nun for a mistress, not that he would have got the reference. Not that you were a nun. A nun is full of piety, and the sin of having a lover provides her with an exceptional frisson that can't be faked. The piety produces the passion. In your case, I think, there was neither. Just simple mechanics.'

'You can think what you like. Was it simple mechanics this morning?'

'I wasn't referring to us.'

'Good. Yesterday was a bit sorrowful. I kept hearing a Sindhi lament in my head as I tried to arouse you. Do you have to leave today?'

'I must. I have to prepare a talk for a conference. I need a few days in the library.'

'That seems excessive. When is your Chinese friend returning from the murder inquiry in Isloo?'

'How did you know about that?'

'I made it my business. My brother says they have no idea who killed the general. It wasn't the usual suspects who are blamed for everything these days.'

'I never thought it was, but why are you so interested?'

'Because you are, and I feel linked through you. I thought if I discovered something you could pass it on to your friend. What my brother did say was that General Rafiq had several mistresses.'

'A crime of passion?'

'Always possible and not just in beloved Fatherland. And there will be another one if you ever turn your back on me. I like you.'

'Remain calm. We're both matrons and must preserve a certain decorum. No reason to regress to our teen years. Sorry, that doesn't apply to you.'

'When will you be back?'

'Within a fortnight.'

'Should I buy an apartment in Paris or London? Has to be a big city. '

'Berlin.'

'So I can leave you in peace to take a Chinese mistress in London. No way. I'm buying an apartment in London. Prices are dropping more and more each day, and Alice has sighted a suitable buy.'

I sat down and shook her.

'Listen to me carefully. Jindié is a friend from the past who lives with Zahid, another friend, whom I once wronged. She is not my mistress.'

'She will be soon. Of this I'm sure. Let's not argue. We'll both know when it happens. As a matter of fact I prefer Paris. Let's go and see apartments today.'

'In the Fauborg St-Germain?'

'Why not? I want something in the Latin Quarter and wouldn't it be fun if I found something nice on the rue de Balzac. And which of Stendhal's novels should I read first?'

'Difficult. Buy them all and toss a coin. How lucky you are to read them in French. I love them all, but if you put a gun to my head I'd say *Lucien Leuwen*. That and the two best-known ones need to be reread every two years, and at my age every six months. One always learns something new. I would also strongly recommend his thinly disguised memoir.'

'By the time you return I'll have finished them. I read very fast.'

'Does understanding keep up with your pace?'

'Does insolence keep up with the charm?'

'Rewrite.'

She was serious enough about buying a flat, and we spent a few hours in various streets looking at available property. She liked one on the rue de Bièvre, and when I pointed out that Mitterand and a Polish Marxist intellectual had once shared the street, adding that Balzac's favourite eatery was here, she became agitated. The agent was rung. The apartment was huge for such a small street, but she would have friends to stay over and would be entertaining regularly. There was no haggling. She would pay the asking price. The agent gave me an astonished look as if to ask whether she was serious. I suggested that he close the deal quickly before she saw something on the rue de Balzac.

'Well, that's settled. Now should we go and inspect some antique furniture?'

🔎

Her living room was especially large, and I suggested that the space above the fireplace might be a home for Plato's unfinished masterpiece. She screamed.

'Hai Allah, never. Never. It's a frightening painting. You haven't even seen it. Anyway it's too big for this apartment or any other. It should be in a public space.'

'Where is it at the moment?'

'At our Sind home, I hope, carefully covered with muslin sheets to dry it properly. He was worried that local hoodlums might raid his studio when news of his death became known. All the other paintings are in a warehouse. This last one is now at home. We need a museum in Europe or North America to give it a home, and someone like you should write an explanation. It really needs one. Can you think of a title?'

'Canceristan?'

'Don't be silly. Something simple and nonprovocative, like Unfinished . . .'

'Last Thoughts in a Dying Country?'

'No. I visit regularly, and Fatherland's death has been predicted far too often.'

'Dying Thoughts in the Last Country.'

'Shut up. One more try, and then I'll—'

'Artistic Structures of Political Meaning in an Unknown Country. Unfinished, 2009.'

'Brilliant. That will be the title. In fact, given that you haven't seen the work, it's pretty close to the mark and sounds obscure. "Unknown" in the sense of being unknown to its rulers. Yes? Good.'

I received a kiss on the cheek. It turned out that she was the sole executor of Plato's estate, and she gave me complete authority to negotiate the sale of ASPMUC to a serious modern museum wherever I wished. She would arrange for it to be photographed and have slides posted directly to me.

'Unless you want to just fly over and see it.'

'Not this month, but I might do that sometime. Always helps. In any case the curator of whichever museum takes it will certainly want to see it before the purchase, or at least send an expert.'

'This book you're writing. It isn't just about Plato?'

'No, and it's not a biography. It's fiction.'

'Allah protect you.'

'No reason for Allah to be upset. I'm just sad that Plato will never read it. He was one of the sixteen people I was writing it for.'

'Am I included?'

'Plato and I went back forty-five years. I've barely known you a week.'

'I feel I've known you a long time, and the book was my idea. I will be one of the sixteen. Let the figure remain.'

On the train back to London, I thought mainly about Plato, since I had been asked by a daily paper to write his obituary. His life had rarely been untroubled or happy till Zaynab offered him a haven. But nor had he died a physically or mentally broken man, like so many of his wealthy peers whose lives had been led without a trace of generosity or compassion, men who had justified, for petty gain, some indescribable horrors of the modern world. Plato died with his pride and self-respect intact.

One summer evening in Lahore we were discussing the fate of Islam in the West. Plato first mocked the nostalgia and sentimentality that prevailed on the subject – a sure sign of total ignorance, he remarked. Zahid backed him up, and when another friend said that the decision by Muslims in al-Andalus to eat pork in order to survive was a crime, Zahid defended their right to eat cow dung if necessary in order to survive. A strange, sad smile prefaced Plato's response.

'It's one thing to eat pork in order to survive. I would have done the same. But they wanted us to swallow our history, our culture, our language, our entire past, and all that is not so easily digestible.'

THIRTEEN

On the twenty-fifth day after the murder of General Ilyas Rafiq, commanding officer of the Special Services Assault Battalion, I went to have dinner with his mother-in-law. Incapable of stomaching any further hypocrisy, Jindié had refused to stay for the *chehlum*, the fortieth day after burial that concludes the ritual of official mourning. She left Zahid to console their daughter and returned to London. Her offer to bring the grandchildren back with her to give them and the widowed Neelam a break had been turned down.

The meal she served, unlike the story that accompanied it, was on the skimpy side, a bit too healthy for my tastes, but all I wanted to know that evening was who killed Rafiq and why. No real evidence had emerged so far – though this tiny fact has yet to spoil a good story from circulating in Fatherland. According to Jindié, each of his colleagues suspected different people with varying motives. I rubbed my hands together in delight. It was a classic Fatherland conspiracy. Three versions were floating in cyberspace, she told me, and any of them could be true, but she no longer cared. As far as she was concerned, her son-in-law had been a reprobate and had come to the bad end he deserved. Yet another *Rashomon* moment for our debased elite, I thought to myself. Assassins are rarely uncovered in Fatherland, which adds to its many charms.

The first and most-believed account linked the death to the machinations of a fellow general, Muhammad Rifaat, who commanded a garrison in a crucial town on the edge of badlands where drone-rockets rained down regularly on the villages and the streams had turned red. Reputedly, the two generals, close friends since their school days, were sharing a mistress, Khalida 'Naughty' Lateef, the spirited spouse of a junior officer desperate for promotion. Naughty Lateef's charms had on one occasion led to fisticuffs between the two men, and all this in the presence of fellow officers. Adultery, especially with the wife of a junior officer, and breach of discipline were both punishable offences.

General Rifaat, who had not provoked the assault, had been officially reprimanded, a black mark that presaged early retirement to a foreign embassy, Kazakhstan or, if he was lucky, Austria.

General Rafiq was reprimanded in private by his chief and told in strong language that such clashes were unseemly. Nothing more. He was an important component in the local 'war on terror' and a regular at the US embassy in Fatherland. An angry General Rifaat decided that this state of affairs was unacceptable and planned a private revenge with the help of his old schoolmate, General Baghlol Khan, a weak-kneed Pashtun, in command of the Inter-Services Intelligence but famed neither for his own intelligence nor for anything else, except obeying orders from his superiors. Baghlol loathed Rafiq because of departmental rivalries, but there were a few other reasons as well. The latter, soon after taking command of the Assaulters, as his battalion was known, had uncovered two ISI plants amongst his senior officers. He ordered them to be returned immediately to their base with his compliments. These took the form of some choice insults, including a throwaway reference to the ISI chief as General Camel's Arse, not an indigenous epithet but one which Rafiq had first encountered as a young officer during his days in Saudi Arabia many moons ago, when Fatherland soldiers defended the kingdom against internal threats. News of the sobriquet had spread, increasing Rafiq's popularity with the soldiery. Camel's Arse was what they thought as well.

Given this history, General Baghlol Khan was only too happy to respond to a personal request from his old friend General Rifaat. He called in one of the officers whom Rafiq had insulted and sent back; together they prepared a crude but effective trap. Naughty was brought in to ISI HQ and told that unless she did what she was asked to do, her husband, Major Lateef, would be provided with ISI videos showing her in action with at least three generals. She was shown clips from all three videos, in which she played a starring role. A stunned Naughty fell into line. She rang Rafiq and arranged a rendezvous. Her task was to lure him into making a few unsavoury remarks about the amorous adventures of their boss, the chief of army staff, whom Washington was plotting to remove for reasons unconnected with this sordid affair.

Rafiq, in a relaxed mood, was only too delighted by the unscheduled rendezvous and happily provided Naughty with a salty account of their chief's amorous exploits, with exact details of the localities in each city where his many lovers lived, houses that therefore required round-the-clock security, diverting some of his assaulters from the war against the terrorists. How could he have guessed that Naughty had a hidden recording device attached to an orifice she knew he had yet to explore? Through this tiny device, a nose-ring, the entire conversation was monitored by Rifaat's chums in the ISI, who, unsurprisingly, were aware that everything said by Rafiq was true. Meanwhile, in case the encounter became so passionate that the ring fell out, a secret video camera had been set up, which filmed the entire afternoon. Some of this unedited material was sold by ISI operatives in the thriving porno-markets all over the country and played exceptionally well in the war zones, where men were starved of affection.

Baghlol went to the chief of staff and played the tape. General Sohail Raza became livid. Not because of the women. That did not bother him at all, but because of the potential risk to his own life. Rafiq was confronted and fired that same week, but Sohail was fond of this brash general who reminded him of his own youth and he knew that in a similar situation he might have behaved in exactly the same way.

He offered General Rafiq a sinecure: head of a key commercial sector of the military-industrial complex where he would have double the salary he had enjoyed as a serving general, with regular kickbacks from potential contractors in the West that would triple the doubled salary. In addition, there was a large mansion attached to the job that he could, of course, buy at a reduced price as he approached his retirement. There was nil responsibility, since all the key decisions were taken by rocket fuel experts and other specialists. Rafiq, by now in a blind and stupid rage, refused what was, after all, an extremely generous offer. His pride was hurt. He felt he was being unfairly punished and he knew who was behind it all.

He resigned from the military on his bare pension, nothing compared to what he had been offered, but sufficient to feed a hundred poor families in Fatherland each month. After a few weeks of sulking in his tent and then numerous visits to the imperial bunker in Isloo, Rafiq wrote a letter to his most senior contact in the Defense Intelligence Agency at the Pentagon. It was sent in a top-security code from the bunker. The general was immediately summoned to DC and interrogated at length.

He had not simply broken ranks but divulged an important state secret to Fatherland's fair-weather ally, a nation that many inside the armed forces considered more an enemy than a friend. The information he provided was explosive. Generals Rifaat and Baghlol were accused of having leaked to the enemy secret plans for his battalion to assault terrorist encampments in the border zones. On three occasions, he told his minders, his highly trained, hand-picked soldiers had been ambushed and killed by the terrorists. He suggested that the DIA carry out its own investigation into the two generals concerned and left behind a carrier bag full of clues and evidence. Not surprisingly, seeing that they were funding Fatherland's army, the Pentagon decided to act swiftly. This was, he had told them, not so much a question of breaching a country's sovereignty but a necessary audit to protect imperial financial interests in bad times. He hoped they were touched by his concern.

When news of this treachery reached its intended targets in Fatherland, the targets decided to eliminate General Rafiq and discredit him in the country at large as a traitor. They did, and the mechanics of how they did are of little concern. This was the end of the first version.

'Does it sound credible to you, Dara?'

I shrugged my shoulders. 'That whole world is so murky that anything is possible. If General Rafiq actually did what this version alleges, then I think the theory is believable.'

'That's what poor Neelam thinks. She's convinced it was an army decision.'

'Just so that we can exclude them, what are the other two possibilities?'

The first of these, which was virtually the same as an official briefing given by the army to select journalists, suggested that the death was a well-planned Talibu execution. Rafiq had been known as a no-nonsense general, closely linked to Western intelligence agencies. His team had targeted and killed a number of senior Talibu commanders, and once they discovered that he was no longer protected by the military, they got information on his regular movements from Naughty's husband, Major Lateef of military intelligence. And they made no mistakes. The Talibu, according to Jindié, are a special squad of the Taliban whose task is to penetrate Fatherland military and police. They are intelligent, beardless and usually dressed in Western clothes and dark glasses. When one of them was captured and tortured, the US officer supervising his interrogation complimented him on his clothes and remarked to the torturer that people now dressed like that in Malibu. The prisoner replied angrily in a West Coast accent, 'We are Talibu, not Malibu.' That was how they discovered the existence of this special unit, or so they claim. The prisoner gave no more information and was killed.

'Well?' said Jindié when she finished.

'Can't be ruled out.'

'No. Except that one of the Talibu visited Neelam in secret and swore on the Koran that they were not responsible.'

'Could be disinformation. And the third?'

'Too stupid for words, but believed by many people Rafiq used to refer to contemptuously as the common herd. They say it was the Americans.'

I snorted with delight. 'I wondered about that. Usually it's the first answer. And it can't be denied that when it comes to procuring assassinations here and elsewhere they find some very clever pimps.'

'Yes, Dara, but it is ridiculous in this case. The whole world knows that Rafiq was one of the staunchest pro-West generals in the country. Three British intelligence people came to our house and sat in this room to offer Zahid and me their condolences before we left to attend the funeral. Why should they kill their own? Oh, you are joking. I'd forgotten that side of you. Last time we met you were so proper. Have you had enough to eat?'

'No.'

She burst out laughing and that reminded me of our youth. We moved from the kitchen table to the living room. I wanted to talk about her diaries and related matters, but she was worried about her daughter.

'What makes them so religious, Dara?'

'Philandering husbands, a desire to cling to something in a world dominated by money, pure desperation?'

'By that criteria I should be in a nunnery . . . but we'll discuss that some other time.'

'When did Neelam move in this direction? Your diaries suggested it was while she was at school in Washington.'

'Yes, but she got over that particular variety. Her best friends were two African-American kids from Muslim families. When she went to Vassar, which is now mixed, by the way, there was no trace of any of this in her life. She seemed happy. Suleiman says she had a Chinese boyfriend who wasn't religious at all, and everything seemed fine.'

'Where did she met Rafiq?'

'At our house in Washington, I'm afraid. He was a military attaché at the embassy. Zahid invited him to address a gathering of Fatherland Physicians for Bush. Rafiq said he would not come unless it was a mixed gathering. So wives and daughters and nieces and female hangers-on were present. She and Rafiq liked each other. He asked permission to see her. Two years later they married.'

'Then it must be to do with him. Did you like him?'

'No, but she did. Neither Zahid nor I were keen that she marry into the army.'

'It must be Rafiq-related. Doesn't make sense any other way. Have you asked her?'

'She would never tell me. She's become an alien as far I'm concerned. We had an old woodcut of our Sultan Suleiman of Yunnan. It belonged to Elder Granny and was probably inherited from her mother. Neelam had it framed and still treasures it, but Dù Wénxiù's sultanate was never like what she imagines Islam should be and how it must impose itself on society. I said that to her once and she snapped back like a little dog. Sultan Suleiman was defeated because he wasn't a true Believer; he allowed people too much freedom and that is corruption. I lost control at that point and slapped her face. She gave me a triumphant smile and left the room. I know it was stupid of me. What really makes me angry is the way she's bringing up those children. They're being indoctrinated. The boy is ten and is told not to talk to girls. The girl aged eight is being taught how to wear the hijab. Is she crazy? No wonder Rafiq went elsewhere for his pleasures.'

We discussed Neelam for a few hours without reaching any conclusion. I was about to leave when I remembered something. What, I asked her, had she written in the destroyed section of the diary that had so upset the teenage Neelam? Might that have prompted her conversion? Jindié coloured slightly.

'It's simply an account of our youth, of how close we once were and of my love for you. Some of it may have been expressed in strong and emotional language. I really can't remember now except that I headlined it with an old saying: Fame is sweet, but youth is sweeter.'

'Surely that can't be a Chinese proverb, or have you substituted "youth" for "venerated ancestors". As we know, they're sweeter than everything else, a sentiment I'm beginning to appreciate more with each passing year.'

'It's Roman, not Chinese.'

'Now they always did appreciate young men. There must have been something in what you said that upset young Neelam.'

'She thought it was a secret from her father. Zahid was a sensitive and loving father. I have no complaints on that score. He told her all about the story of his friendship with you and that he knew about us long before we were married. I thought all that was good for her. Her parents were very open. I shouldn't have destroyed those bits. I was in a temper.'

As I rose and thanked her for the healthy meal, she asked if I wanted to stay. There was a comfortable spare room and we could carry on talking. I asked for some coffee. There was none. But when it was midnight she did offer me a glass of red wine.

'Why did you continue to stay with Zahid after he had become a

Republican? The anger in your diary surprised me, but there seemed to be no follow-up.'

'The children . . .'

'After the children had left home?'

'Perhaps because I had nowhere else to go. Sometimes I've bitterly regretted my decision.'

'Jindié, how could that ever be a reason for someone like you? What an absurd idea. You could have lived comfortably anywhere in the world, and very comfortably in Lahore or Dali.'

'Even though Zahid has changed a great deal, sometimes he is very much like you. He said almost exactly that at a very bad period in our relationship and made it clear that I would never be in need. It was when he suggested that we separate that I changed my mind.'

'Just to be difficult?'

'Partially. There was no other alternative, and by then I had got used to living with someone who did not mean much to me. I used to send his money to the Democrats and Ralph Nader. Everything changed after 9/11. He learned his lesson.'

'Did he really save Cheney's life in 2000, or is that another Fatherland myth?'

'It's true, but he was part of a team. He was so boastful. The children didn't speak to him for a month.'

'That was a good enough reason to walk out.'

'Within twenty-four hours of 9/11, Cheney instructed his staff to make sure that Zahid was removed from his medical team. The Muslim name was enough. He came home that night looking like a beaten dog. We sold everything and left for London some months later. Did you know that he literally ran into Anjum by accident?'

'These things happen. Who would have thought I would have met you again? Or him. Where did he meet Anjum? In Isloo?'

'No, in some sweet-sounding Norfolk town. He was at some exclusive medical conference and had gone out for a walk by the sea. She recognized him. Zahid was stunned. She was wearing a skirt and blouse and a cross round her neck.'

'What? She became a Catholic? What happened to that idiot she married?'

'Alcoholic. Useless. Infertile. Impotent on every front. All his business projects failed. The last was an attempt to link up with an Irish building firm to build roads in the interior of Sind. Work was slow. They lost the contract. The chief engineer was staying with them. Anjum left Fatherland with him. He turned out to be a non-drinking Catholic fundamentalist linked to Opus Dei. Are they anything like the Falun Gong? Can you imagine? He forced her to convert, attend church every Sunday and make regular visits to the confessional. Zahid said she was so miserable that she started weeping as the horror stories poured out of her.'

'Why didn't he offer her refuge in Richmond?'

Jindié laughed.

'He did, but she said her husband would track her down. She was really scared of him. That upset Zahid greatly.'

'Just as well she dumped him when she did.'

'Why? They both might have blossomed. I'm sleepy.'

'You can't stay up all night?'

She started laughing. 'Too old now to spend a night with you in the garden.'

'Neither of us is young. It's pointless deceiving each other or exaggerating what were strong but youthful emotions. I still haven't forgotten that you screamed *Hsi-men* at me. What were you doing reading the *Chin Ping Mei* at that age?'

'It was at home, a very old edition in my father's collection. Both Confucius and I used to read it in secret, but carefully, so that the volumes weren't damaged. No self-respecting Chinese teenager in those days could admit to not having read some of it. At least in our language, it's very funny as well as erotic.'

'True, and even in translation, but how do you explain that there is not a single character, male or female, one can identify with?'

'The anonymous author probably belonged to some obscure religious sect which saw human nature as evil and unchangeable.'

'A bleak view of humanity.'

'Not at all surprising in sixteenth-century China, where corruption, extravagance and the use of women as pleasure machines had affected everyone. There was a reason for the author to remain anonymous. The sex that Western readers enjoy so much was joyless. It was part of the degeneration of Chinese society and that is what he was exposing.'

'Jindié. I'm not sure the author described lovemaking as joyless. Exploitative, male-dominated, but not joyless.'

'It appeared so to me.'

She left the room and returned with one of her books.

'I want to read something to you. It's by Hsun-tzu, who was very hostile to the argument of Mencius that human nature is essentially good, but becomes corrupted by society.'

'I agree with Mencius.'

'The author of *Chin Ping Mei* didn't. He agreed with Hsun-tzu that man's disgrace is but an image of his virtue. Listen: "Meat when it rots breeds worms; fish that is old and dry brings forth maggots. When a man is careless and lazy and forgets himself, that is when disaster occurs." He was attacking the rulers of the time for their refusal to accept moral responsibility.'

'A universal disease as far as rulers are concerned, then and now. I'm still not too convinced by any of this . . . I wonder how my old friend Confucius-your-brother would have interpreted the novel.'

'It's obvious. A degenerate work reflecting a degenerate age. That was the Maoist line on everything classical during the Great Proletarian Cultural Revolution.'

I wondered which of the men who'd led the Chinese revolution to victory had read the novel. Mao would certainly have enjoyed it, and some of his later life gave the impression of being modelled on that of Hsi-men, though the fictional character never had to contend with a tough-minded wife like Chiang Ching. I never liked her, but I couldn't help admiring her poise and arrogance as she confronted her prosecutors in court before being sentenced to a life in prison after the collapse of the Gang of Four. It contrasted well with the demeanour of broken Bolshevik intellectuals in the Stalinist show-trials of the Thirties, confessing to 'crimes' they had never committed. What had our Lahori Confucius made of it all? His testimony would really be something. I willed him to be alive. Did Jindié think he was? She shook her head.

'I think he must have died under a false identity.'

'I feel he's still alive and keeping an eye on us from afar. Just a feeling. Pure irrationality. Is your son Suleiman still in Yunnan?'

'Yes, I'm going to see him next month. I've never been, you know. Time to go and bid farewell to the ancestors. Want to come? Zahid would be very happy.'

It was a tempting offer and I promised to think about it.

'China is going through a remarkable cycle in its history. How will it end?'

'Don't know. Sometimes a nation grows more in a decade than in a century, but there have been so many decades and centuries in the Chinese past that prophecy is impossible. If I can I will accompany you to China. There is nobody else I would rather be with in Yunnan.'

'I will accept that as a compliment.'

I graciously declined her offer of the guest room, though grace is not generally regarded as one of my virtues and is frowned upon as an affectation in most of the Punjab.

'It was a really nice evening, Jindié. I'm really happy we finally spent a night together without quarrelling.'

She kissed my forehead. 'Why did you decide not to stay? Frightened of being raped by me disguised as Hsi-men?'

'I just don't like waking up in a house where there is no coffee.'

She pushed me gently out the doorway.

I drove back to North London just as dawn was breaking. Whatever the time of year, this has to be the nicest time of day to be awake in London, just before the big city wakes up. I crossed the river at Kew, stopping for a few minutes to see if a house I'd shared with friends after leaving university was still there. It wasn't, and, slightly disappointed, I drove on and was home within fifteen minutes. There are advantages to living in an early Victorian square within ten minutes of St Pancras station. Novelists and bachelors share this in common: both are permanently at the mercy of capricious impulses. I espressoed myself two coffees, shaved and showered, left a message for Zaynab on her machine asking her to get some croissants, rush-packed a bag, adding a few books, earphones and my iPod, and walked to the station. At six-fifteen in the morning I was on the train to the Continent.

FOURTEEN

The croissants were cold by the time we finished making love, but dipping the cold edge of one in a bowl of milky hot coffee can sometimes be an equally sensuous experience. Zaynab Koran, née Shah, having lived in Paris for over a month on her own, provided me with an emotional account of her social life.

'I'm not sure I made the right decision, D. I love this city and I love French culture, but something's happened. Have you heard of a Fatherland woman called Naughty Lateef? That's what she calls herself.'

She was flabbergasted when I described Naughty's recent adventures in Fatherland. She repeatedly shook her head in disbelief.

'She's writing her memoirs, and they've started promoting her already. Let me show you the magazine.'

Naughty had made the cover of *Feminisme Aujourd'hui*, a journal that had not crossed my path before and was largely full of ads for perfume, lingerie and related goods. Naughty, herself an Isloo Hui, was the cover story. Prior to this, I'd had no idea what she looked like, but the image on the cover did not come as a surprise. The modesty implied by the Armani scarf covering her head was immediately negated by her two friends below, proudly jutting forward as if to say, 'Look, look, we have them in Fatherland too.' Her looks were typical of Fatherlandi starlets who disgrace an already abysmal cinematic tradition: a fair skin, brown eyes with a tinge of green or blue eyes with a ring of brown, a toothpaste-ad smile, wavy hair, big breasts and a saucy expression.

This was what undiscerning males from the high command of Fatherland's armed forces required for rest and relaxation; and all in all it was best their needs were fulfilled by indigenous commodities. It avoided the trouble of importing Eastern European call girls, whom the fall of Communism had made available in very large numbers to the rest of the world and who now cluttered the hundred or so brothels in Kabul and numerous five-star monstrosities in the Gulf.

The pretty wives of the more obedient junior and not-so-junior officers were regarded as fair prey, occasionally to be had with the full agreement of husbands eying a rapid promotion or a sinecure in the military-industrial enterprises and pleasantly surprised that their wives had turned out to be such lucrative investments. This was the world so well described in the anonymous *Chin Ping Mei*. The Fatherland high command was littered with Hsi-men types, who their juniors were only too happy to mimic.

The interview with Naughty spanned six glossy pages. She was masquerading as a wronged Muslim woman, describing her oppression in lavish detail. The number of times she had been forced by different men, totally against her will, the tears that followed each experience and how when she had complained about this to a religious scholar, he had looked at her with anger and said, 'Women like you should be stoned to death.' Fiction, thinly disguised as fact for the European market, especially France and Holland, where the premiums on this sort of material were high. She informed the reader that she was working on a book for a giant German conglomerate and its North American, French, British and Spanish subsidiaries.

It was not that wronged and oppressed women were in short supply in Fatherland – though their sufferings were not exclusively the outcome of religious oppression – but Naughty was not one of them. I couldn't wait for her book. The fiction was so blatant that it was bound to generate a response. I couldn't help chuckling at market fashions. Fake anti-communism and Holocaust memoirs had become popular a few decades ago, with publishers justifying these faux biographies as an attempt to grapple with a unique experience of horror, rather than seeing them for what they were, tawdry attempts to exploit a historical tragedy in order to appease one's bank manager.

Now it was open season on Islam. Any piece of rubbish was fine as long as it targeted the followers of the Prophet, preferably rubbish from women with pleasing exteriors, who would be easier to market in the West. I could see why Zaynab, forcibly married to the Koran, was seriously upset by Naughty's dramatic entrance on the European stage. Zaynab had a real tale to tell, a story that had the Holy Book at its centre and the uses made of it by cruel and rapacious landlords to oppress their sisters and daughters. She had never spoken about any of that in public when she was in Europe. She told me she had no desire to fan the flames of prejudice.

Zaynab threw the magazine in the kitchen bin. 'Let it putrefy happily in the company of rotting vegetable matter and discarded eggs past their sell-by date.'

'Why are you so angry? Naughty's just trying to assert her independence and make a bit on the side. Not the first nor the last to do so.'

'Perhaps not, but do you have any idea how bad things are in this town? At three dinner parties over the past fortnight, and with very different types of people, the minute they realized I was brought up a Muslim, the same question was pointedly repeated and usually by very nice, cultured people and always with a charming smile: Why does your religion insist on female circumcision? I was enraged by this absurdity. Where on earth have they got that idea from? I was polite the first few times and said that as far as I knew the millions of Muslims in Indonesia, China and South Asia had never suffered from this practice. It was restricted to parts of Africa and had tribal origins. Christian women in those areas were also mutilated. No injunction in the Koran or the traditions that I know so well demands it. And I was quite proud that this was so. I was unchallengeable. The third time it happened I did raise my voice. If men can be circumcised, why not women? It was a sign of our equality. Anything a man could bear, so could we.'

'And?'

'Shock. Horror. Till they realized I was being facetious, and then I let them have it. I really did. This last dinner party was in a very proper, polite, even haute bourgeois household. Still they asked. The level of ignorance was so toxic that there was a moment when I thought I'd drop my poison capsule in the host's wine.

'To change the subject, I inquired whether anyone at the table was a strict believer, since I certainly did not qualify. Two young men, both Normaliens, admitted without a trace of shyness that they were practising Roman Catholics and, to the embarrassment of their parents, they put up a staunch philosophical defence. I asked about abortion. They were opposed. Divorce and contraception were issues that could be discussed, but this was not a romantic reverence for religious tradition. It was the real thing.

'So they're all doing religion, I thought to myself. And France, like Italy, despite pretensions to the contrary, is a Catholic country. The veneer of the Enlightenment is wearing off very fast. Why just attack us? *Munafiqeen.* Hypocrites. You can't imagine what a relief it was to escape from all this and return to bed with my Stendhal. You were so right. I love him, and he writes at such a pace that you read him with the same rhythm. Why the soppy look on your face? Am I wrong? I'm glad you're back. Can't you move here? I mean travel from Paris to wherever you go to give your lectures, instead of from London?'

I had never imagined I would someday hear Zaynab defending the faith with such vim, but then Euro-crassness had that effect on many Muslims, believers and unbelievers, who now lived and worked on the Continent. A month in this city had revived her spirits. I knew she had been extremely depressed by Plato's death and by her inability to stay behind and watch him suffer and die. But she was recovering, and rapidly. It was this quality in Zaynab, her refusal to sham in order to please, as so many of our acquaintance did, that I found so attractive. This quality had created the affinity. From the very first time I met her I had been struck by her lack of affectation, whether we were alone or in company – as we were about to be that night, since she had invited a dozen people to dinner at a restaurant situated conveniently close to the entrance of her apartment. That's where we normally ate, since – like many other women of my acquaintance – she was not one of nature's cooks. It was time for a confession.

'Zaynab, I have no idea whether or not Balzac ever ate here. I just made that up to expedite your decision on the apartment.'

She laughed, her eyes darting a few flames in my direction. 'Hai, Allah. That is so funny. I became excited when you told me. After I had come to know the people who own the place I decided to share this information with them. They were so thrilled that they put a large portrait of him in the entrance hall, as you'll see tonight, and also a quote from *Le Père Goriot* on the menu. Dara, they're thinking of changing the name to *Le Père Goriot*. What should we do?'

'This is how history is written these days. Leave it be. But let's suggest that *Eugénie Grandet* might be a better name for the place. It's a merciless assault on stinginess and might encourage their customers to spend more. A number of apposite quotations from that could be found to embroider their menus and enhance the impact. They're doing it all to increase custom. Making money. A true homage to Balzac.'

'How should I introduce you to the other guests? I don't mean what you do, but . . .'

'What we do?'

'Something like that. One of the Frenchmen is married to a fading beauty from Karachi, so whatever is said will reach Fatherland. Of that we can be sure. It's awful how I'm picking up your stupid jargon.'

We discussed the issue for far too long. Alternatives were considered and discarded. Zaynab often indulged in the most rash judgements, a trait not unrelated to her early years of enforced piety and isolation.

'I could say you're my brother-in-law who's visiting for a few days.'

'Does the Koran have a brother?'

'You fool. I meant my brother's brother-in-law.'

'You mean your sister-in-law's brother.'

A fit of giggling temporarily immobilized her. I suggested a simpler solution: I would be just another guest. This would avoid any unnecessary rigmarole. Agreement was reached. A phone call in the afternoon from the fading beauty was a relief. An emergency had arisen and she and Jean-Claude had to go and comfort their son in Lyon. Zaynab was two guests short, and this worried her. I suggested one of my nonfiction publishers. If Henri de Montmorency were in town he would be fun and she would realize that Paris still contained critical minds, even more disgusted with official culture than she appeared to be. He was available. He had a new young Tunisian woman, Samira, in tow and they would happily join us for supper. There was a tiny glitch. He had agreed to meet a Chinese author writing a book on Shanghai for a drink and they might be a bit late.

I suggested he bring his Chinese author along to dinner. Suddenly the party began to feel more promising. Zaynab had originally organized the dinner to be polite, returning the hospitality of the Islamophobes who had fed her over the past month. She knew this had all the makings of a dire evening and that since she was the hostess, sitting through it in disdainful silence, a satisfying option on other occasions, was excluded.

In fact, the evening proceeded smoothly till Henri de Montmorency and his party arrived. Samira had not bothered to dress up, which surprised some. The Chinese author graciously beamed at us all. It was Henri who became argumentative early on, just as we were busy consuming the first course. He announced that he had just returned from Gaza and began to speak of crimes and atrocities that were being committed by Israel. Even at the best of times this is not a subject greatly appreciated in polite society in Paris. One of the women present, the wife of a liberal news-paper editor, excused herself and we heard her being loudly sick in the lavatory. Her husband rushed to her help as silence reigned at the table. Then the couple returned, the journalist apologized for his wife, who was not feeling well, and they left.

Henri, whose surname concealed his Sephardic origins, of which he was immensely proud, remained unrepentant. 'This is not the first time, you know. She was sick at another dinner party where I was present a few years ago. That year I was returning from Jenin. I don't think she's really sick at all. It's an act of protest. The minute I saw her I knew that a mention of Gaza would send her straight to the toilet.'

We carried on with the main course. Another of her guests, who worked for Credit Suisse, asked me where I was staying. As I was thinking of a suitable hotel, Zaynab interrupted.

'At my place. And not in the guest room.'

'Ah', said Henri, 'you are lovers. Very pleased. Very good news, Dara.'

Till then the Chinese author, Cheng Chiao-fu, had remained silent. I looked at him more closely. He smiled. I was sure we had met somewhere.

'What book are you writing for Henri, or is it a secret?'

'Henri thinks it's on a famous banking scandal in Shanghai that led to three public executions. That will be a small book. I'm working on a much larger book, on the history or, more accurately, the sociology of festivals in China. There are so many of them and their origins have always interested me. The existing work on them is not good.'

Chiao-fu's English was perfect, not a trace of any Chinese accent, but before I could question him, Zaynab attempted to engage Henri's companion in conversation.

'Do you work for Henri?'

'You could say that I work on him.'

We were just finishing at this point, but not wishing to hear more in this vein, Zaynab's other guests pleaded the constraints of time and left us. There was a relieved burst of laughter from her. A more relaxed atmosphere prevailed. It was only ten, and more wine and cheese was laid on the table. I asked Chiao-fu whether he'd studied in Britain or the United States.

'Neither.'

'Where did you learn English?'

'I can't remember.'

The way he said that was familiar. I looked at him more closely.

'Do you think we've met before?' he asked. 'That might be interesting.'

'Do you mind removing your spectacles?'

He did as I asked and I was almost sure. I spoke to him in Punjabi, using a phrase that he had often deployed in the old days.

'You dog, Confucius, you cold-hearted catamite. Where have you been all these years?'

He answered in Punjabi. 'Who are you? Have we met?'

'We met in Lahore. I knew your parents and Jindié. She lives in London now.'

He looked blank, and something none of us had considered as a possibility was now a certainty, unless he was fooling. But it soon became clear that he had lost his memory, at least partially. I carried on speaking to him in Punjabi, and he replied and asked questions.

'Did you give up physics?'

'I don't know. I did economics at Beijing University.'

Zaynab saw that I was close to tears. She said, 'Confucius, do you remember Plato?'

'Yes, I think so. He made me laugh. What happened to him?'

'He died a few months ago.'

'I'm sad to hear that. And you knew him, too?'

Henri had immediately realized that what was taking place was serious. I explained rapidly in broken French who Chiao-fu really was and was told in return that he was regarded as one of the top economists in the country, but had been sidelined because of the scathing criticisms he had made of the direction in which China was headed. I couldn't restrain a few tears. Something of the old Hanif Ma–Confucius had stayed in him. What happened to this boy? Whose identity had he assumed or been given and in what circumstances? His confusion was now palpable. The fact that he could suddenly speak a totally different language that he'd had no idea was in him had shaken his self-confidence. I asked whether I could ring his sister and inform her.

'Later, please. Let's just talk now. In Punjabi.'

Zahid and Jindié arrived the next morning and we all met later that day. Confucius was still bewildered. He didn't recognize Jindié, but accepted rationally that she could be his sister despite her stumbling Chinese. She would often revert to Punjabi, reminding him of their childhood, using mixed Punjabi–Mandarin phrases from their past that were known only to them. Occasionally he would smile, his only tiny flicker of recognition. More would take time. I could see that she had been crying and attempted to comfort her.

'Thank you for finding him.'

'Pure luck.'

'But you were convinced he was alive.'

We embraced warmly. 'Go with him to Beijing and find out more. Stay for as long it takes, Jindié.'

'I'll write and let you know.'

I shook hands with Confucius and said farewell in Punjabi. 'We will meet again, Confucius. I'm so happy that Zahid and I are not the only remaining survivors of the table at college.'

'Was there someone we used to call Respected?'

Zahid and I screamed in tandem. 'Yes!'

'Why do you call me Confucius?'

'I'll let Zahid explain all that in great detail to you. I look forward to your book.'

The intense affection that Jindié felt for him could only have heightened the pain she felt when it became obvious he did not know her. What did he know? Did he remember his Maoist days? Was the past a total nonstarter? It couldn't be if speaking in Punjabi had reminded him of Respected. Perhaps it was all inside him waiting for an opportunity to return to the surface. Zahid was confident that some of it would be recovered, though the shock or accident that had caused the loss of memory in the first place must have been a very long time ago. And that would be a problem.

I returned to the Rue de Bièvre exhausted. Zaynab was out and I switched on the computer to read about memory loss. Nothing definitive. Too many variables. One interesting statistic, however, revealed that in sixty percent of the cases studied in California, memory had largely or completely returned.

I had seriously considered going to Kunming and Dali with Jindié and Zahid, meeting young Suleiman and discovering what was left of the monuments from the time of the rebellion. How much of the Dali Forbidden City still existed? Had the Manchu, like the Red Guards a century later, wreaked their revenge on the architecture as well? It would all have to wait now. Confucius had become the centre of her world.

The next day was the first real spring day of the year. Paris was caressed by deliciously warm breezes; Zaynab and I walked virtually the whole day. She had heard about Jindié and me, Zahid and his life from Plato, and clearly in some detail. Now she turned towards me, looking slightly worried.

'I think Jindié still loves you.'

'*Aflatuni ishq*. Platonic love.'

'Our Plato didn't think so. Did he ever tell you that when he was being discovered thanks to your help, she would contact him to ask about you and your life?'

'He never told me. It was obviously too trivial to be repeated. In any case it means nothing. I am fond of her. I like her. Nothing more. She and Zahid are quite close in some ways and their life has developed a rhythm that suits both of them. It happens to couples who've been together a long time. You look vexed.'

She did not reply, and I wondered whether this had anything to do with us. I asked her.

'I suppose it does, in a way. When we first became intimate I had no idea what I really felt about you, but now I've got used to you. I miss you when you're not here, and that is not good. What do you think?'

'I think we need to find you a boy toy. A vigorous young stallion who can escort you all over the world. A jockey capable of riding any mare. A Plato-style chauffeur, but young and virile.'

'Be serious, Dara. I'm not joking.'

I could see numerous obstacles to any permanent arrangement, but I could also see the attractive side of what she proposed. I had got so used to being on my own and enjoying what I did that a complete break in my old routine was unappealing. Perhaps we could be together for long weekends, and more if we wanted, but I could also see that, after a lengthy interval, fate was offering a new possibility on a platter and that, too, was pleasing.

'Let's talk about this later and see how we should proceed. As you know, I've become attached to you.'

'Not so attached that I am invited to stay in your London flat.'

'Let's go tomorrow. Come and see it for yourself.'

'Are you serious?'

I was, and then I also remembered that neither of us had informed Alice Stepford of Plato's death. That evening I rang her in New York. She demanded to know why we hadn't told her. I though it best to be truthful.

'We forgot.'

She became vituperative, but then calmed down and wept sensibly.

'Has there been an obituary?'

'Two, in *Art Monthly*. Both good.'

'I meant the *New York Times*.'

'No.'

'I'm going to write one. And I assume that Zaynab is the executor and all the paintings now belong to her.'

'This is true, Ally.'

'Alice. Good. He did a nude of me once. Usual stuff. Huge balloon-shaped breasts with all the other accompaniments. Could you tell Zaynab that if it hasn't been sold I'd like to buy it off her? Don't like the thought of it hanging anywhere. I might e-mail you for some details of his youth, but otherwise I'll write mainly about his work.'

Which she did, introducing Plato to an art public that he had neither known nor coveted. He was the only one of my friends who, in all the time I knew him, showed no interest — negative or positive — in the affairs of the United States, or any desire to visit it. This lack of curiosity annoyed me, and when I reprimanded him he would contemptuously shrug his shoulders, but never offered an explanation.

✆

meta

We may return later to the impact of Ally's obituary, but in the meantime Zaynab is waiting for me in the restaurant to hear my views on our future. I thought of all the things I liked about her, some of which have already been listed. Another quality that I appreciated was her incapacity to make small talk and to give her undivided attention to people she did not like or value. Better not to speak than maintain a pretence. And though she was in her early fifties now, she had retained a girlish quality, largely with the help of her mischief-filled eyes, and this belied her age. All these traits could not have been the result of her unique upbringing, or other unfortunates in a similar position might have benefited equally. Nor was there a trace of bitterness in her. She did not suspect people she liked of base motives or jump to embittered conclusions regarding their actions. I'm sure that is what Plato saw in her, too, and why he adored her in the way he did.

My hesitation was purely selfish. I wanted no further disruptions in my life and I was fearful that this might happen, which was why I had devised a compromise formula that might suit us both: weekends and holidays together and every third week a change of city. As I entered the restaurant the first thing I noticed was that the portrait of Balzac had disappeared from the wall. Zaynab sat at her table near the window, smiling. As I joined her she pointed at the menu to indicate that the Balzac quote had disappeared as well. What had happened? That catamite Henri de Montmorency had happened. He had returned one lunchtime and informed the Spanish proprietor that the place postdated Balzac's death and this was not a street much visited by the novelist in any case. I should have alerted Henri to the joke, but he had written a highly regarded history of Paris and probably would have become cross with me. History was sacred and woe betide those who took liberties with it. We tried not to laugh. Zaynab whispered that she had told them it was an honest mistake on my part.

We talked and she appeared perfectly happy with my solution, as long as she could stay with me in London. Why should that have been a problem? She gestured as if to imply that I knew. I was genuinely puzzled.

'Don't you keep London pure for Jindié?'

It was jealousy. I burst out laughing, repeated what I had said before, and explained why I hadn't stayed in the guest room in Richmond and the excuse I had offered Jindié. For a minute I was the subject of a fixed and profound gaze, and then she burst out laughing.

'I know how fussy you are about your cursed coffee. That may well have been the real reason as well. So there were two reasons for not staying. Now I'm convinced.'

She had more wine than usual that night and at one point was overcome with a giggling fit, to which she was sometimes prone. This time there was no apparent reason. Finally she spoke.

'I have been sworn to total secrecy and if this appears anywhere I'll lose a very good friend in New York. She'll never forgive me. It's about a professor from our parts.'

'Which parts did you have in mind?'

'Geographical. In this case, South Asia.'

The story concerned egos in academia. A leading professor in the literature department of a university in the Midwest had been invited to Harvard some weeks ago, where she was due to receive an honorary degree, followed by a banquet at which there would be speeches. Her best work was behind her, but it had once helped her acquire an enormous reputation and a cult following for reasons that even at the time – it was the height of the postmodernist wave in the late Eighties – could be only partially justified. Subsequently she had languished, producing books that her students were compelled to read but that were not part of course lists on other campuses. The New York universities, in particular, had ignored her recent work and had stopped inviting her to lecture. For that reason, the honorary degree at Harvard and the fanfare surrounding it had come at a good time for her.

During the dinner, at which Zaynab's friend had been present, the guest of honour was ignored by most of the old men at the table. This lack of attention upset her greatly, and she burst into silent tears, which went unnoticed, and then began to weep loudly. Everyone present fell silent; now she was the centre of their undivided attention. A kindly retired professor in his eighties put his arm around her to ask why she was so upset.

'Well, it's like this,' said the visitor. 'After lying fallow for a long time I acquired a young Egyptian lover last month. All went well till yesterday, when he refused cunnilingus point-blank because of his religion. I just thought about it and that made me cry.'

There was pin-drop silence. She looked appealingly at the gathering and pleaded for some expert advice. 'Do any of you know why the Coptic Church forbids cunnilingus?'

I laughed as Zaynab finished. It was the one of the more original and comprehensible utterances that I'd heard reported of this particular professor in twenty years. And just before leaving the restaurant, I think I managed to convince its hirsute proprietor that whether or not Balzac had literally eaten at this location was irrelevant. His spirit now hovered over this entire area, if not the country as a whole, and he should reinstate the portrait and the quotation. The Spaniard promised to give the matter serious consideration.

Later that night we agreed that as Plato's friend and possible biographer, I would accompany Zaynab to her family estates and study his unfinished masterpiece.

'I've told you I hate it, D. If your opinion is the same and the work is without any intrinsic value, let it stay at home. Why inflict it on the world? Plato would have respected the decision.'

Sleep did not come easily that night. Every so often Zaynab would sit up, turn on the lamp and question me. 'D, what was that stupid Punjabi song that Plato used to sing or hum and which had quite a funny first line but was otherwise conventional?'

I remembered. 'The first line was Plato's contribution, and the rest of the song was early Bollywood, vintage 1958, I think.'

'"The sight of your breasts sends me to sleep." Stupid Plato.'

Half an hour later: 'Are stupid people generally more happy than more intelligent ones?'

'Zaynab, it's nearly two in the morning.'

'So what? Why, can't you sleep? But first please answer my question.'

'How the hell should I know? Make a list of your family members and answer your own question.'

'I know some really stupid ones, but that's not my point. What I mean is whether or not they even understand the concept of happiness.'

I turned off the light and took her in my arms.

FIFTEEN

Six months later, when I returned to Paris, it was difficult to ignore the fact that Naughty Lateef had taken the city by storm. Her book was out. It had been sold to every large publishing corporation in the world. The advances had been modest, since the industry was in severe crisis, but for this book subventions had been promised by various foundations and cultural organizations to cover the losses. Posters with Naughty's image were everywhere. She had changed her name to something that was both user-friendly and exotic. She was now Yasmine Auratpasand. The market would respond well to that, with a tiny bit of encouragement from the publishers' marketing directors. Their shrewdness and cynicism would both ensure good sales and, much more importantly, project the author straight into the world of celebrity. Unlike her male equivalents, she did not need any medical help in the way of a hair transplant or what is unappetizingly referred to as a nose job. Naughty was a healthy Punjabi girl with rustic good looks. All she required was some work on her English diction, but not too much, and on her overeager smile, which she was asked to make a touch more refined, a bit more modest, just enough so that she did not seem to be enjoying her new status quite as much as she actually did. The mediacrats were instructed to go easy on her, at the same time making sure that she became an overnight celebrity. That was important, since she needed to be used to justify, in the sweetest and mildest manner possible, every Western atrocity in Muslim lands requiring justification and simultaneously help to prepare public opinion to accept future crimes. What must be avoided was too early a comparison of her writing with Voltaire's. That claim had seriously discredited a previous operation of this sort, and Washington had been forced to step in and transport the heroine in question to the safety of a right-wing think-tank. Perhaps in six months' time the phrase 'there is a touch of Diderot in her work' could be suggested to Jean-Pierre Bertrand, the host of Orinico.com, the travelling book show aired on France 2, which was filmed on a cargo plane and sponsored by the eponymous company.

The interview with Naughty in *Le Monde* had been conducted or, if readers will pardon a homely truth, written, by one of Zaynab's dinner-party guests, who, like most senior journalists in the Western world, wrote copy as imaginative as any of those gallant captains who enlivened the sixteenth century with tales of adventures in unknown worlds where they killed countless brigands and a vast number of heathens. (Those stories in their day had inspired or provoked hundreds of satirical and, sometimes, extremely vulgar sonnets, which were secretly admired by many.)

In our twenty-first century, a Muslim woman's real virtues cannot be appreciated on their own, but like the adventurous captains' have to be spiced up with stories, imagined or real, of courage in the face of over-whelming odds – in her case, of Islamist tyranny. And since the struggle against this tyranny is led by humanitarian politicians and generals with high collateral from the Western world, they and their global network of media acolytes become the final arbiters of what these women's books are worth. Zaynab, an unsung Muslim heroine of valour, had followed Naughty's antics with a sense of horror, but also with growing admiration.

Now she looked at the clock and rushed to switch on her television to Arte. 'It's the only thing left worth watching . . . sometimes. There were more serious debates on Fatherland TV networks during the military period. Not now.'

'What are we watching?'

'Shhh.'

Arte had decided to broadcast a live double interview with Naughty and a critic of hers, a hijab-clad Maghrebian Frenchwoman. Their two points of view were to be offered to the viewers as an either-or choice. Zaynab would not let me switch it off, nor would she allow me to leave the room. The show was live, she said, and anything could happen, which I strongly doubted. Very rarely are these things left to chance, and unforeseen spontaneity is muzzled the moment it rears its unwelcome head.

The silk-shirted interviewer sharing a bit of his hairy chest – it was the ubiquitous Bertrand – introduced the two women in a husky French voice. I preferred reading the German sub-titles.

'Yasmine Auratpasand, of course, is familiar to you. Her struggle for enlightenment in a dark world has inspired us greatly. In the right corner is Yusufa al-Hadid, a young schoolteacher who has published a slightly undiplomatic criticism of Madame Auratpasand's work in *Le Monde Diplomatique*, where else?'

He attempted to amuse us with his boxing-match terms, also meant to assure us that he was only the referee. His task was to separate the combatants if the fight became too rough, to prevent any fouls, and to pose a new question whenever he deemed a round completed. To set the tone for this new objectivity, he showed the audience a ten-minute film on Naughty's world and the society that produced her. Beards, bombs, horrific footage of Taliban touts flogging a woman, statistics of honour killings, 'balanced' by interviews with a few good people in Fatherland, mainly women, who pointed out that most women who were put to death were killed in the family and not by fundamentalists. Then interviews with many bad people who wanted more wars, supported the drones, and accepted with sad faces that the collateral damage was a price that had to be paid for freedom. I wondered whether they would be saying that if their families had been wiped out. Intercut with all this were images of Naughty in peaceful Paris, reflecting on the difference between the two worlds. Wonderful stuff. Just like a boxing match whose outcome has been decided in advance – as long as the fall guy sticks to the bargain. I assumed that in Yusufa al-Hadid they had found a particularly obtuse young Islamist who would knock herself out, since Naughty had to stick to her script and was incapable of a killer blow. I was wrong.

The young woman with the covered head began to speak. In a deceptively gentle voice, she congratulated the director for giving us a film from which all unpleasant images of Parisian cops harassing black people had been eliminated. This could not have an easy accomplishment in 'our Paris'. Why had they filmed Madame Auratpasand exclusively in the arcades? Bertrand concealed his irritation with a patronizing smile. She was, of course, entitled to her opinions, because France was a free country. This remark, of course, implied that al-Hadid was not French, but some other, unspecified, nationality. Then he began posing his intelligent-sounding but banal questions.

Naughty had been effectively tutored and carefully rehearsed. Her French was improving daily. At one point she said, with a sigh, 'What a joy it is to read Diderot.'

Bertrand gushed, 'I must confess that after reading your own work I said to Justine, my wife – a famous opera singer, by the way, and a great fan of your work – that I think we have a new talent amongst us. A woman from a war zone with a touch of Diderot.'

The camera lingered, first on his chest and then on hers. Before he could resume, Yusufa interrupted in a calm and reasonable voice:

'Excuse me, Madame Auratpasand, but would you mind sharing with us which of Diderot's works gave you such joy?'

Poor Naughty was flummoxed, on the edge of panic. She wiped some sweat off her face and sipped some water. Bertrand stepped in adroitly.

'You told me before that it was the *Story of the Nun.*'

'Yes, yes', said a grateful Naughty, 'that's the one. Brilliant, brilliant, very brilliant.'

Yusufa persisted. 'I like it, too. Which character did you most identify with?'

This time Bertrand was prepared. 'We can discuss Diderot another time. Now I want to ask, Madame Auratpasand, whether you have ever worn the burqa.'

She nodded, as a sad look came over her face. Zaynab hoped a few tears might follow, but they were held in check, though her eyelashes flickered in an attempt to squeeze something out.

'I was forced to wear it by my father when I went to school. I felt badly constricted. It was as if my brain was being compressed. After I was married my husband did not insist on it, except when other men, strangers, came to our house, but not when I went shopping.'

Bertrand turned to Yusufa.

'I started wearing a hijab only when it was prohibited in French schools and some municipalities threatened to make it illegal in public spaces. Now I quite like it as a gesture of defiance, or should I say freedom?'

'Oh', said Naughty, who had clearly not understood the reference, 'I am sorry that you are compelled to wear it. Don't you feel its oppressive weight on your mind? Stifling, crushing your thoughts?'

In response, Yusufa recited a verse whose effect was so hypnotic that it even silenced Bertrand for a few seconds:

> *I said to my rose-cheeked lovely, 'O you with bud-like mouth,*
> *why keep your face hidden like a flirtatious girl?'*
> *She laughed and replied, 'Unlike the beauties of your world,*
> *In the curtain I'm seen, but without it I'm hidden.'*
> *Your cheek can't be seen without a mask,*
> *Your eyes can't be seen without a veil.*
> *As long as the sun's fully shining,*
> *Its face will never be seen.*
> *When the sun strikes our sphere with its banner of light,*
> *It dazzles the sight from afar.*
> *When it shines behind a curtain of clouds,*
> *The gazer can see it without lowering his eyes.*

Naughty was moved, even though she was not meant to be. Her unscripted remarks might have destroyed her.

'So beautiful, Yusufa. So beautiful. Did you write the poem?'

'No, no, it's Jami.'

'Ah, Jami,' said Bertrand. 'The Arabs used to produce such good poetry.'

Yusufa corrected him. 'He was Persian, and died in 1492, not long after the fall of Granada.'

As far as Zaynab and I were concerned the young Frenchwoman had knocked out both Naughty and the referee. The rest of the interview was composed of set pieces, but Yusufa's spirit shone through and Bertrand was discomfited and clearly annoyed with himself. The researcher who had found Yusufa was bound to suffer his wrath.

As we went down to eat, Zaynab pointed out another triumph. Henri de M. had been defeated. The eatery had reinvented itself as Eugénie

Grandet's, and as we entered I saw that the portrait of Balzac was back on the wall, together with framed covers from many of his works. And the menu was once again emblazoned with a quotation.

Zaynab now confessed that Henri had asked her to write a short book on Naughty's rise in the world for his small but select publishing house. She had agreed. And she had met Naughty.

'How did you manage that?'

'I wrote a fan letter stressing our affinities and she wrote back suggesting we meet.'

'Deception.'

'Pure and simple.'

'The results?'

'I have the whole story, but Henri is joining us soon, so you'll have to wait. It will be boring for you to hear it repeated.'

I did not have to wait too long. Henri walked in and laughed as he saw how the place had been transformed. 'This one you have won,' he acknowledged.

He, too, had seen the Arte interview and expressed his delight at Yusufa's performance. He would try to contact her, to judge whether or not she had a book in her, but in the meantime he was banking on Zaynab to lift the veil on Madame Auratpasand. 'Her response to the Sufi poem must have worried her minders.'

I pointed out that it was a tiny lapse and they would soon correct it. If anything it had humanized Naughty a little. They could use that to their advantage. Henri took out that day's *Herald Tribune* and put it on the table. There on the front page was Naughty, flanked by Bertrand and some of the pioneers in her own field, who included an uncongenial and bloated novelist, permanently high on his own fame or shame, whichever way one looks at it, who wore a crooked smile for the cameras while his beady eyes were unashamedly turned in the direction of the well-stroked

Naughty mammaries (or *mammas,* as they are affectionately known in Punjabi, and immortalized as such, at least for his friends, by Plato's song line in their honour).

'She's on course for two or three prizes this year,' said Henri, with a maniacal laugh. 'What will be the contents of your book, Zaynab? And when can I expect a finished manuscript?'

'The contents are obvious. It's her story as she told it to me. In her own words, but with explanations by me where necessary. In a phrase, the unvarnished truth.'

Had Zaynab actually taped the conversation?

'Yes, and with her knowledge.'

I was astonished. 'She trusted you completely?'

'By the end she did. And we were wrong. She's not a monster. Could have become one, but held back.'

Henri, ever sceptical, inquired whether Naughty was aware that this material she had provided might be published.

'As you will see in the transcripts, I informed her of this possibility and she agreed with a nervous laugh. Her only stipulation, also on tape, was that I warn her well in advance. She's entranced with her new land-scape, but has few illusions. I have to confess that I liked her. She hasn't an ideological bone in her body and knows only too well that she's being used, as she has been all her life. She wants the truth for her children, who will not speak to her at the moment. Bertrand wanted her to go big on this aspect of the operation: her courage is measured by the disaffection of her children, whom she has had to discard. Diderot and Medea in one. She refused. If her children were mentioned in any newspaper, the whole deal was off.'

'This is remarkable,' said Henri, after he had digested the information. 'We'd better make copies of everything, and I will consult our lawyer when we're ready. This could be explosive.'

Zaynab handed him three copies of the transcript and three CDs.

'You are a real professional, Madame Koran.'

As I read the transcripts the next morning I, too, thought that Henri de M. had an excellent book on his hands. Naughty's stories about everyday life with her husband and the generals, an unremitting account of moral, political and financial corruption, was of much greater interest to us than to Western readers, but her account of how she had been head-hunted by French Intelligence and seduced into her new role was a fascinating insight into the murky world of modern war propaganda. It had always been the same game, but new conditions and new enemies required new methods, and the land where the Enlightenment was born was perfectly situated to carry them out, much more subtle at it than the wooden-headed Dutch and Danes, who were rash and crude in their methods.

Naughty had given Zaynab a detailed version of exactly what had happened to her. She had named names. The name of the charming young Frenchman, fluent in Urdu, Pashto and Persian, who had first established contact with her after General Rafiq was killed; the names of his colleagues at the embassies in Kabul and Isloo, who had informed her that her life was no longer safe. They had intercepted secret messages and the terrorists had even hired a hit man to kill her. Later she thought this couldn't be true, since she had, unwittingly, done the insurgents a favour. They had hated Rafiq. But by then it was too late: she was already settled in a hideout near Rambouillet, receiving crash courses in French and elocution lessons to improve her English. At least she would never regret that side of the operation.

Then M. Bertrand entered the transcripts in the guise of her creepy television tutor. He taught her the tricks of his trade and while doing so made a sudden pre-emptive strike on the poor mammaries. She fended him off, but he never apologized, just shrugged as if to say, I'm a Frenchman and you know we all love women. She wasn't unused to behaviour of this sort in Fatherland, but the comparison between her favourite military lover and Bertrand would certainly not enhance the latter's reputation.

If her account wasn't simply a set of prudent falsehoods, then the principle reason why she agreed to the entire operation was financial. She had already netted a million dollars for the book and hadn't had to write a single word except for her signature on the contract drawn up by her agent. The book was the result of a collaboration between a well-known Fatherland journalist and her French counterpart. They were paid for that only, but with the collateral money she had coming, Naughty confided to Zaynab, by the end of the year she expected to net a cool two million euros. This would enable her to live independently wherever she chose and perhaps even create the basis for a reconciliation with her sons, whom she now wanted to educate abroad.

It was a situation in which morality had played no part on any side. Personally, I doubted whether it would be possible for Naughty to live in Fatherland again after all the publicity, but stranger things happen all the time and, who knew, perhaps Zaynab's interview might help, but only if the new book caused the scandal we hoped for.

Many people today know all about these goings-on, yet literary and other hacks fall into line without a word of protest, concealing reality under a veneer of fine words like 'civilization', 'freedom of speech', etc. Of those who are willing to write the truth, most reveal only a very small part of it, masking their revelations with such obscure metaphors and ambiguous language that the end result is tedious to decipher even for those of us who know; for others, it is simply unreadable. There is more than one deadly plague raging in the world today, but few can call the ills that beset us by their right names.

〰

Zaynab was working on her manuscript, and I was getting restless. She had some way to go. The interview had been conducted in a mixture of Urdu and English, and now had to be cleaned up and translated into French, after which Henri would read it and decide its fate. Meanwhile Zahid had e-mailed me saying he was back and wondering whether we might meet up one of these weeks. The present seemed as good a time as any. Zaynab protested feebly, then agreed, insisting only that she wanted me present when Naughty came for a meal next weekend, after returning from her triumphal tour of that Mother of all Fatherlands that is the United States of America. I promised not to miss this key G2 summit, the conference of two new authors. She hurled a sandal in my direction.

The next day I went to see Zahid and met Neelam, who had arrived for a short stay with her children. She looked at me curiously, but was perfectly pleasant. I made my condolences. The children said salaams. The mouth-watering scents emanating from the kitchen were from the meal she was preparing for all of us. Zahid and I went for a walk in Richmond Park.

On Confucius there was still no positive news. He remained in a confused state. Zahid had left China soon after seeing Suleiman in Kunming. His son was thriving and showed little interest in returning to the world of finance, which had already provided him with sufficient wealth to live without lifting a finger for the next twenty years. He was deeply immersed in history and was studying various phases of the Chinese Empire after the sixteenth century. Jindié was in Beijing for the duration. She couldn't leave her brother, and Confucius had a large apartment where both he and his wife had made Jindié very welcome. It was obvious that Zahid, a provincial Punjabi to the core, did not really wish to discuss China. He was worried about Fatherland.

'But we're always worried about Fatherland. Has there ever been a time when we were not?'

He insisted that in our youth we had had high hopes and that in retrospect all those summers in Nathiagali during the Fifties and Sixties didn't seem so bad. I reminded him that while we were mooning after girls in the mountains, radical students we knew were having icicles shoved up their backsides, political leaders and poets were in prison and the debacle of East Fatherland was hovering in the background.

He agreed. 'But compared to later . . .'

'If we get into relative values, old friend, we're sunk. I mean you and me. The country's already down there.'

'You heard about Jamshed?'

I nodded. Our quondam friend had bought his way to high office and then been gunned down by a gang hired by the father of a young woman that both he and his son had raped. Jamshed was dead. The son was holed up in Dubai. Some newspapers maintained it was the terrorists, but nobody believed them.

'Did you feel anything? Be honest.'

I shook my head. 'Nothing at all. I was indifferent. Compared with Plato he was worth less than a pigeon dropping.'

'Same here. And yet, this was a guy who was constantly in our company, Dara.'

'Half a century ago and in another country.'

'Old friendships die, but some can be revived.'

'Like ours. Though had we been friends at the time of your Republican deviation, harsh words might have been exchanged.'

'Had we been in touch and close, that deviation might never have happened. It was herd instinct. Jindié nearly left me over that and the kids became angry and alienated. It was a blip. Nothing serious.'

'And operating on Cheney?'

'Don't you start . . .'

We started laughing. Then I reverted to the days of our youth and demanded a complete account of life with Jindié. At first he resisted, but the magic of the Punjabi language got to him and he began to talk. Most of it I knew from both of them, but he was frank. The relationship had worked on many levels but never physically. He had no idea why, but he was sure it would have the same with me or anyone else. Women who enjoy sex can enjoy it in different ways with different men. Obviously, he argued, it is more intense with someone you love. The opposite holds true, too. Some women don't enjoy making love.

'I'm sad to hear that, Ziddi . . .'

'It's the first time you've called me that in almost fifty years.'

'Did you ever ask her why?'

'Did you?'

I was slightly taken aback. 'How could I?'

'I think you could and should. She might tell you if there's anything to tell. I had always assumed that all young women are waiting for passionate love, but Jindié wasn't one of them.'

'Dai-yu,' I muttered.

Zahid was familiar with the novel. Jindié had forced him to read it in the early days of their marriage, and he had enjoyed doing so. He still thought of that novel. 'And please don't say it's the only novel I've ever read. In case you're interested, I even read one by you. Even though it was set way back in the past, I thought I recognized some old friends.'

He agreed that there was a great deal of Dai-yu in Jindié. The swirling of passions but inability to fulfil them. No wonder Bao-yu had gone for the maids in such a big way.

'He never went for anything in a big way. He waited for everything to happen to him.'

'He reminded me in some ways of Anis. Remember him?'

'How could one forget him? I know he was a friend of yours, but he was so affected that I never really liked him. Even the way he walked. As if there were something stuck up his arse. I was polite to him only because I knew your families went back a long way.'

Poor Anis. Zahid's view of him was quite common. It was also unfair.

'Listen to me, Ziddi. It wasn't his fault his father sent him off to an English public school. Allah knows what happened to him there. There was an incident and he was expelled. He was gay. Had he been born ten years later it would have been fine. His mother was a paranoid lady. Spied on him when he returned. Bought girls for him. It became too much. Unable to face life, he removed himself from the scene in the only way he knew. Suicide.'

'They were pampered kids, Daraji. They had everything. If he wanted men, what was the problem? Is Fatherland short on this front? I didn't know him as well as you so I can't say much more. How's Zaynab?'

'She's well.'

'Just well? Not thriving, not passionately in love with you, not successfully moving you from London to Paris? She's just well. I see.'

He always used to make me laugh. I did so now, but said nothing.

'If you think the news hasn't spread to Fatherland, you can think again. Everyone knows that you and Zaynab are together. I used to envy the fact that you had done your biological duty and returned to being a bachelor. It seems I was wrong.'

'We live separately, but strike together. And, since you asked, her intelligence matches her beauty.'

'Of course. How could it not? How could you go just for beauty?'

As luck would have it, at that very moment my phone buzzed with a text message from Zaynab:

When pleasure has entirely run its course it is clear one sinks back into indifference, but an indifference which is not the same as before. This second state differs from the first in that it appears we are no longer able to take such delight in enjoying the pleasure we have just experienced . . . but if in the midst of pleasure we are wrenched away from it, suffering will result.

I showed it to Zahid, who gave an appreciative whistle.

'You've struck gold.'

'She didn't write that. It's from Stendhal, whom I know you haven't read.'

'At least she knew where to look. You seem happy and relaxed. The children well?'

'Yes. And the grandchildren.'

'What did you think of Jindié's notes on China and her diary?'

'Both were incomplete, but the China material was gripping. I was looking forward in the diary to a few salty references to our youth, but they had been destroyed.'

'I read them. They weren't that hot. I keep telling you that she's not a passionate person.'

'Shut up about that, and anyway I'm not sure your assessment is accurate on that front. It's too late. How many nurses and fellow doctors did you find to make up for Jindié's deficiencies?'

'Not that many.'

'Nothing serious.'

'One could have been, but Jindié moved swiftly and put a stop to it. The details are dull.'

'She told me about Anjum and your chance meeting in Norfolk.' He stopped walking. We found a bench.

'Dara, that was truly depressing. She was a complete wreck. She looked like a very old Christian lady, with a stoop. Remember when we first started going to Nathiagali? There used to be old English ladies who were nice to us. They couldn't bear returning to England. They were old but still full of life, active, going for long hikes. Anjum was the exact opposite. It wasn't just that her appearance was shrivelled. She had dried up inside. I felt very sad when she told me her story. Her first husband an alcoholic disaster, the second a teetotalling religious maniac. No children from either.'

'Why didn't her sisters fly over and rescue her?'

'I asked her. She hasn't told anyone where she is now. She gave me her address and phone number, but only for emergencies. She's the one in an emergency. Anyway I e-mailed Nazleen, her younger sister, and gave her the details. She must be taken away from this monster.'

'And the old flame?'

'That went out in the last century when I received reports of her family life. A scene out of a Russian novel.'

'Which one?'

'Bastard. Dog. Catamite. Should I try Dostoevsky?'

'Good guess. You were saying?'

'When I heard what was going on from mutual friends, I did make one attempt to see her.'

'Pre- or post-Jindié?'

'Pre. I drove to Sahiwal. We met at a prearranged spot and I followed her car to some godforsaken place. A tiny stream and a few trees is all I can remember. We talked for a few hours, but she was not prepared to walk out on the drunkard, who often assaulted her in and out of his cups. There were no children. I couldn't understand why she didn't leave him.'

'Oh, I can. Shame at having failed, fear of parental displeasure, a society scandal, all of that affected her, but there was a basic problem that you avoided discussing with me, and when I hinted at it on one occasion, you told me to shut my mouth and gestured that if I didn't, you would.'

'I don't remember, but what was it?'

'She wasn't that bright. I'm sorry, but it's true. She was very beautiful, she could hold her own at social gatherings, but apart from money and being a society wife there was nothing else. She twittered nonstop about her holidays abroad, like a squawking parrot. A cheerful little birdbrain. Nothing more. Affluence had made her obnoxious. You got so angry when I suggested you ask her if she had ever read a book. And finally, desperate and feeling hopeless, she jumps into bed with some idiot Irish engineer who offers salvation, but not of the variety she wanted. I wonder what you would have done with her.'

He became thoughtful.

'I don't know. Perhaps you're right. Sometimes I think if she'd had children and come to the States it might have worked out.'

'Suburban bliss as the solution. Is that what you think? Other women like her, all leading empty lives. She might have fitted in. You're right. She would have learned to cook and bake and everything she made would have been so delicious, and then one day she would have realized it was all going nowhere with you, since you were permanently at the hospital, and run off with the first guy who made a pass. It might have been better for her, but what about Ziddi Mian? You would have cracked, boy. Gone to the dogs. Jindié may not have turned you on, but she was a good mother and extremely sharp-witted. You were never bored.'

'True, but she's been a bit rough on Neelam, which reminds me that a chicken biryani is waiting for us at home. Jindié said on your last visit you complained nonstop about her cooking.'

'She meant her noncooking.'

'Neelam is a great cook. Even you will admit that.'

We walked back to the house.

'What have you done with all your properties? Four locations? Four homes? Why did you do that?'

'My accountant did on my behalf. Two were gifted to Neelam and the other two to Suleiman. I think Neelam has sold the beach house in Miami.

We kept an apartment in New York, which you're welcome to use whenever you wish.'

Jindié's description of her daughter had given me the impression of a young born-again fanatic wedded to her refound faith and uninterested in the rest of the world. This was not my opinion, and not just because she was a wonderful cook. The way she dealt with her children, addressed her father and put me at my ease was admirable. There was much of the young Jindié in her.

After the children had gone to bed the three of us sat in the living room, which was marred by a grotesque deer head, which had escaped my notice on earlier visits and which I now pleaded with Zahid to remove. He did so on the spot and took the antlered object out of the room. In his absence Neelam became much more forthcoming. I had not raised the subject, but she spoke of Jindié with great affection and said her mother's life had been neither easy nor particularly happy.

'She wanted me to have the life she never had, and when I fell in love with Rafiq she never tried to stop me, but I knew she disapproved. He was too brash, too full of himself, and my mother's instincts told her I would not be happy with him. Unfortunately, this turned out to be true. I never told my parents even a quarter of what happened. Late nights fuelled by alcohol and women. Drunk before the children – that I could not forgive. His women ringing home nonstop and pretending to be friendly to me. Army life. I made a terrible mistake, but mercifully the children came early. They became the only thing I cared about. Now they're older. I was planning to leave Rafiq and told him so the week before he was killed. Mom was horrified when I became religious, but believe me, it was the only way I could cope with life. The children needed a set of rules, and in our country, as you know, there are few role models. So I turned to the Prophet. Mom thinks I'm a fanatic, but that is not true. I needed Allah to deal with Rafiq and his friends.'

'Who killed him?'

'Not the Taliban or the Talibu or any group like them. That's clear enough. It wasn't suicide terrorism, but a clinical operation, like the one Abu performed on Dick Cheney. Everything carefully planned. No traces at all. He was killed by his own people, for telling the Americans too much. That horrible Naughty Lateef is worse than a prostitute. They do it for the money. Have you seen the way she's been picked up by the West? Are they that stupid? She could never have written that foolish book. She's illiterate.'

I wondered whether I should tell Neelam about the goings-on in Paris. Instinct sounded an alarm. I refrained, saying only, 'She's being educated.'

Neelam burst out laughing. 'I suppose that's good.'

'Neelam, it's not for me to say, but is there no way you can make friends with your mother again?'

'You can say what you like. I think you're the only person she regards as a close friend. She adores the children, and that is always an important bridge. I will try. I'm taking the children to Beijing to see their Uncle Suleiman and meet Great-Uncle Hanif Ma. My son wants to learn Chinese. That will make Mom happy. Why didn't you and she work out?'

'I was never the marrying kind. You look disapproving, despite your own marriage and how you describe your mother's life.'

'It was not a disapproving look at all. Nobody told me that.'

'Were you upset at reading about me in her diary?'

'Did she say that? It's not true. I was touched and began to ask why she had married my father. It was she who overreacted and tore the pages up. She was in a real state. I was not shocked at all. If anything, pleased – but I did have a few questions.'

'Dai-yu.'

'That *Dream of the Red Chamber*. She's read it at least a dozen times. It's her Honoured Classic.'

Mention of the Holy Book made me think of Zaynab and her dinner guest. In a few days I would be seated at the same table as the woman who had altered Neelam's biography, possibly for the better.

'Neelam, what are your plans? I hope you have some project.'

'Nice you asked. I did law at Washington State. I'm qualified, you know. Never practised, and that was another reason for Mom's anger. Now I'm studying Islamic law. The sharia courts will need a few women lawyers to defend women and I hope a few women judges as well, like in Iran. And I'm going to start work soon.'

I suggested that she might consider working in ordinary courts as well, just in case work opportunities in the others dried up. Quite a few Sunni theologians would argue against women being permitted to practise.

'Possibly, but we can organize a special Sunni NGO to pay them off and find other theologians to overrule them.'

Her cynicism was pleasing.

'It's getting late. Sure you won't stay? The bed is very comfortable and there's an en suite bathroom.'

'Is there any decent coffee in the house?'

'Of course. My father can't do without it and will make you an espresso or whatever you want for breakfast. Just stop him boasting too much about it. We've all heard his coffee stories a million times.'

'Then, I'll stay.'

SIXTEEN

I detected a slight panic when I embraced and kissed Zaynab. It turned out that Naughty, sounding strained and distant after her US tour, had asked to bring her publicist-agent to dinner tonight. The auguries were bad. Zaynab had been firm in her refusal. It was a private occasion, she told her interviewee. After several agitated exchanges, Madame Auratpasand, as we should now have been referring to her but couldn't, had agreed to come alone as long as the meal was at home. Her publicist did not want her to be seen in a public place unless photographers had been arranged and there was at least one other celebrity present.

Zaynab had asked Eugénie Grandet's to prepare a meal in advance and deliver it half an hour before her guests arrived. Apart from Naughty, the only other person invited was Henri, who had expressed a desire to see the monster from close up.

It was barely midday, but I was despatched to go and buy some wine. Zaynab was distracted, and the reason for that was obvious, at least to me. She had, not unnaturally, developed a great deal of sympathy for

Naughty and had begun to see her exclusively as a victim. My attempts to wean her from this view had been rebuffed. Henri, too, was sceptical, which was why he had been invited to supper.

Naughty was late, as celebs are supposed to be, but it was her attire that surprised all of us. She wore a loose tracksuit made of some indefinable dark green material and a white silk headscarf that she pulled off and threw with abandon on the sofa. We smiled. Then I complimented her on her clothes.

'Very patriotic of you to dress up in Fatherland colours.'

'Deliberate, deliberate,' she said in a funny accent, as if trying to cultivate a nasal twang. 'My publicist in the States also does makeover jobs on Fatherlandi politicians. He told me I should wear Fatherland colours. Just to show I support our government against terrorism. I wore this on the *habshi* lady's show. Copra Freedom. Very popular show. Miss Copra advised me not to wear white brassiere underneath green top.'

'That was an intelligent suggestion by Mademoiselle Freedom. So you switched to a green brassiere during the advertising break, Madame Auratpasand?'

'*Oui, Monsieur.* Copra has bras of every colour just in case the guest is wearing one that can be seen. Many families and children watch Copra Freedom show.'

As we sat down to dinner, Naughty looked uncomfortable, but a few restorative glasses of wine relaxed her a great deal. When Henri praised her interview and her courage, Naughty decided to hurl her first grenade. After a slight pause, she asked politely, '*Quelle interview, Monsieur?*'

Zaynab erupted, 'Our interview, Naughty!'

'Oh, that one. I thought that was just informal, Zaynab. By the way, Jean-Pierre Bertrand wants to write my biography for very big New York publisher.'

Before Zaynab could speak again I addressed Naughty in Punjabi.

She appeared delighted and replied in a *potwari* dialect of the language, much sweeter and softer than the Lahori version. I shifted to *potwari*, the language of my childhood, because I preferred it and still spoke it when visiting northern regions of Fatherland. Naughty grabbed my arm and dragged me from the kitchen into the living room, where the following conversation transpired in dialect.

'Listen, kind sir. You explain it to the lady. I can't allow her to publish the interview. I know I agreed, but in America they loved me. Look, dear sir, I'm just a village girl. I only went to school for five years. Captain Lateef was a distant relation. My father gave me to him because he didn't want a dowry. I just want her, he told my father. Never treated me well. He gets home from the office and drags me to bed. "Open your legs, girl. Hurry up." Then he mounts me like a dog, and after his business is finished he goes and bathes and says his afternoon prayers. That was life with him for ten years. Two children I gave birth to, and then a kind lady said to me it's better get your tubes tied. Or this man will just make you a machine to produce sons.'

I asked who the lady was, and Naughty's hitherto untroubled face became clouded with anxiety. 'Such a kind lady. She suggested I learn some English and helped me do it. I'm filled with shame. She was General Rafiq's wife. He first saw me when I was having English lessons with Begum Neelam. One day he sent his car for me. I thought the car would take me to Begum Neelam. It took me to a small hotel in Isloo. General Sahib was waiting for me. He talked a lot, asked many questions and then touched my breasts and said they were nice. So I opened my legs for him. Lateef knew. He said, "Open your legs for the general, you prostitute. It's good for me."'

I asked whether her legs had been opened for other generals and if so, how many.

'Three, including the big chief, but Rafiq, may he be safe in heaven, was the only general who talked to me. Asked afterwards how I felt.

What gave me real pleasure. Rafiq was really a very kind man. The other generals made me betray him. Once I betrayed him, my life was finished. What could I do? That's when I met the Frenchman.'

Once again I interrupted her and asked with as much delicacy as I could muster whether the Frenchman, too, had asked her to open her legs. Her response was accompanied by raucous laughter.

'No, no, sir. He liked boys. He worked hard on their bums. But he was very kind to me. His name was Gibril, like the angel. Please, sir, please ask the lady and the French monsieur to forget the interview. If it is published, my life will be finished.'

'Have you told anyone about this interview?'

'Only my American publicist, Mr Jonathan. He said if the interview was made a book it would be the end of my career. He was very angry. Then I said there was no contract. I had not signed anything. Then he became happy. He wants me to go to Israel, where my book will be published in six months. Sir, is it good idea?'

'Very bad idea. Listen to me carefully, Naughty. Don't demand anything of the French publisher now. Tell them you'll think about it and decide in a few months' time.'

She agreed. She had sent Lateef a great deal of money for their two sons and had been invited back for a family get-together later in the month, but it was to be a private visit. No publicity at all. Before we rejoined the others I couldn't resist one last question.

'I saw a photograph of you in New York. Did anyone in the photograph ask you to open your legs?'

'The French television guy tried again. I said no. The bald writer pursued me like an animal. I finally agreed but his tablets didn't work. He made all sorts of promises to get his way. He would review my book in the New York Book Review and New Yorker Book Review and many other things.'

Back in the kitchen, Naughty did as I had suggested and feigned indecision. The rest of the evening passed peacefully, except for the constant ringing of her cell phone. Finally she said her publicist was waiting in a wine bar for her with other people. She left.

Zaynab was now thoroughly disillusioned. 'Your conversation with her is on tape. Henri suggested we tape everything.'

I was astonished and reprimanded them.

'I do understand a lot of Punjabi', Zaynab volunteered, 'but what language were you speaking? Most of it was incomprehensible.'

❦

Ordinary people measure satisfaction in a variety of ways. A chef who knows he forgot to include some key ingredients in the dish he has just served will not be pleased with the result, regardless of the plaudits received from every customer. A writer may be delighted with her own work, regardless of anything the critics might say. For celebrities there is only one measure. The amount of exposure they receive in any given week in the media, the number of paparazzi skulking in hidden places hoping for an unusual photograph, all this feeds the insatiable desire for publicity that has become, for so many, the transplanted heart of an empty world.

Celebdom is the summit of ambition today and is pursued at whatever cost. It's a world peopled by actors and sportsmen and a few writers and certain politicians who are devoid of any principle except an insensate obsession with multiplying their wealth and fame. Their marketing and publicity advisers work overtime to ensure that our leaders get enough exposure on celebrity talk shows or in the company of other suitable celebs. The appeal of reality television lies in its insistence that anyone can become A-list overnight. Fellini's brilliant parody of the jet-setter's world in *La Dolce Vita* has been superseded, but in ways that would not have surprised him in the least.

Naughty's example was a single case in point. Who can blame her for being seduced by the glitter and the cash, when others a hundred times more intelligent and already multimillionaires in their own right were just as desperate to be known to a larger world? This, I suggested to Henri, was the book he should really be commissioning, with the interview as an appendix published in the public interest.

Henri waged guerrilla war against the spirit of the age. He had published stinging essays on the political culture of his own country, some of them written by him. Now he agreed that this was the best way to publish the book, as a combination of polemic and oral history. Both parts should be exactly the same length to emphasize their interdependence, and which came first could be decided later. Zaynab was not convinced. The interview had to be the heart of the book, and the rest an introduction or an epilogue. There was no changing her mind on this structure. She won the argument. It had turned out to be a convivial and productive evening after all.

Once we were alone, Zaynab's customary curiosity took charge. She wanted every detail of the Richmond conversations. To her annoyance I would provide only a bare summary. But Neelam's role in the saga of Naughty's rise surprised both of us, and confirmed my impression of her as a warm-hearted and intelligent person, not unlike her mother.

Zaynab had begun to miss Fatherland. The memory of Plato had become blended with all the other events in her life. She wanted to see how he had left the painting that she had seen in its early stages and disliked. She had found and kept a scrap of Plato's writing, a diary entry or memo. It was unheard of for Plato to write, so this must have been about something he wanted to paint at some stage.

✺

Weak Smile: A short talk with I. M. Malik, March 2001.

Malik came with paintings because I refused to go to his neat, tidy studio that I've always hated. There we used to crowd into the middle of the room, and he would light the place with five huge spotlights and display his paintings. Most of them were examples of bad landscape art: mountain streams with a deer watching from above, pine trees and hills with monkeys, portraits of the famous and the rich and copies of countless other paintings that already existed. I stopped going and when he rang I asked him to bring his new wares to my place. He wanted an honest opinion. Malik was an intelligent critic and I always wondered how someone like him who understood other people's work extremely well had so few insights into his own art. His admirers, and there were many, claimed that his finest work had been done in pre-Partition Lahore in the 1940s, when the city was known as the Paris of the East and intellectual and artistic life had peaked. What use was all that now?

Before I let him open his case I said, Malik, if they're money-makers, let's not waste time. He cursed me and insisted they were good and wanted me to see one in particular. I agreed. looked at it. Really bad. Purely decorative and would probably grace some wall in a vulgar mansion in Defence. He looked at me. I smiled weakly. He said, 'I know you think it's ridiculous.' He waited for my response. I managed another weak smile. 'You don't like it?' Finally I said, 'No. It's a very bad painting.' He got angry. 'The trouble with you is that you enjoy being out of harmony with the times.'

I replied: 'An artist should never be in harmony with the times even if they accord with his beliefs. An artist must always look ahead, live on the edge. Otherwise art would become predictable.'

'You think all my paintings are bad?'

'*No. Some of the earlier ones were good. Very good.*'

'*You've always spoken the truth. Like a true friend.*' I did not say anything, which was a mistake because it encouraged him.

'*My last painting sold for fifty thousand dollars in Miami. I am a painter in residence in different countries each year. I've won six prizes. My new work is not as bad as you think.*'

I smiled weakly.

This was the inner core of Plato, and the memory moistened my eyes. I remembered his weak smile well. He hated pretentiousness in any form. Even at our table in the college café in Lahore all those years ago, if anybody started quoting couplets from the poets to emphasize a point, a habit common to many in that city, Plato would smile weakly, wait till they'd finished, and his sarcastic one-liner would follow. Why did he have to die? Zaynab came and sat on my lap. She was missing him too.

'Don't go back just yet,' I pleaded as I stroked her face. 'Fatherland is at its most dangerous at the moment. Incessant troubles and unparalleled violence, and your brother is a senior government minister.'

She promised to think about it, but I knew she wanted to leave Paris for a while without moving to London. I was beginning to understand her changes of mood and her capriciousness. She was feeling restless. Where did she want to go? She didn't know, but I could decide. Did she like the sea? Only if it was wild. Not to swim in but just to walk along the beach watching the fury of the waves. I explained gently that this would be torture for me. To be near a sea one cannot enter is like being married to the Koran. She laughed, signalling a change of mood.

'OK. A sea you can swim in and I can watch.'

'Zaynab, can you swim?'

Her face disappeared behind her hands.

'You can learn.'

'Too late.'

'We're going where there's a teaching pool and the sea. I'll teach you and it won't take long. It would be one thing if the Koran fell in the water, but if I got cramps I'd need you to swim.'

A week before we were to leave for Greece, there was an agitated phone call from Henri.

'Switch on the news. I'm on my way.'

Naughty was dead. Her face was being displayed on every channel. She had disappeared from home two days ago. Her former husband and sons had alerted the police, since her passport and belongings had been left at home. The boys, both in their late teens, beardless and wearing T-shirts and denims, were shown weeping copiously. Their father, in uniform, looked drawn and stressed. Her body had been found that day, hacked to pieces and stored in a sack. The police chief told reporters that the killers were probably surprised at their work, or they would have burned the body.

Tears poured down Zaynab's cheeks as she watched the news footage. Yet another medieval episode in Fatherland, but this was not a religious murder. That much was obvious to anyone who knew the place. Had it been carried out by a hard-core Islamist network they would have filmed the murder and distributed the video as a warning to others who might be tempted down the same path as poor Naughty. Henri arrived and was clearly agitated. For him the real killers were those who had recruited her to their cause, but before he could expand on this, Zaynab interrupted him. 'Henri, I know the country well. This is not a political murder carried out by religious fanatics. It feels like something else, I don't know what, but they will find out. With three generals in the picture as her lovers, military intelligence will want answers.'

Henri was now convinced that Zaynab's interview with Naughty should be published on its own, with the voice tapes made available to the media. The global networks had been giving the story of her murder massive coverage, strongly hinting that it was a punishment killing by some terrorist group angered by the success of her book in the West. Colonel Lateef, her former husband, had adopted this refrain on every news channel. The boys, unabashed at meeting the gaze of so many curious journalists, told Fatherlandi television that if the police were unable to track the killers, they, as her sons, would avenge their mother's death. Nobody thought it fitting to inquire what exactly they meant. Meanwhile posters of the martyred Madame Auratpasand appeared on billboards in every European capital, and T-shirts with her image made an appearance in the duty-free shops at Fatherlandi airports. All that was missing was Detectives without Borders to enter the country and nail the killers.

While this tsunami of emotion and hysteria was drowning other stories in the mediasphere, Editions Montmorency, in a sharply worded press release, announced the Auratpasand interview book. This unleashed a new barrage of interest, but Henri was not prepared to sell serialization rights even though the offers came in millions. He was an old-fashioned publisher and wanted the book to be the only point of reference. The market vindicated his decision. Advance orders in France reached the hundred thousand mark.

In the face of all this, the police chief in Isloo maintained a calm dignity, and the immobility of his facial expression became the subject of bitter comment in much of the global media. Given such a fearful tragedy, how come the chief investigator showed no emotion? Were Fatherland's police indifferent to the crime?

Then, exactly two weeks after the outrage, the unjustly traduced Isloo police called a press conference at 8.30 am that was relayed live on local networks and fed directly to Al Jazeera, CNN and BBC World. There was a stunned silence when the much-maligned policeman, in a calm and still emotionless voice, began to speak.

'Ladies and gentlemen. Early this morning we made three arrests. Colonel Lateef and his two sons, Ahmed Lateef and Asif Lateef, have been charged with first-degree murder and are in police custody. The Fatherland Army has authorized me to say that Colonel Lateef has been stripped of his rank and cashiered. He is no longer regarded as a serving officer and can be tried as a civilian. I have nothing more to add at this stage.'

Since there was worldwide interest in the affair, the impeccable behaviour of the Isloo police surprised and pleased most people in Fatherland. None of the three accused was tortured. The evidence was circumstantial, but deadly. Naughty had signed three separate cheques for a million dollars each to the three men, but even though her account was in her new name, Yasmine Auratpasand, she had signed them *Khalida Lateef*. Asif Lateef later admitted that when he questioned his mother regarding the discrepancy, she had sworn on the Koran that this was the only signature the bank would accept. They believed her, but she turned out to be cleverer than all of them. Had she perhaps suspected the foul play they had planned? Their mistake cost them their lives. Asif Lateef told the court the murder had been planned as an honour killing. Their mother had disgraced them with too many men. They had invited her back purely in order to despatch her.

'In that case', asked a judge, 'why were you so interested in the money? You were her only children, so you would have inherited it automatically. Since your guilt is no longer in doubt, it is in your interest to speak the truth.'

But the sons would not implicate their father. His version was that he came home and saw they had killed her, and since they were his sons he felt obliged to help them. Police evidence contradicted that story. Three different knives had been used. All three were found in the sack. and the fingerprints of Colonel Lateef had been identified on one of them. Why had they killed her so brutally? The colonel had rifles and two pistols in the house. A single shot would have sufficed. Once again, it was Asif who provided the explanation. All three had to kill her, and this was the simplest way. A bullet was too quick. They wanted to punish her for the shame she had brought on the family. The judgement was delivered promptly and the sentence was carried out the following week. All three men were hanged.

✺

The saturation coverage given to the murder, of course, contradicted all earlier speculation, but memories are short in the West. Inconvenient truths can be brushed off any fiction. When Editions Montmorency published the interview book with an acerbic introduction by Henri, it was virtually ignored. Despite not being reviewed in the bulk of the media, the first edition of book sold over two hundred thousand copies, and foreign rights were bought like hot *gulab jamuns* at the Istanbul Book Fair, where Henri had organized an auction.

A few radio stations played extracts from the tape, and that was the sum total of on-air publicity. Jean-Pierre Bertrand was nowhere to be seen. The celebrities who had clustered around Naughty in Paris and New York did not wish to be associated with her after her death.

Madame Zaynab Shah was referred to in *Marianne* as an oral historian, which was news to everyone except me. The book appeared in English, but the New York friends of Diderot chose to ignore its presence. It did not receive a single review, but, as in Paris, sales were brisk. What surprised us all was that Naughty had made a will before returning to Fatherland. In the case of her death, her sons would inherit her apartment in Paris and everything else. If, for whatever reason, including predeceasing her, this was impossible, her entire estate was bequeathed to

Editions Montmorency, with the stipulation that they produce three titles a year that were translations from Punjabi.

I was surprised and pleased to receive a phone call from Neelam. 'Just got back from Beijing and heard about Mrs Lateef. Then I got a copy of the book. It's a very good interview. Please congratulate Zaynab *khala* from me. What an awful end to her life. You know it was I who taught her some basic English.'

I told Neelam of my meeting with Naughty and how she had told me the same thing and had sung Neelam's praises and expressed remorse for having helped to wreck her marriage.

'Let's forget that now, Uncle Dara. Allah's will must be done. The good news is that Mom and I are friends again after almost fifteen years. I told her you stayed at our house and praised the coffee even when I had asked you not to. It pleased her a great deal. When are you visiting Isloo? Soon, I hope.'

Slowly everything was falling into place, some of it in the most gruesome fashion possible and some of it in a way that restored a degree of tranquillity to friends and their children. What would become of Zaynab? I had few doubts that our love and friendship, as pleasant and restorative as it had been, could not last too long. I had books to write. She wanted to build an art museum in Sind where ancient and modern works might be shown together. Mohenjo-Daro on the ground floor, Plato near the top. She had talked about this a great deal, reigniting my old fascination with Mohenjo-Daro and the civilization of which the city had been a part in 3600 BCE. Replicas of its stern-faced priests and exquisitely shaped dancing girls are looking down at me from a bookshelf as I write these words. I'd always thought of writing a novel set in that period in the region, but events had intervened and finally the back burner itself had collapsed. Was it time to revive the project? Perhaps, if only to demonstrate that sanitation and the distribution of food was more advanced then than it is in Fatherland today.

Zaynab knew the state museums were badly funded, run by corrupt bureaucrats, and that as a result many artefacts were already in Western museums or private collections. She was determined to build her own museum. She pressed me repeatedly to become its director, but I could not be part of this project. I could not replace Plato in her life. I told her so and she hugged me tight, but made no attempt to convince me otherwise. We both knew that it was time to move on, and although our friendship was secure for ever, when we would next meet and what we would do were questions that could not be answered. On one issue alone was she intransigent. We had to see Plato's last painting together. On this there was no dispute.

'Your initial instincts were correct, Zaynab,' Henri told her at dinner the evening Naughty's will was made public. 'She was not a complete monster. Part victim, part monster. That is what this world does to people. Dara, what should we do to thank her for the bequest? A Yasmine Auratpasand Prize sounds exploitative and false.'

'Let me think.'

Late that night I did think, and while Zaynab was sleeping peacefully, I thought that a school for girls in the village where she was born, and in her real name, to avoid stupid publicity, might be a possible solution, with scholarships for study abroad guaranteed for the top two students each year. Both Henri and Zaynab agreed. Zaynab would speak to her brother to expedite matters. Henri would talk to a friend on how best to invest the money for such a purpose. Meanwhile a Punjabi list had to be organized for Henri's publishing house, and I promised to suggest six books for it: three classics and three modern novels.

'I wish we could simply call it Naughty School for Girls,' said Zaynab with a gleam in her eyes after Henri had left. 'But I fear that might be misunderstood by some of our bearded friends.'

SEVENTEEN

Dear Dara, I've attached Jindié's report, as promised, on her first three months in Beijing and a trip to Yunnan. I'm now quite hopeful that all will be well in the long run. Remember that song you and Jindié would play all the time when you visited our house: Muddy Waters singing 'Everything's Gonna Be All Right'? The music of my life is more organized than that, but I'm singing again. The attachment accompanying this e-mail I have been compelled to edit, since it would fill a book on its own, and so I have left out long descriptions of Beijing, a satirical account – whose ferocity both surprised and delighted me – of Jindié's visit to the Ethnic Culture Theme Park, entered from a detour off the Fourth Ring Road, of which road, too, she has much to say. Jindié's daily impressions of Beijing and her lyrical description of Dali and Yunnan deserve to be and will, no doubt, be published on their own, though not in the *National Geographic*, since there is not a trace of exoticism in what she writes. Without altering or adorning the simple style of her prose, I have merely shortened the text to concentrate on the development of the characters we already know and the appearance of others necessary to our story.

All best,
Your old friend Confucius.

Dear Dara,
I did not return to Beijing with my brother, but spent a few days in London first preparing for the journey. Zahid knew a number of neurologists and we met two of them together. They pointed out that in memory lapses, it is normally old memories that have been submerged; whether or not they can be brought back to the surface depends on the person concerned. They were impressed by Hanif's (please accept the use of this name even though you and other friends always think of him as Confucius) total recall of Punjabi, and one of the neurologists said he had not encountered a case of this sort before. He advised us to constantly call Hanif by his name when speaking Punjabi and Chinese. The recall of Punjabi, both of them stressed, was a sign of a submerged memory. It would take time and patience.

Hanif picked us up at Beijing airport and drove us home, pointing at new buildings and naming their architects. He lives in a huge, comfortable apartment built about five or six years ago, close to the financial quarter. His wife, Cheng Yu-chih, is in her late forties, short hair, very well dressed and fluent in English and German. She works as an economist in some government department.

While he showed Zahid the apartment and then took him to the basement to inspect the health centre and swimming pool, I told Yu-chih our story. She was not as surprised as I thought she'd be. Hanif had told her that we were friends he had met in Paris, but that we might be related to him as well. Yu-chih explained that he was slowly trying to build a narrative of his life before his collapse, and since his return from Paris had told a number of people that he had been born in Lahore and had recently met his sister.

She also said he talked in his sleep in strange languages and occasionally used such archaic words in Chinese that she had to consult a dictionary. Now this began to make sense to her. She'd wondered who the old couple were that he had introduced her to once as his parents but who never came here and whom he rarely visited. Yu-chih had thought that he was ashamed of them because they were retired factory workers. This was a common phenomenon in all the big cities, so she had not questioned him too much on the subject. 'When a country has changed its identity so completely, is it surprising that many of its citizens do the same?'

I like her very much. She is honest and intelligent.

When the two men returned, I said 'Hanif, I really like your wife.' The name startled him.

Then Zahid repeated it and he turned on us. 'Why do you call me by that name? In Paris one of your friends called me Confucius, and now you call me, what did you call me?'

'Hanif!'

'It's not a Chinese name.'

I nodded, but did not push him any further. Later Yu-chih asked me whether our family was Hui. I told her we were Hui from Yunnan, but when we settled in India some of our community took traditional Arab names from our ancestors as well. My parents and I had Chinese names, but they decided to call my brother Hanif. She sat down on the bed with her head in her hands.

'Dear sister, Jindié, the reason I asked is because your brother is always cursing the Hui in Beijing, sometimes using very bad language. I always reprimand him, but even his body language becomes aggressive. He will never accept he is Hui. That will be the biggest shock for him. I haven't dared tell him that my family in Shanghai are Hui. We are not religious at all, but my father, a surgeon, is proud of his heritage. Sometimes I take him to Oxen Street because it has the best noodles in town. It's in the Hui area and he always looks at them strangely. Once he asked offensively for pork and got an offensive reply in return. "Go and fuck a pig," he said before I drove the car away. I did shout at him afterwards. He talked more rubbish. "The first Hui who came to our country said they would return to theirs. They're still here twelve centuries later. They should go home." I asked whether all the minorities should return and reminded him that the Tibetans are desperate to do so but we won't let them. His reply was very strange. He said: "The others can all stay. Only the Hui. They should go." He doesn't mind the Muslims in Xinjiang. They can stay as well. Just the Hui in the south. The intermarriages in the south between Hui and Han were so strong that for centuries the only distinguishing feature was the pork taboo and prayers.

'Many Han thought Mohammad was just like Confucius for the Hui. Perhaps my dear husband hates hybridity. I just don't know. None of our friends talks the way he does.'

All this came as a shock and I was very distressed. Slowly, I unpacked my suitcases, thinking all the time of how to unpack Hanif's mind. I had brought a lovely old photograph of our parents and Younger and Elder Granny posing in front of the Zam Zam gun, which used to hang above the mantelpiece in our Lahore apartment. I now hung it on the wall in the living room. Then I placed a photograph of all of us just after my wedding, with Hanif dressed in an *achkan*, wearing a turban and grinning, in the kitchen. Yu-chih nearly fainted when she saw that one, but said nothing.

Zahid knew some Chinese physicians from international conferences and through them we found an excellent neurologist. I told her everything, including the outbreak of Hui-phobia. Dr Wang agreed to see him, but only after a month. She thought that with proper stimuli his memory could return. If the Punjabi language had been unlocked, then anything was possible. She wanted to know if there had been an accident, and said I should go and meet the couple he thought were his parents. All she would do was put him under a scanner to see if there had been any physical damage. The rest was up to us.

Hanif and Yu-chih would both leave for work early, and Zahid had gone to Isloo to take Neelam and the kids to London for their holidays. I was left on my own and went out to explore the city. Oxen Street was packed with people. I walked to the mosque and looked inside. Nobody cared. I found the best noodle stand in Beijing. It was marked *qing zhen* (halal); another sign said 'no pork'. They were very good noodles. When I told the owner, who was all of twenty-five years old, that I was a Hui from Fatherland, he was very welcoming. Wanted to know how I had landed up there. His uncle, a Chinese naval engineer, was currently in Gwadur. Had I been there? I shook my head. He told me he was a secular Marxist but also Hui and observed minority holidays to honour his Arab ancestors. He said that since Gulf money has been coming in to help repair the mosques and build a few new ones, he had noticed an increase in mosque attendance. He winked. 'I think some go for free food and clothes.'

Yu-chih took a day off work and drove me to an old part of the city to meet the couple Hanif thought were his parents. They live in a cluster of small houses near the outskirts of precapitalist Beijing. They must be in their late eighties. They welcomed us warmly and offered some tea and very sweet biscuits. They told their story openly; there was no subterfuge at all.

Hanif had been a very close friend of their son's, and the boys often stayed with them in the late Sixties. The boys were members of a group of Red Guards that called itself From the Periphery to the Centre Proletarian Group for World Revolution. One day there was a clash, either with another group or with the Lin Biaoists in their own group. They could never get the details, but it ended with their son, Hsuan, being killed. Hanif picked up his friend and carried his body home. His own head was bleeding and he fell unconscious. The old couple began to weep at the memory of Hsuan, and both Yu-chih and I hugged and stroked them till they grew calm again. He had been their only child.

They had called an ambulance and Hanif was taken to the hospital, where he recovered consciousness but had no idea what had happened. He was sent back to their home in an ambulance. After the political turbulence had subsided he entered Beijing University, gaining admittance as the son of a working-class couple. The university authorities themselves were recovering from the chaos of that period. They were aware that Hanif had suffered a severe memory lapse and didn't press him on details of his prior schooling or anything else. He was given new papers in his Cultural Revolution name, Chiao-fu. He was a brilliant student, always coming home with good reports. Then he went to Shanghai and Hong Kong to work and only recently had he returned to Beijing. Once he started working he had sent his 'parents' money every month, often accompanied by clothes and expensive food parcels. He never talked much after Hsuan's death, but was always dutiful. It was Hanif who had assumed they really were his parents. They never corrected him because in a way he had become their son. Once he saw a photograph of Hsuan and himself with red bands on their heads and asked them, 'Is that my brother? What happened to him? Why did he die?'

They'd had no idea of where he came from or they would have written us. They looked in his case and found only a Chinese passport with the name he uses today. No address book, no other identifying papers of any type. Nothing. It was like that during the Cultural Revolution. Getting rid of identity cards was regarded as an act of liberation. We now have as complete a picture as we are likely to get till his memory returns.

At home he looked at the photo in the kitchen, the one of my wedding, and didn't recognize himself. Neither Yu-chih nor I said anything, but I've noticed him staring hard at the other picture, of our parents and grannies.

When I'm alone I often speak Punjabi to him and he replies, usually with a smile in his face. Once he said, 'This is a very funny language. I remember a joke we used to repeat.' He had used the words 'I remember', and this made me shiver with joy, but I kept calm and asked him to tell me the joke. 'It's quite stupid, but funny. Someone says to the bichu booti (the stinging nettle-like plant that you must remember from our Nathiagali outings), "How is it I only see you in the summer? Why do you disappear in winter?" The bichu booti replies, "Given how you treat me in the summer, why are you surprised I prefer to stay away in the winter?"' I didn't find this amusing, but Hanif laughed so much that I joined him. He alternates between this mood and one where he seems very tense, as if dragons were fighting in his head.

My boy, Suleiman, has arrived from Yunnan. He is living in Dali but travels all over the province. My child, whom I thought we had lost forever to the financial world of futures and derivatives, has returned home. Hanif was touched by his presence and heard the stories of his adventures in Yunnan with some delight.

But it was Suleiman's earlier life as a stockbroker in Hong Kong that really interested his uncle. Where he had worked, how much money he'd made and what had made him leave that world. Both Hanif and

Yu-chih nodded a great deal as Suleiman described how hard he had worked, how he had no time to think of anything else except rushing to a club after work each day, drinking with his friends, watching television and going to bed early so he could wake up at five and be at work an hour later.

Alone with me, Suleiman confessed that he was in love and showed me his girlfriend's photograph. She was a postgraduate student at the university, a few years younger and, like him, studying history. Which mother is ever satisfied with her son's choice? My first reaction was that she was far too pretty and I could not make a judgement till I met her. There was a photograph of both of them on a boat in the lake in which she was laughing. I liked that more than her pin-up pose. And I had always thought that Suleiman would marry a nice Punjabi girl. When I said that, he responded, 'Yes, just like the nice Punjabi general who made Neelam so happy.' I asked him so many questions about her that he lost his patience. She was in Beijing with her family for the next week and I could meet her. So, I thought, all this has been well planned by the young couple. But before I met You-shi, there was a tiny earthquake in our lives. The tremors had been there for weeks.

One morning when Suleiman and Hanif were in the kitchen together, my son saw the old wedding photograph and burst out laughing. 'Uncle, you look good in Punjabi clothes. Just look at you.' Hanif paled. He looked at the photograph carefully. He left the kitchen and knocked at my door.

'Jindié, are both our parents dead?'

I nodded, and we both sat on my bed and wept. We talked that whole day. He wouldn't let me tell him his life story, but instead asked questions. I would answer them and he would ask more. He was piecing it all together for himself.

'We are a Hui family?'

'Yes,' I said firmly.

'From Yunnan?'

'Yes.'

'Our great forebear was Dù Wénxiù?' He began to smile. 'I think it was Plato who named me Confucius, or was it Dara?'

'Plato died a few months ago, Hanif. And Dara you met in Paris a few weeks ago. It was he who rang us.'

'I will ring him later. Now I have to choose between three names. Hanif would be best, I think, but all my official documents say Chiao-fu. And Confucius reminds me of our young days in Lahore.'

The silt in his head was being dislodged. Too many memories were coming back at the same time. Suddenly he began to weep again and said we had to go to the home of his adoptive parents. He drove fast, cursing the Beijing traffic even though his car was too big and part of the problem. The old couple were pleasantly surprised. Hanif burst in and hugged them.

'I remember everything. My friend Hsuan, your son, died saving my life.'

And the story poured out. They had been attacked by a rival faction of Red Guards, who had denounced them as lickspittles and running dogs of Soviet revisionism, supporters of the traitor Lin Biao and US imperialism. Then they had taunted Hanif. You are no Red Guard. You are a Hui pig. Pigs can't be Red Guards. Repeat after us: I am a Hui pig, not a Red Guard. Hanif had refused to repeat this, and they had charged at him with staves and knives. He had been hit several times on the head, but as they charged him once again, young Hsuan put himself in the way and died from a single hammer blow to his head. Seeing what they had done, the rival faction disappeared. All Hanif could remember was lifting Hsuan on his back and walking and walking and walking. The old couple wept. So many tears during these days. Then Hanif said to them: 'Why are you living here? I have a large apartment. Come and live with us. Or I will find another apartment near us for you.'

They refused to leave. They were proud of having been workers at a time when it was a good thing to be, and besides, they said, it was here that Hsuan had been born and died. They did not wish to move away from him. We had bought food along from a restaurant on Oxen Street. Hanif described the area. 'Our people lived here for centuries.' Had his revulsion for them been caused by the taunts heard just before Hsuan died? Who knows? Now we all sat down and ate together. I couldn't help asking the old people what they thought of Mao. The old man spoke first: 'He forgot where he came from and headed off for a different past.' His wife was less objective: 'I think back now. Hsuan was always saying that Chairman Mao was fighting the capitalist-roaders. He was right about them if nothing else.' I looked at Hanif. He was smiling. 'Both of you are right, my parents. He was also right about fighting the Japanese bandits as well as the KMT. Our present leadership prefers Chiang Kai-shek to Mao, without realizing that they wouldn't be where they are without the Revolution. But I can see why they're nostalgic about Chiang.'

As he drove back, he talked about Hsuan a great deal and was full of self-reproach for not having done more for his parents. I told him that they certainly didn't believe he had been inattentive. The next few months were truly joyous. I had not felt so happy for a long time, in fact, not since the start of the evening in the Shalimar Gardens in Lahore forty-six years ago. Yu-chih is the most adorable sister-in-law one could ever hope to have. She adjusted to Hanif's identity without any problems and even shamed Hanif by reminding him, to his mortification, of the Hui-phobia that his amnesia had brought to the surface.

I discussed Suleiman's life with them, and we invited You-shi to dinner. They came together. She still seemed too pretty and a bit too aware of it for my liking, but as her shyness wore off and she began to speak I melted. I was happy for them, and Suleiman, noticing the softness that had suddenly come over his mother, smiled the whole evening. Hanif asked whether she had told her parents. Both the young people started laughing. Before I arrived, Suleiman had often spent the night at her place and clearly in her bed. You-shi's parents were both university professors and were happy to go along with whatever the two of them decided.

'We'll get married when we want, Mom,' said Suleiman. 'There's no pressure on us here. This isn't Lahore or London.'

There was nothing more to say. Soon Neelam arrived with the children and stayed a week. She, too, it would appear, loved You-shi at first sight, and they became inseparable. You-shi took charge of the children and went with them to horrible, ugly theme parks but also to the Forbidden City, which will, I'm sure, soon be sold off to some billionaire as private property once the crisis subsides a little. Perhaps Zhang Yimou can buy it and make it the centre of a pulp film industry. There are things that still make me angry, which surprises Hanif, who always regarded me as apolitical.

I decided to leave my brother and sister-in-law alone for a while. Their house had become a hotel. Suleiman and You-shi took me to Dali and then Kunming. On the way to Dali they told me that they lived together in an old apartment overlooking the lake. The 'old apartment' is tastefully furnished and very comfortable. They live and behave as if they were already married, but I never discuss these matters with them.

I walked by the lake often, thinking about the past. One day, even though it was sunny and warm, I found myself shivering. I was overwhelmed by emotion, remembering Elder Granny's stories about this place. I walked a great deal that day, trying to imagine what Dali must have been like when Sultan Suleiman was alive. I looked at the people and wondered whether their forebears had been among those who had stood in the streets and wept on the day of the surrender. My thoughts were constantly interrupted by the noise of traffic and car horns. Many tourists visit this city without being aware of what took place here only recently.

After a week, we went to Kunming and visited the museum. Here another surprise awaited me – something that I had never even thought of since I wrote a brief account of the historical events in this region for you. Naturally the story of the rebellion is all here, but presented in neutral terms. Very factual, even though I couldn't help but feel that the massacres in Dali that took place after our defeat were underplayed. Perhaps time and all the deaths China has suffered since then have blunted their sensitivities about the earlier past. It seems different when you view history far away from the country where it is taking place. Often you can see some things much more clearly, but also lose sight of others, from a distance. When I view the lake in Dali from the window of the 'old apartment', I see it glimmering in the sun or its colour changing when it's cloudy, but till you go on the lake you can't see that it has become polluted, or spot the occasional dead fish that floats to the surface.

As we were leaving the museum I happened to mention to the curator that we were direct descendants of Dù Wénxiù. The old man's face lit up. He dragged all three of us to his office. He was literally trembling with excitement. I couldn't fully understand the reason for this till he opened the visitors' book. This was normally the preserve of visiting dignitaries, and Arab names littered the pages. What he wanted me to read was the following message:

'We are the descendants of Dù Wénxiù. Our great-great-grandmother was sent by Sultan Suleiman to Cochin China. She settled there as a trader, with her child by him, and was pregnant with another. They all survived. If any other descendants ever visit this museum and read these lines, please get in touch with us in Ho Chi Minh City where we have always lived. There is another branch of the family that moved to California after April 1975, but we do not maintain any contact with them. These are all our phone numbers and my name is a Vietnamese one: Thu Van.'

Now I was trembling. The curator ordered some tea. I explained our roots to him and he asked for all the family photographs to be copied and sent to him as well as the letter the sultan's sister in Burma had written to Elder Granny. They wanted to display them in the museum. The news of this unexpected discovery caused a big stir in Beijing and in Isloo. Everyone's first impulse was to hop on a plane to Ho Chi Minh City, but before any of that could happen I had to make the phone call. Would Thu Van speak English or French? They must have stopped speaking Chinese a long time ago. I wanted Hanif next to me when I made the call. I don't know why, but I wanted him to help us decide what to do. Suleiman was a bit upset and suggested wisely that I wait a while and let the news sink in properly. After all, there was no reason to hurry. We knew where they were. I think he was also concerned that too many shocks were not good for his mother.

Zahid, when I rang him, understood my needs better. I should discuss it with Confucius. Strange how Zahid won't call him Hanif at all, and, secretly, Chiao-fu would rather be called Confucius. I had already noticed that whenever there was a call from Zahid and once from you, Yu-chih would shout, 'Confucius! Phone.' And he would come running with the big grin that I remembered so well.

So I flew back to Beijing, and Yu-chih collected me from the airport. She had never known Chiao-fu/Hanif/Confucius so relaxed and happy.

They wanted to adopt a child and had begun to make inquiries. The old couple were fine and they saw them every weekend. More than that she didn't say. She let Hanif tell me that he was fed up with his job. He didn't like being an economist and was going to suggest to Henri that instead of writing a sharp academic-style critique of the pitfalls inherent in the Chinese economy or a sociological study of festivals, he now wanted to reconstruct the path from 1949 to 2009. He would call it 'Capitalist Roaders and the Road'. When I looked at him critically he grinned. 'Don't ring your husband and the one you wanted as your husband just yet. I'm not reverting to any crazy Maoism. I know what all that cost this country, and unnecessarily. They destroyed our hopes. I know that better than most. So it will be very critical of the Great Helmsman, but also of those who came after him. Those who ordered our soldiers to fire on the students in 1989, those who crush peasant uprisings today just like the campaign to rid China of fleas during the Communist period. And those who buy radical intellectuals like we do noodles in Oxen Street.' I was relieved to hear all this, and I think he will write a good book. He certainly knows both sides. Perhaps Henri should be alerted to the change of plan.

I did ask whether if Hanif gave up his job they would be able to afford the life they were used to now, just on Yu-chih's salary, a question that provoked only mirth. Like Suleiman, his uncle had played the financial market and accumulated if not vast at least sufficient wealth to live comfortably for the rest of his life. I asked whether he would have gone in this direction had there been no memory lapse. He did not know. Perhaps he would have come back to Lahore and returned to physics. How could he say?

I am still old-fashioned enough to be slightly repelled by this, but both Suleiman and Hanif insist (funny how similar they are in so many ways. My mother used to see it, too) that they exploited the system more than it did them and now they will pay it all back in projects that help people. Suleiman, in particular, is in a state of permanent shock at what he is seeing in Yunnan and elsewhere in the country, the effects of belated industrialization on the ecology of this country. 'Animals are dying, Mom, and people are being treated like animals, except in theme parks.' This passionate manner of feeling and expressing feelings is common to both uncle and nephew.

With Hanif seated next to me and listening on the other phone, I made the call to Ho Chi Minh City. Thu Van answered. I asked what language would be easiest for her. She repeated the question to me. She spoke five languages, including Chinese, and worked as an official interpreter. I explained who I was and that I was ringing in response to her message. Her screams could be heard in our kitchen. Then she shouted the news to her mother. She wanted to get on a plane and come over immediately with her mother to see us. We could come to them the following year. There was no stopping her, and so I gave Hanif's details and said we would pick them up at the airport, but reminded her to bring as many old photographs as possible of the family. They did not put us to the trouble of either picking or putting them up. They arrived within three days and stayed in a hotel they had always used before. They brushed aside all formalities. We looked at each other, but there was no resemblance. Thu Van's mother did remind me slightly of Elder Granny, but this could just be my overly sentimental and charged imagination.

I had brought my family album to help Hanif. Each side of the family devoured the photographs of the other. On seeing one of my mother at the age of twenty-four, both of our Vietnamese relations laughed with delight. She was very similar to Thu Van's grandmother. We compared the two side by side. It was the same family. Of this there could be no doubt. Then they unwrapped a large framed sepia photograph of 'our honoured matriarch', in Thong's words. So this was what Li Wan had looked like. She was old by then. The photograph had been taken in 1898. The location was the Saigon studio of a French photographer, Guillaume Boissier, whose name was prominently stamped on the photograph itself. She was approaching fifty, but the beauty and the authority on her face were only too visible. This was a copy made for us, and I will bring it back with me. I love her face. Sultan Suleiman had met her when she was only eighteen. How lovely she must have looked then, and how mature she must have been to play the role she did at the time. There was nothing like this in our family. We had no photographs of Elder Granny's mother. My mother said some had been taken by an English photographer in Calcutta, but they had disappeared.

Hanif asked whether there were any other documents, but both women shook their head and Thu Van's and her mother's eyes became sad. It emerged that there had been papers, including a manuscript written by the honoured matriarch herself, an account of the Dali sultanate and the uprisings in Yunnan, together with her journey to Cochin China and what she had subsequently achieved. This existed but was owned by the family in California. As I imagined, they had split during the long war in Vietnam. One branch, the one with the archive, had collaborated first with the French and later the Americans. And not just collaborated but provided names of the resistance and betrayed the whereabouts of Thu Van's uncle a few months before Saigon was liberated in the spring of 1975. The uncle was a leader of the resistance in Cholon, a Saigon suburb. He knew the date of the final assault and a great deal else, but revealed nothing. He was tortured to death.

This concludes the memorandum from Beijing. The postscript below concerns only us.

Postscript

Neelam told me how much she liked you, and that was pleasing. She also said that you and Zahid were bonding again and that she heard you laughing together in the manner of Punjabi schoolboys. Hanif will now, no doubt, become part of all that. Since he must have told you that the big problem in our lives was my lack of passion – this was a regular complaint – let me now confess something to you, and don't be shocked if it challenges your image of me as Dai-yu, which was also reported by Neelam, who told me she agreed with you. Just to stop you thanking your stars for sparing you an ethereal, spiritual beauty who felt nothing physical and lived in her dreams, let me tell you that I had two lovers at different times in my life. One didn't last too long and it's hardly worth mentioning him. The other I enjoyed physically a great deal and also liked as a person, but not enough to break up my family for him. That affair lasted most of the time we were in DC. I trust that you will not impart this information to anyone, neither my husband nor my brother nor either of my children. The secret must die with you, as it will with me.

You're wondering who this person was, and I will tell you. He was a Tanzanian agronomist I met in the library at Georgetown. We became friends and I learnt a great deal about Africa from him. One day it happened. And, dear friend, were I to describe the heights that my passion reached you would be the one shouting, 'Hsi-men, Hsi-men.' The others I can excuse, but you knew that the *Dream of the Red Chamber* was not the only novel that I had read. You knew that I was busy reading the Chin Ping Mei at a young age. So why am I Dai-yu? Why not Meng Yu-lo or another character like her from *Red Chamber*? I often told you that Zahid was a nice man, but I never felt passionately about him. What's so unusual about that in a marriage? It's the story of the institution, is it not? He pleasured young nurses. I was pleasured by a middle-aged African professor, but I played the role of Hsi-men. Zahid, as we Chinese-Punjabis say, could see a bee defecating forty miles outside the city, but tripped over an elephant on his own doorstep.

I hope you didn't believe him, but knowing how male camaraderie operates in a Punjabi milieu, I fear you did. You might have discovered the truth for yourself had you not insisted on coffee for breakfast. That opportunity, alas, will never come our way again.

EIGHTEEN

I sent Jindié an appreciative e-mail praising her prose to the skies and suggesting a publisher for her musings on Beijing and Yunnan. 'As for the postscript', I wrote, 'I'm delighted to hear you have enjoyed life to the full, though I hope not as fully as Hsi-men Ch'ing, despite your invocation of his name more than once. As for the rest, all I can say is better a middle-aged Tanzanian agronomist than a rapidly aging Punjabi writer who lacks the vigour of youth.'

Zaynab had returned to Fatherland and was asking me each day to set a date so that Plato's painting could be brought to the house and unveiled. She promised this would not be done till I arrived. Did I think we should invite someone else as well? For Zaynab to ask that meant she already had someone in mind, and even as I was wondering who this could be and from which continent, the phone rang.

'Alice Stepford here. Is that you, Dara?'

'Has Zaynab invited you to her country mansion?'

'Have you decided a date?'

'Think carefully, Alice. Fatherland is a mess. Americans are not safe there.'

'Let me know the date, when you've decided it, and the flight from London so that we can synchronize watches. Speak soon.'

A frivolous e-mail exchange with Zaynab followed this call:

Good idea to invite a few other people. What about Zahid and Confucius, who were close to him in his Lahore days, as well as Ally Stepford? z.

Will you provide security for the Stepford mistress? D.

You mean your ex-mistress. Why have you gone off her? z.

Could Yu-chih come as well, since she has to be shown Lahore? D.

The party was growing by the minute. Zaynab rang an hour later.

'Master of the Universe, have you decided on a date?'

'Mistress of all you survey, what's the weather like in Sind? Any storms in the offing?'

'Dara, stop fooling. I've got e-mails from all your guests thanking me for the invitation and glad that you invited Mrs Confucius along as well. Ally, my only guest, said you were distinctly harsh and rude to her.'

'Is there a helicopter service from Karachi Airport to Thanda Gosht Yar, or is it called *Sain*ville now?'

She suppressed a giggle. 'Behave. Unless you send me dates by tomorrow morning I'll unveil it on my own.'

And then one day we all arrived in Karachi. Zaynab's brother had thoughtfully organized a helicopter, and we were met off the gangway by flunkeys. The Confuciuses had already arrived. The flunkeys took our passports and escorted us to the hotel's VIP suite.

'Why not VVIP?' I asked one of them.

'Permission only for VIP today, sir.'

'Was the VVVIP full?'

He tried not to smile.

In the VIP room the Bride of the Koran herself, looking ravishable, greeted us. I had missed her. The sun had done her good; she was a few degrees darker. She embraced Alice with a show of real warmth. Then she gave Zahid a salaam from afar and completely ignored me. I embraced Confucius with genuine delight and was introduced to Yu-chih, so well described by Jindié. Breakfast awaited us. It consisted of tinned and slightly mouldy orange juice, which I warned the others to ignore, but Ally ignored me and downed a tumbler of the foul stuff. An hour later she was looking distinctly peaky. The juice was followed by some deliciously stale chicken sandwiches, withered by the overnight heat and not restored to life by the early morning humidity or being sprinkled with water. One sniff and it was obvious that turpentine had been used as a butter substitute. When I pointed this out, Zaynab collapsed in laughter. She asked if we could have a word alone in the neighbouring prayer room.

'Are you sure your husband isn't in there?'

Inside she lost control and just roared.

'Will you please behave yourself? I know you're in one of your stupid moods, but preserve some decorum. Please try.'

I kissed her on the lips for a very long time. She broke loose; we adjusted ourselves and joined our friends. By the time the helicopter was ready we were in normal Fatherland mode. Zaynab had her head well covered, and, I was pleased to see, so had Alice. She looked very fetching in a maroon Sindhi scarf embroidered with silver stars. I put on my dark glasses. 'To hide his mocking eyes,' I heard Zaynab whisper to Alice. The helicopter was well prepared and we were handed a bottle of water each for the forty-minute hop to Pir Sikandar Shah's helipad.

'In case you're wondering why there are no parachutes, it's because you can't jump from a helicopter,' I said to nobody in particular. As the blades began to whirr, I noticed a momentary look of concern on Alice's face. At this point Zaynab put on her dark glasses. Conversation is always difficult on helicopters, but was more so in this one because the guard accompanying us had forgotten to bring the noise-cancelling earphones on board. I took out mine from my hand luggage and listened to a violin concerto that came to an end just as the helicopter landed on the baronial estates of the Shah family.

Pir Sikandar was at an emergency cabinet meeting in Isloo. His personal assistant and sundry retainers greeted us on landing. Zaynab was surrounded immediately by four maids, and she, Yu-chih and poor Alice retired to the women's quarter, no doubt for massage and bath respectively. Lucky things. We were taken to our guest cottages, with mine the closest to the house. I was greeted by a refrigerator overloaded with Murree beer but demanded fresh lime juice without sugar and a jug of tamarind juice with ice and honey. We men showered, and then Zahid and Confucius knocked on my door. I offered them beer. Both preferred the tamarind concoction. Confucius appeared slightly bewildered.

'I hope they haven't kidnapped Yu-chih for too long.'

Zahid asked whether I had been here before, to which the answer was no. Neither of her brothers was known to me. Most of my Sindhi friends were writers and poets and painters, and I reminded them that it was to see the last work of one of these that we were here.

'Plato was a motherfucking Punjabi,' muttered Confucius, in the language he had just mentioned.

'Glad you're back on side.'

He grinned. 'I want my wife back.'

Lunch was eagerly awaited by all, especially those who had travelled on Fatherland Airlines, but even the Beijing Two were starving. It was served in the pir sahib's dining room. His wife and kids were in Europe, and Zaynab had to play official hostess. A very elderly gentleman had joined us, a great-uncle who had helped to create Fatherland but whom nobody remembered was still alive. We had no doubt on that score. He drank a couple of beers and ate a healthy portion of each of the seven or eight well-prepared dishes that had been placed before us. When I asked his age he said 'ninety-two' in a lively voice. Nobody was disappointed with the food, but the presence of this elder had a slightly inhibiting effect on the conversation.

Every evening, he would lead the prayers in the tiny mosque on the estate, for a congregation of two dozen servants and about fifty serfs who were rustled up to keep the old man happy. The prayer was followed by an improvised exhortation to the assembled to be good Muslims and say their prayers; occasionally he would tell them not to interfere sexually with animals. Such acts had not been sanctioned, and they confused the lesser species. When the service was over his jeep would bring him straight to the house for a Patiala peg of whisky before supper. This daily disjuncture between theory and practice appeared to have kept him alive. Nor was he ungenerous. One reason the servants and serfs didn't mind him all that much was that he was too old now to demand one of their wives for the night and besides he was doling out money to whoever said they were in want.

He was, of course, a dreadful bore, but this could be said of most people who reach such an age.

During supper that night he remarked, 'Unless our politicians are led back to decent principles within ten years, we will have a bloody Communist revolution, and all these estates will be distributed to these donkeyfucking peasants.'

Confucius could not remain silent. 'The same will happen in China, except they fuck pigs, not donkeys.'

The old man roared with delight. Usually nobody spoke to him. Zaynab signalled me with her eyes, but I had no idea what she wanted. Later she told me that it was a rule at the table that nobody should ever answer Great-Uncle. I thought this excessively mean, but she had that don't-argue-this-one-with-me look in her eyes. I told her that her injunction would genuinely shock Mr and Mrs Confucius, because they came from a culture where ancestors were literally worshipped, including by many Hui. She was not impressed.

'Young man', he said now to Confucius, who was in his mid-sixties, 'I thought China *was* bloody Communist.'

'No, sir. They're capitalists now and conquering the world with their commodities.'

'Bloody good show. Did they bump the Communists off?'

'Oh no, sir. The Communist leaders became capitalists.'

This puzzled the great-uncle, and, aware that his presence annoyed Zaynab, he did not speak again till the dessert was served. This was a sensational rice pudding, exactly the correct consistency. Great-Uncle posed a question that none of us had yet asked.

'I was told there was an English lady with your party. Where is she?'

Zaynab was forced to announce that Alice was indisposed and had retired early. I was sure that the rusty orange juice that none of us had touched had rotted her insides, and the deadly desert diarrhœa germ, permanently in search of an opening, had scored a majestic triumph.

The old man mumbled something sympathetic. 'I had no idea she was ill. Otherwise I would not have worn my dinner jacket.'

None of the rest of us had dressed for dinner, but we had not packed any smart clothes. As we were leaving, I was handed a note by a retainer. It gave me instructions for the rest of the evening. When everyone had retired at about ten p.m. and the guards were pretending to patrol the perimeters, two of Zaynab's maids came to my room and wordlessly escorted me to their lady's bedchamber.

'I am a ruined man, Zizi. If we're discovered I'll be killed and you'll be married off to twelve volumes of the hadith as a punishment. Paris is one thing, but in this holiest of holies where you were married to the Holiest of Holy Books, there can be only one punishment.'

'Stupid man. Take off your clothes and get into bed.'

'Are you not going to dismiss the maids?'

'They've seen better things hanging in their time.'

'I thought we were breaking up.'

'I've told Alice she has no cause for anxiety. I'm sure she'll be fine. And please stop winding her up. Did you know she was a distant relation of the Napiers?'

'I'm taking my clothes off.'

'I'm waiting.'

'The Napiers of Napier Road in Karachi? It should be called Peccavi Road.'

'It's nice you're in this bed.'

'I feel a poem coming in my head. Where once a candle stood to light the Koran, a peasant entered and replaced the candle with his own . . .'

The maids turned out the lights and retired to the adjoining room.

'Has Alice got diarrhœa?'

'I can't find your candle.'

'I'm perfectly happy.'

'I'm returning to Paris soon. It's irritating never to leave the house without a maid. These two are well trained. One was married to the peasant who replaced the candle, but he died a few weeks ago.'

I felt keenly aware that our relationship was about to undergo another change.

At five in the morning, the maids woke us up, helped me dress and returned me to my official quarters. Fifteen minutes later the muezzin called the faithful to prayer, but old Great-Uncle didn't stir a muscle. Two hours later we were all having breakfast.

NINETEEN

At nine forty-five we moved to the big hall, an unusual structure that stood on its own, at a slight distance from the old house and the new additions. It had originally been built as a covered market so that the horse dealing took place in the shade and the animals could be thoroughly inspected before being bought or sold. Improvements in keeping with its later function had been made in the nineteenth century. Beasts of a different sort assembled here now. Local landlords, usually men of harsh and violent temperament, met here regularly to discuss common preoccupations, mainly brigandage of various sorts that was supposedly plaguing the countryside. For many centuries peasant brigands had constituted the only serious opposition to the vile rule of their masters, who had long forgotten that the origins of their own fortunes, as is the case with great families everywhere, lay in theft and pillage on a grand scale.

When these outlaws were caught and punished, ordinary people felt great sympathy for them; songs and ballads about their deeds remain part of Sindhi folklore. They had defied authority, and for that they were honoured. It was rumoured that this hall had briefly been used as an execution, or rather a strangulation, chamber: those caught stealing were brought here and the life was choked out of them. Not all of them were men.

This was also the hall where the landed gentry of the region had met in the nineteenth century and decided that since the British conquerors had occupied Sind with such superior force, any resistance would amount to collective suicide, and their heirs would be punished by being deprived of their property. Thus, it was unanimously agreed, collaboration was the only way forward. Great-Uncle's grandfather had been the moving force behind the decision. The landed collaborators had prospered. As the British prepared to leave India, they advised their old friends to transfer their loyalties to the Muslim League and the new Fatherland. They did so and continued to prosper.

Such was the historic location where Plato's last work was going to be revealed to a handful of his friends. We arrived soon after breakfast and began looking at the old photographs that adorned the walls, including a very fetching one of the then-young great-uncle on horseback and attired in polo gear. We were interrupted by the slow march into the space of a team of ten brawny peasants, five on each side of the huge painting. They carried it in and placed it against the wall. More retainers rushed in to help uncover it. Plato would have found this both amusing and repulsive, but homilies were redundant, for had he been alive we wouldn't be here and the work would not have existed in its present form. It was the artistic equivalent of his last will and testament.

Zaynab was becoming impatient. 'Get the paper and cardboard off and open, open. Hurry up.'

Alice had recovered sufficiently to be present, and in case of an emergency there were six toilets attached to the hall – one for each of the big families who convened here in the old days. Zaynab desperately wanted MoMA in New York to host the first exhibition: hence her determination to bring Alice over to Jam Thanda Gosht and her irritation with me for 'ragging Alice'.

Yu-chih, no doubt wondering why Confucius had dragged her to this place when she could have been sightseeing elsewhere, was trying not to look bored, and failing. The rest of us were impatiently awaiting Plato's message to the world. Once the cardboard and brown paper had been removed, we saw that it was not one painting at all, but a huge triptych. Each panel was painted in different colours. I insisted that we should see each in turn, with the other two turned temporarily to face the ancestors on the walls.

The first panel was what Zaynab had seen at an early stage. 'The horror, the horror' had been her first reaction, and she had fled to Europe thinking that Plato was on the verge of insanity. The 'horror' was undoubtedly present as the core of the painting, but it was much changed since those early drafts. This was the Fatherland panel, the one he had told me might trigger an upheaval in the country. The cancers destroying it were painted as living organisms with tentacle-like attachments that were competing with each other to occupy the whole body. I had never seen anything like this before, from Plato or anyone else. It was certainly original. The colours used to paint the cancers were strange combinations of blood red and pus yellow, but each was given individual features.

Zaynab wanted me to explain each section in turn, though Plato's message was clear enough. 'It may be tedious but it's necessary', she had insisted the night before, 'in order for Alice to fully understand the complexity of the painting.'

Ally only knew the young Plato's work, which was not difficult to understand, not even the folio of 1964 etchings. So, I complied – as I usually did with Zaynab's demands. The first panel, I said, could simply be titled 'The Four Cancers of Fatherland'. These were lurid and surreal depictions. No subtleties, no mysteries to explain here. Plato loved leaving clues in his obscurer work, but had not bothered with any in this panel. The malignant cancer that had sprouted three siblings was shaped like an eagle. Stars and stripes in a state of cancerous decay were tattooed on the back of an Uncle Sam, like so many welts. The face of Uncle, watching the eagle with an approving smile, was unmistakable. It was Barack Hussein Obama, the first dark-skinned leader of the Great Society. The newest imperial chieftain was wearing a button: 'Yes we can . . . still destroy countries'. Plato's image was designed to be crude, I thought, but was it accurate? Alice had become nervous and fidgety as she scribbled furiously in her notepad, a clear indication that the arrow had hit the mark.

Was this the first critical entry by the art world? I could hear the syco-phants hard at work reassuring liberal opinion that Plato could be safely ignored. He was a marginal painter, not a celebrity with over twenty prizes to his name. I. M. Malik was a much greater and more important artist from that country and was already working on a portrait depicting the president as Saint George fighting an Islamist dragon breathing mushroom clouds. Commissioned by a private collector, it had already been booked into seven museums on the strength of the idea and Malik's formidable reputation. But which painting would last? This is a question usually avoided by toadies, who can only live in and for the present so as never to be on the wrong side of history. Adept at sniffing power in every sphere, which is part of their trade, they shift effortlessly from one poste-rior to another. Plato had nothing to fear from their judgement.

The second cancer, painted in blood red and khaki, appeared to be saluting the first. Or was that simply my imagination? I moved back. I was right. He had not wasted much time on Fatherland's army and had painted the dictators it had given the country in garish colours. They were devouring bits of the dying country as if keeping the chemotherapy at bay. That must have been in Plato's mind, though not everyone present accepted my interpretation. Zahid thought it was far-fetched, but Alice and Zaynab agreed with me. One of the despots was crumbling and different bits of metastasizing material were floating in the air. The chemo had disintegrated at least one tumour. It was all a bit too much.

The green bomb-shaped blobs with beards were the jihadis, shown in slow separation from the previous two and developing a life of their own. But who were these five bloated figures with linked arms, all of them defecating gold coins, with each figure's outstretched hand cupped under his neighbour's buttocks, making sure that the enriched droppings fell on it, until you got to the last figure, who was eating the gold-shit with such vulgar abandon that his face was lathered with it? An odd nose, a typical display of teeth, a populist wave identified this gang as poor Fatherland's much-despised politicians.

The colours used in this panel matched the intensity of the work. Looked at from a distance it was stunning, but the closer one got to the painting the more horrific it became. What gave this section real depth, however, was not so much the satire, which was obviously strong, but the wall of humanity with which the painter had encircled the canvas. Zaynab had not seen this in the first draft. Plato must have finished it not long before he was taken to the hospital to die. The people on the edge were part-hedge, part-fence, men and women not unlike the ten who had carried the painting into this hall an hour ago and were waiting patiently in the hot sun outside to take it away again.

The people in the painting are also waiting. Why are they waiting? What are they thinking? Portraying them as a wall, Plato is stressing their collective strength. They are many, the cancers are few. What are they waiting for? For the interlinked cancers to reach them? Each face reflects a different form of pain, resignation, anger, despair. I'm reminded of his very first work, the Partition etchings, but this is different, for these people are not simply victims. Their passivity masks their strength. We may be poor, their faces appear seem to be saying, but our dreams are pure. There is no blood on our consciences. Perhaps there should be some. Did Plato feel that too, during his last days, as he fought against time to finish this painting? Some figures have one hand behind their backs. Is the artist implying the existence of concealed weapons? Will the last attempt to save Fatherland come from below and sweep every malignancy away? I don't know, but that is what I would like to think was in his mind, a last utopian shout. Was it, Plato?

There are a few smiling faces on the canvas, representing innocence and hope. Infants being suckled by peasant Madonnas, one of them with a tiny mole below her breast, intended to remind us, or perhaps me, of Zaynab. The babies are unaware of what lies ahead, like so many who once thought that Fatherland was the future. This is Plato's stunning farewell to the land to which he was forced to flee as a refugee more than half a century ago.

We sat in silence for a while, contemplating the work. Alice spoke first. 'Very brilliant. No doubt about it. His best work. Very brilliant indeed. Some atrophy as they age. He improved with every year. Problems: MoMA won't take Obama-as-cancer. They would if the picture were by a very famous artist, but Plato has only recently become known in the States.'

'Don't tell them,' said Zaynab. 'Let them interpret it as they wish.'

'There is no other interpretation. That's where the power of the painting lies, Zaynab.'

Yu-chih, who had barely said a word since arriving in this backwater, entered the fray. 'It's universal. Any gallery with a curator who knows what constitutes artistic merit will not turn this painting down. The Horse Thief is a very large new gallery in Beijing. They would exhibit this tomorrow. I hope slides are being prepared.'

'Westward or eastward, Zaynab?' I asked in a whisper. She looked at me pleadingly. I turned the Fatherland panel to the wall and displayed the next. This was in classic Plato colours. The entire canvas was covered in waves of blue, turquoise and dark green. We were confronted with a turbulent ocean. Please, I thought, no mermaids. Don't do it, Plato. In the centre of the painting was a large shell-shaped island with six men surrounding a single woman. Plato had clearly had to restrain himself from painting her as a mermaid. The paint used to cover up the tail was in a slightly different shade, and his death had prevented any further retouching. Five of the figures, surprisingly, were painted almost in Socialist Realist style. Only one, like the sea, was surreal. I moved close to examine the subjects and recognized each one. The others followed suit, and a guessing game began. Everyone knew Kemal Ataturk, though his portrait was the only surreal one. The famous hat, the cryptic smile, the cigarette, the tilted face were all his, but what lay below? He was dressed in tights and his legs were posed in a fantastic pirouette. Rudolf Nureyev or a whirling dervish? The choice was ours. I had no idea that Plato had ever been interested in Ataturk, so this was a surprise – or was he trying to imply something that is often discussed in Istanbul but never written or painted?

The other figures were also from the world of Islam, but of a very different time. Intellectual dissidents, like the man who had painted them, and for that reason heroes who had thrilled his artist's blood. A blind poet is seated at the feet of the others. On his lap lies a famous work that was, in fact, the only parody ever done of Zaynab's husband, and that, too, in the twelfth century. How we have progressed. The poet, Abu Ala al-Maari, is conversing with fish and birds. Watching him with kindly, amused and protective expressions are three men in robes and turbans, each clinging to his own best-known work as if someone were threatening to snatch it away from him. These three were old friends I had introduced to Plato thirty years ago, when he was in his most nihilist phase regarding the faith of his forebears: the great scholars of al-Andalus and the Muslim world, Ibn Hazm, Ibn Sina and Ibn Rushd. The last man, and I chuckled with delight, was the Sicilian geographer Muhammad Idrisi, showing them all his map of the world. I introduced these figures to the others, with Zaynab nodding a bit too vigorously, as if she already knew – one of her few irritating habits, because she only did it when she was surprised but did not wish to admit to her lack of knowledge.

At first the single woman puzzled me. Whom had Plato intended? Then I noticed that the uplifted arm had a sleeve with an Arabic inscription: *Allah, I am fit for greatness and stride with great pride / I allow my lover to reach my cheek, and I grant my kiss to he who craves it.* But it was the hand that seemed odd. It had six fingers. Sixer. It was Wallada! A tenth-century poet in Cordoba who maintained a salon, not far from the Great Mosque, that was the site of many heated debates on art and literature and where gossip-carriers reported each day on the latest goings-on in the city. Sixer was the insult she had publicly hurled at her lover, a truly great poet, Ibn Zaydun, whose love poetry is taught to this day in Arab schools and universities. Zaydun had betrayed Wallada's love by seducing her maid, and subsequently moved on to young men. The poem she recited against him in public lacked literary merit – unlike her epic in defence of gossip, which only survives in fragments – but was repeated endlessly at the time for its shock value, and poor Ibn Zaydun became known in the city, indeed as far afield as Palermo and Baghdad, as the Sixer:

> They call you the Sixer,
> Your life will leave you before this name does;
> Sodomite and buggered you are, let's add
> Adulterer, pimp, cuckold and thief.

There were ruder epithets as well, but 'Sixer' remained stuck to the poet till his enshrouded corpse was lowered into the mud. This panel was obviously 'The Good Muslim'. I had realized my attention had been so concentrated on the main characters that I had missed a few important details. Just below the surface of the sea, death was lurking in the shape of shark-like creations, a few with long beards. But it was Alice who made the discovery of the afternoon. What I had assumed was just a cloud turned out to be a man's face. Alice swore loudly that it was James Joyce and repeated the name with incredulity. We inspected the cloud from every distance, and seen from where she was standing, just a few feet from the painting, it was obvious she was right. There was also a number, and Zaynab immediately understood.

'His first and last present to me was a well-worn edition of *Ulysses*. The Arabic numerals obviously refer to the page number.'

She had to go herself to fetch the book, since the maids could not decipher English titles. All present insisted they had read it, though I knew Zahid and Confucius were definitely lying, unless Confucius had read it during the memory-lapse period. It turned out he had, and Yu-chih informed us that there were two Chinese translations, the older of which was more loyal to the original. Given that some people find Joyce's later work incomprehensible, I wondered what the Chinese translation might be like. How could JJ possibly be made to work in another language?

An excited Zaynab had found the page and was going through each line. Then she found it and screamed. 'It's Stephen Dedalus. He's just been reflecting on the mathematical discipline of the medieval Arabs, and in particular algebra – al-jabra – and its symbols. He sees them as "wearing quaint caps of squares and cubes", but listen to this: ". . . imps of fancy of the Moors. Gone too from the world, Averroës [Ibn Rushd] and Moses Maimonides [Ibn Maymun], dark men in mien and movement, flashing in their mocking mirrors the obscure soul of the world, a darkness shining in brightness which brightness could not comprehend.'

How had I missed that? Was he in Trieste already when the thought occurred? Thinking of the tortured history of his country, his continent and his religion, he had remembered another world. Clever, clever Plato. The panel was unanimously awarded a new title, 'The Obscure Soul of the World'. JJ's tribute to an exterminated civilization as recovered by Mohammed Aflatun, deceased. He had never mentioned it to me or to anyone else.

What could the last section of the triptych contain? There was a sense of expectation as we crowded close to examine the work. It was very different from the previous two. This was personal. It consisted of four large and six small panels. Each contained a portrait or a miniature. These were painted short stories. Two small self-portraits of Plato, one showing him as a young man, his face filled with pain, and the other as an old one, with the cancer-ravaged features of the last period. There was the table in the college café in Lahore, around which we were all grouped in the shadows of a pipal tree, with Confucius the most obviously recognizable. Satire had crept in here, with the more reflective types wearing spectacles, the talkative triumvirate with tongues hanging out, and me, licking my spectacles clean. The most straight-laced portrait, and yet funniest for those of us in the know, showed Zaynab covered from head to toe, a pious look on her face, sitting cross-legged on a *takhtposh*. Lying next to her was the Holy Book. She was holding an unlit candle. The fact that it was unlit was remarked on by everyone. Zaynab and I did not dare look at each other.

'It must mean something, Dara,' said Yu-chih. 'You must have some explanation.'

'Of course there is,' I said, racking my brains and trying not to laugh. 'It's obvious. Even though Plato was not religious, he was understanding of our faith in his last days. You cannot show a lit candle next to the Honoured Classic. The light emanating from the Book is all you need.'

Zaynab sighed with relief. The rest applauded. There were a few vintage Plato paintings. In one, a dwarf with upraised sword was guarding the pudendum of a crowned lady while a crowned male was happily helping himself to her behind. The Punjabis present roared with delight. Plato was reminding himself and us of the famous impromptu remark that had once reduced an entire theatre to helpless laughter and projected its author onto a larger frame. Alice had not heard the story and – by now fully recovered from her stomach problems – laughed without restraint.

A satirical miniature depicted Jindié and me sporting in Mughal costume in the Shalimar Gardens, below the marble canopy, though I had been given a few Chinese features. I'm lying with my head on Jindié's lap playing with a flower. Sweet birds fly above. A dropping from one of them is headed straight for my face. A sitar player, who looks suspiciously like Plato, is strumming away below us. One of Jindié's breasts, something I have yet to see, was delicately displayed, causing a bit of embarrassment to her brother and husband. Then I noticed that it wasn't simply that. A tiny portion of my anatomy was peeping out in hope. Zaynab gave me a quick glance, pretending she was coughing to cover her giggle, and said, 'I think this is my favourite one in the last panel.'

'Oh, no,' said Yu-chih. 'It's too obvious. The unlit candle is the one I really like. It's so subtle.'

I agreed a bit too loudly.

Plato's favourite poets were represented, too, and unlike his friends, they had been treated with possibly too much reverence. Here they all were. Faiz, cigarette firmly held in the same hand that is close to his mouth, suppressing the cough that often interrupted his readings. The other hand is resisting the overtures of a society beauty, while in the background Plato's wall of humanity has been miniaturized from the first

painting; their faces, filled with agony, plead for something. A homage
to Faiz's most famous poem, whose first line, 'Lover, do not ask for that
old love again', is the prologue to verses that explain why he should not.
Not because the poet has found another lover, like poor Ibn Zaydun, but
because 'there are other ailments in this world outside the pain of love'.
Like the pain of oppression, felt by the poor.

And here is Sahir Ludhianvi, from Plato's old city in pre-Partitioned
India. He was not recognized by any of the others, and I only knew him
because we used to recite his poetry all the time as young men. It was easier
to grasp than Faiz's, didactic, and had a Brechtian ring to it though it has
survived less well than the work of the great German poet. An explanation is unavoidable. Why is Sahir standing with his trousers at his feet? He
is facing us with a mischievous look on his face and a drooping little penis.
We can't see his naked backside because he's busy showing it to the Taj
Mahal, which is being photographed by the tourist hordes. One of Sahir's
sharpest poems is a response to his beloved, who suggests a rendezvous
in the moonlight outside the Taj. The poet's reply is at once moving and
brutal, denouncing the monument as the indulgence of an emperor who
used his wealth as a crutch 'to make fun of the love that we, the poor, feel'.
How many died building this absurdity, asks the poet of his lover. Ever
think of them? Were they never in love? Were their emotions less pure?
In Plato's portrait, the Taj is cracked from side to side, and the cracks, tiny
impressionist blobs, are painted in similar colours to the cancers depicted
in the first painting. As for the penis, here Plato is suggesting, accurately,
that the poet suffered from an ailment like that of the man who painted
him. I did not mention this, though Ally and Zaynab exchanged a quick
look.

The last three figures are much-loved Punjabi poets from the seventeenth and eighteenth centuries, presented as tribunes of the people. It is
the triumvirate of Waris Shah, Bulleh Shah and Shah Hussain, more holy

for many Punjabis than the most devout preachers of any religion. No portraits of them were ever made. Plato paints them as angelic Punjabi peasants: Waris Shah is rescuing Heer from the wedding palanquin; Bulleh Shah is frowning at mosque and temple and reprimanding mullah and Brahmin, done in miniature. And Shah Hussain, who publicly flaunted his male Hindu lover Madho Lal in the streets of Lahore and wrote love songs for him, is shown naked in his arms, but not in bed. They embrace in the streets of Lahore as an admiring public, similar to the faces in the wall of humanity in the previous panel, watches the pair. Plato's imagination here rested on fact. When Shah Hussain died, the mullahs ordered that his body be left to rot in the sun, since he had breached Koranic injunctions. It is written that tens of thousands of the poet's admirers defied the mullahs. His body was publicly bathed and shrouded in the red colour he loved and buried with great fanfare and singing.

The title for this panel did not require too much thought: 'My Life'. It was over.

Lahore – Pelion – Sardinia – London
2006–2009

3312260870002
kale. 12

#9H9YNIV7C9M

Laus